THE PERFECT HOME

A Novel

DANIEL KENITZ

SCRIBNER

New York   Amsterdam/Antwerp   London

Toronto   Sydney   New Delhi

Scribner
An Imprint of Simon & Schuster, LLC
1230 Avenue of the Americas
New York, NY 10020

First Scribner trade paperback edition January 2025

SCRIBNER and design are trademarks of Simon & Schuster, LLC.

For information about special discounts for bulk purchases, please contact Simon & Schuster Special Sales at 1-866-506-1949 or business@simonandschuster.com.

The Simon & Schuster Speakers Bureau can bring authors to your live event. For more information or to book an event, contact the Simon & Schuster Speakers Bureau at 1-866-248-3049 or visit our website at www.simonspeakers.com.

Interior design by Jaime Putorti

Manufactured in the United States of America

1 3 5 7 9 10 8 6 4 2

Library of Congress Cataloging-in-Publication Data has been applied for.

ISBN 978-1-6680-6387-3
ISBN 978-1-6680-6389-7 (ebook)

For my parents, Scott and Mary

Part One

THE MALFUNCTIONING MAN

CHAPTER 1

DAWN

A fuse has blown inside me. I'm sure of it. If it made noise, it would be like a firework: a pop, a sizzle, then silence. There was a cramp in my side two nights ago, which I assumed was gas. But gas doesn't land you in the office of a fertility specialist. Something else is wrong. Something inside me, something critical and egg producing, has become overgrown with a dark spot that the doctor has found. A polyp. A tumor. An alien tentacle.

Yeah. I'm a bit of a worrier.

Sensing this, my husband tightens his hand around mine. Wyatt is always hot-blooded. I like how I can squish his veins, watch them roll and wriggle like snakes under the skin.

"Dawn and Wyatt Decker—fancy meeting you here again." The doctor plops two folders on her desk and smiles, pleased with the joke she must tell every couple. Jokes are strange coming out of her. Small and spectacled with a pinpoint chin, she looks like a woman who would shush you at a library. "Well, then. Dawn. How's the irritation?"

Not nearly as bad as the anticipation. Three days of rubbing my unoccupied belly in the mirror, circle after circle, like some healing spell. Three days of Wyatt humming Brahms's "Lullaby" in the shower.

I eye the folder on her desk and give Wyatt's hand a squeeze. "Irritation's totally gone," I say.

The doctor chuckles. "That's good. Because we put you through the wringer the other day."

That's putting it lightly. Three days ago, the tests hit me like a marathon rerun of Sex Ed. Uterus, cervix, fallopian tubes, ovarian fossa. Did you know ovaries are technically gonads? I do now. I am thirty-one years old and I just learned I have gonads. The process of oogenesis—egg making—is an assembly line of follicles and oocytes. I don't like knowing this much about myself. There are too many moving parts, too many things that can go wrong.

"Yeah. Not like this one." I throw a thumb Wyatt's way. "What did you have to do again, honey?"

Wyatt's cheeks flush. "It's not as pleasant as it sounds. I felt like a monkey in a zoo."

"I won't touch that one," the doctor says.

"Good," Wyatt says. "I've touched it enough."

In spite of ourselves, in spite of where we are and what news we're waiting on, all three of us laugh. God, I love this man. He could defuse an atom bomb with a smile.

She opens the folder. I try to read upside down. *Dawn Decker. 31 years old.* It's hard to make out the rest, so I assume it reads *BIG OL' UGLY TUMOR ON HER BUSTED BABYMAKER.*

Pop. Sizzle.

Silence.

"Moment of truth," she says. "So, Dawn."

I hate how slowly she paces her words. How she isolates my name in its own sentence, like she's about to announce I've been expelled from school, like my ovaries have been caught smoking weed after second period. Isn't that always how it is for women? We're judged on the health of our wombs. No matter how much I want children, my success—in my eyes, in my mother's eyes, in everyone's eyes—depends on the next words out of the doctor's mouth. Women have the wombs and that makes us the Replication Machines. We are never ourselves; we are only the quality of our Machine. Can we have kids? Then our Machine is good, and we are Instagram-worthy. Can we not? Then we are lonely malfunctions. I've raised chickens before, and once the novelty wears off, all people ever want to know is how many eggs the hens lay. It's the same if you're a married woman.

"Everything looks good. You're in great condition to have children."

Relief shoots out of me in hot breaths. Though I hate how much it matters, I am thrilled my Machine is good.

Then the doctor turns. "Wyatt."

He is no longer squeezing my hand. The doctor looks glum as she pulls the second file and opens it. I can only imagine what his papers describe.

"That means it's me," Wyatt mutters as it registers. "It's my sperm."

CHAPTER 2

WYATT

Here's something they don't tell you about your low sperm count. You can feel it between your legs. An emptiness, but not like a hole. Something is *there*, a misrepresentation of the real thing. A meatless burger. A diet soda.

Two hours after the doctor, I'm sitting with my legs closed, chomping my way through a pack of sugar-free gum. Dawn's inside with the crew. I can hear their laughter go mute against coffered ceilings. (Bad idea, by the way, coffered ceilings. They muffle sound and make spaces seem smaller.) I'm outside on the porch of a four-bedroom renovation in Pleasant View, looking the part: calloused hands, flannel button-down, belt loaded with all sorts of fully functioning tools.

On the inside? I'm Caffeine-Free Wyatt Zero. Tastes just like a man, none of the calories.

Isn't that always how it is for men? We have to assign numerical value to what we offer the world. A sledgehammer might be our favorite tool, but the one we use most often is the measuring tape. How much do you bench? What sales did you pull this quarter? How many commas in your bank account? Even your house—the so-called curb appeal—is just a megaphone for the size of your mortgage payment. It never ends; everything about your manhood can be summed up in a number. Your paycheck. Your TV ratings. Your testosterone levels.

Your sperm count.

Turns out that number means more than all the rest. It means we'll struggle. Even if we try IVF, Dawn's poor mother—who's made it clear she wants nothing else in the world more than a grandbaby—would still have to live long enough to see that bear fruit. I feel slightly guilty about that. If Dawn had married someone else, anyone else, maybe she'd be vetting elementary schools instead of spending her mornings in fertility clinics, listening to our specialist verbally spelunk her way through my seminal vesicles and ductus deferens. For most people, children are just the beginning, Mile One in the marathon of having a family. They forget the thousand little miracles that have to take place before the starting line.

I'd do anything to get there with Dawn. To step across the starting line together.

This afternoon, I'm sitting at our latest renovation, off a tarry county road with a bike trail. I'm wrapping up my gum wad when a couple, about midforties, come cycling up the way. The guy's pants are tight. *Be careful with that, buddy!* I want to say.

The husband eyes our whole production: two TV equipment trucks, half a dozen cars, sound cables snaking up the front walkway. He says something to his wife and gestures at me.

This is when I tell you I'm famous.

To be clear: I'm not Brad Pitt or Michael Jackson famous. Restaurants might comp me for the occasional meal, but it's not like crowds form around me while I eat. I'm famous in the way the Property Brothers are famous. Sure, *The Perfect Home* is the crown jewel in the Home & Lawn TV lineup, and I've been on the cover of a few grocery-register magazines, but if you aren't into home renovation, there's a good chance you haven't heard of Dawn and me. Most of the time, my face sets off some sort of internal *Isn't he familiar?* alarm. A lot of people can't put their finger on it until something clicks.

The couple rolls to a stop and the wife squeezes her husband's shirt. It's always the wives who recognize me first. Both of their eyes go glassy.

Click. The fertility clinic dissolves from my mind and my fingers get fidgety. Around my fans, I am a nest full of honeybees. I pocket the gum, wipe my hands, and walk down to the trail.

"Wyatt Decker," I say.

The wife laughs. "We know."

"Biggest HLTV fan in the world, right here," her husband says, pointing his thumb at her. "You're her hall pass."

The wife elbows him.

"Oh, am I?" I ask, eyebrows wiggling.

Then I flash her the pearlies. Right on cue, she laughs, which makes the husband laugh. This sends sugar right into my veins. My show was already in season two when I realized I was smiling so much in public that I should probably invest in it—Invisalign and Dr. Winstrome's $2,000 laser-and-peroxide treatment, though he kept my teeth a few shades under bleach white for a more natural look. It's the same thing I do with the houses on *The Perfect Home*. I never paint a room white—it's always alligator egg or vanilla lace. A subtle, off-white choice, never perfect. You learn quickly on TV that it's better to leave in the takes where you hammer your thumb or drop the end of the coffee table on your foot. It's the reason folks like this couple are comfortable coming up to me.

After a few selfies and a new voicemail recording for the husband ("This is Wyatt Decker. Please leave the 'perfect' voicemail . . ."), they mosey on down the bike path with a story they can tell at their next dinner party. The feeling leaves me wiped clean.

In the house, the AC is off. Everyone—Dawn, Janie (our veteran reality-TV producer), the cameraman, our key grip—is wearing a mask because of all the sawdust floating in the air, the chalk of broken tile. The once-coffered ceilings are now Grecian ruins on the floor.

I clap my hands and everyone turns. "All right! Let's do it."

"Thank God," Dawn says. "Look who got his groove back. Can I stop trying to come up with talking heads now? I'm all out of wordplay."

I slap on a pair of goggles as our cameraman gets in position. In the corner our head contractor hikes up his sagging tool belt. His team handles the real demolition. Dawn and I are the *talent*, much as that word makes Dawn gag, so we only drop in for an afternoon of goggle donning and sledgehammering and mugging for the cameras. Then the demolition crew will settle in and get down to the real work.

Dawn tugs my arm. "You sure you're feeling okay? We can end *one day* of shooting short, if you're not. We're kind of the stars, you know."

"Oh, yeah? Big, sexy TV stars, huh?"

"Noticed you added *big* and *sexy*." She frowns, chewing her lip.

Dawn's always been self-conscious about her teeth. But I need her perfect, janky, full-toothed smile in my life. I bear-hug her and feel her arms go soft in my grip.

"It's the *smile vise*, Dawn. Unless you smile, you will be crushed into a cube and sent to the recycling yard—" I plant a big kiss on her cheek, then stay near her ear, gnawing and making Cookie Monster noises. That finally breaks her. There is nothing better than a full-throated laugh from someone who doesn't suffer fools.

"You win," she says. "You win, you win!"

"The vise *always veens!*" I say—for some reason, my accent has gone full Transylvanian. I turn to Janie, rub my hands together, conjuring up the Reality TV muses, and ask if we're ready to shoot.

I refuse to let this high wear off.

DAWN

With the camera tracking them, Wyatt and the contractor make a show of surveying the same wall they already surveyed off camera. They will find that the wall next to the dining room is load bearing, which is going to give us problems if we plan on sticking to an open concept. It's the kind of scene we need before a commercial break. A little moment of *uh-oh.* You don't have to watch *The Perfect Home* to know this is the oldest trick in the reality-TV playbook.

I don't love coming along for demo days. I'd rather be home fixing myself a soft-pimento-cheese sandwich. But Wyatt says my highest audience scores come when I'm there to rain on his parade, so this became our routine. Wyatt going full Neanderthal on old drywall, me scolding him because I was going to hang some ivy there, him pulling up a leaf and nailing it in, his face a broken mirror of smile and apology. I am the acid to Wyatt's base. For whatever reason, that's the married-couple chemistry America wants in its home renovation.

"So this isn't coming down?" Wyatt is saying, pressing his palm into a wooden beam.

"Not if y'all want open concept." The contractor's East Tennessee accent—think Dolly Parton with a dipping habit—always reminds me how much Wyatt has worked to lose his. "Heck, if I was an inspector, I'd already be on y'all with a *shtop* order."

Then there's a pause, which is strange. Wyatt only lets dead air on the show if it's setting up a punch line.

Wyatt turns to me. "That's you, babycakes."

"Oh! I'm sorry. What was I going to say, Janie?"

"Reset," Janie says to everyone in the room but me. The whole routine begins again. Wyatt keeps his gaze on me, deciding whether to shake his head or smile.

"Sorry." I do a cuckoo sign with my finger. "I just pulled a Myra."

Myra was Wyatt's ex-wife. Long story short, Wyatt caught her cheating on him with his attorney. He immediately filed for divorce, and as soon as they signed the papers, she up and left for South America. Nobody's heard from her since. *Pulling a Myra* is our inside joke for disappearances—literal and metaphorical.

"Lemme think." Wyatt looks at Janie. "You sure this doesn't need something? Now that we're resetting, it feels wrong. We've done the load-bearing thing already. Everyone has."

"The same thing can go wrong in different houses," I say, dreaming of the soft white bread I'll use for the pimento-cheese sandwich. Maybe I'll cut off the crusts.

Wyatt's eyes float miles away. I steal a glance out the window. The late-afternoon light has gone soggy in the summer haze. Our daylight is burning.

"How about this: I'm knocking down some wall as usual. Then what if there's something inside it?"

"Like *what?*" Janie asks.

"Y'all stay put," Wyatt says, sounding more Tennessee than ever.

Tool belt and goggles and all, he walks out the door. This leaves an entire TV filming crew silent in his wake. The life of the party has just left. Despite his usual charm, I can tell there's a sore spot in his mood, a rawness left over from the fertility clinic. He even forgot that we drove here together; now I can't drive home and make myself that pimento cheese.

The *gall* of this man.

Janie walks up to me, scratching her scalp. "Well, since we're stuck here, you wanna do a talking head?"

I groan.

Done well, those insert scenes when one of the actors breaks the fourth wall and speaks directly to the audience feel like interviews, add to the documentary feel. But in practice they're nothing like real interviews. Every punch line is choreographed. If I could cut one now, a direct line between me and *The Perfect Home* fans, it might sound like:

Wyatt's gone to the store and he won't tell us what it's about. You know how Wyatt is.

Cue eye roll. Eye rolls come naturally to me, and that's why I fit in the show. Ostensibly, I'm here for interior décor, for deciding whether a breakfast nook needs an oversized clock hanging above the table. But for every ten questions I get about the show, only one is about décor. The rest are about Wyatt.

After we film a new talking head—I do one of my trademark riffs, complaining to the camera with my hand next to my mouth like I'm telling tales out of school—we wait so long that the crew breaks out into a game of cribbage. But we can't leave no matter how bad the light gets. Wyatt could be back at any moment. Once when Wyatt disappeared to buy a replacement futon for the one he accidentally broke during a shoot, sunset came before Wyatt did, so Janie called it a day and sent us all home. Wyatt showed ten minutes later, texting everyone in all caps, *I WASN'T GONE THAT LONG. C'MON. WE'RE BURNING THE MIDNIGHT OIL.* Turned out he'd driven through half of Nashville looking for the exact same futon. *And* he'd found it.

Looking back, we all felt a little silly for thinking he'd abandoned us. Wyatt would never lose a day of shooting.

I type out a text warning him not to pull a Myra and abandon us for South America, but I've barely hit send when his truck pulls in the driveway. He scampers up to the entryway with a cloth bag dangling in his hands.

"Can we rig a fake wall for us to demo?"

I point at Wyatt's bag. "What'd you get?"

"Antique coins. I went to a pawnshop." Wyatt tapes the bag to the wall, and the contractor covers it with the fake wall we're about to destroy. I slather on a coat of Van Courtland Blue as Wyatt tells us the concept: we're going to stumble upon a bag of coins from the Prohibition era.

"Sounds kinda convoluted," Janie says.

Wyatt shrugs. "First we shoot coverage with windows in the shot, to preserve the light. Next we'll do the indoor shots. We'll add a warm light and hang a curtain diffuser if the continuity doesn't work. Worst case, we transition with a voice-over from establishing, then directly into the shot of me hammering the wall. Someone can curse in the background so we have something to bleep, which snaps the audience to attention, and I say, 'What is *this*?'"—emphasis on *this*—then a shot of my gloved hand as I pull out the bag, saying, 'Noooo way.' Then *bam*, we're into a Lowe's commercial. Couldn't be simpler."

The cameraman scratches his cheek with his mouth open, megaphoning the crackling sound of fingernail on stubble. "That sound plausible?"

"Sure. The house was built in 1932, right? Prohibition. Or is that too obvious?"

A few of us exchange looks of surrender, the tension defrosting from our eyes. No, it is not too obvious. As we film it, I catch myself leaning in behind, sucked in by the moonshine mystery Wyatt's just constructed out of thin air. I forget all about pimento cheese. Pimento cheese can wait. This is better.

If I had to do a talking head:

What else is there to say? In Wyatt We Trust.

CHAPTER 3

WYATT

As I drive us home to Belle Meade that night, I find myself wishing our F-150 were a stick shift. Something for fidgeting. Something a man holds. Anyone who's ever seen my TV show will assume I can drive a stick. I can't. In reality, I am a man who doesn't know what to do with his hands.

"There are options," Dawn says. "You heard the doctor. In vitro. And adoption isn't the A-word, you know."

"I just have this image in my head, babycakes"—even my pet name for Dawn has the word *baby* in it—"you and me, a fireplace, our baby, main page of Modern People. Not just *a* baby. *Our* baby."

"Adopted would still be our baby. And why shouldn't Modern People like that?" She crinkles her nose. "Was this really your first sperm test? I mean, you were with Myra for a while."

"Me and Myra never tried for kids. And we weren't having sex by the end." Flicking on the turn signal, I change the subject. "Want some Chick-fil-A?"

As I turn, the F-150 downshifts for me. The space under my hand is a cockpit panel of seat warmers and cupholders. I am too comfortable, I decide. Too coddled. That's why my sperm doesn't work. My whole life has been on automatic transmission.

At the Chick-fil-A menu, Dawn pulls out her gratitude journal, swipes the leather with a thumb, pulls off the band. The pages she's filled are sweaty and rippled, nearly ruined. That's a classic Dawn trait. Family heirlooms and sentimental things should not be behind glass, she once told me. They're to be ruined with use. And she does use things up. Journals, tennis shoes, credit card points. Dawn once told me a life well lived ends with an empty tank of gas.

"What are you writing?" I ask.

"I'm grateful . . ." She searches. "For all the consequence-free sex we can have."

"We *want* consequences, though. Don't we?"

"Then I'm grateful we didn't need any biopsies. That's pretty awesome, right? Not having cancer?" She makes a smile, sour puckered, the kind only someone with those dimples could make.

I order two Cobb salads and pull to the first window. The poor woman behind the register looks about nine hours into an eight-hour shift.

"That's eighteen thirty-nine . . . *oh ma God!*" The woman flinches, then freezes as she reads the name on my credit card. She blinks, rereads. Just to be sure. "Wyatt Decker."

I grin and point at the card. "I think you're supposed to swipe that."

"Lordie. Look at me. I'm sorry. I got myself all twisted. You're Wyatt Decker."

"Watch it!" I joke. "That's a registered trademark."

"That makes you Dawn," the woman says, shouting into the car now as she hands back my card. "Ease off my man, Dawn. You're always teasin' him about the renovation budget. My man can have any budget he wants."

Dawn's smile is close-lipped. "It's sort of . . . that's for TV. The banter. I don't have any say in the budget."

The woman at the register shoots me a downcast look. "Oh, I'm sorry. You can, uh, go to the next window for your order."

I glance at her name tag. "Listen, Tanya, I don't want to hold up the whole line. But thanks for being a fan! Here's my card—ring up my producer. She'll hook you up with all the swag you want."

That lights her up. I drive to the second window—Tanya's "Thankyouthankyouthankyou" fading behind us—and give Dawn a love tap on the thigh. "You could have been a little nicer. That woman was only trying to get you to smile."

"Sorry. You're so much better at celebrity small talk than me."

"That's the thing. I'm not. You're a hundred times funnier when you want to be."

Dawn makes a show of licking her finger, then opens the journal. "I'm writing that one down. What's today's date?" She scribbles, "'Wyatt finally admitted it today . . .'"

Our French Colonial in Belle Meade stands on top of a hill, the tip of its belvedere tower slicing a baby-blue sky in half. Behind it, a buzz cut of chainsawed oaks speckles the backyard. Dawn and I had to clear it of trees and huckleberry if we wanted a backyard—a true backyard for red rover games and long Hail Mary passes. That was where the playhouse would go, once we had the rest of the trees cut, but now I wonder if I should call and cancel the tree guys. Right now, the only thing that's out there is the toolshed we erected on an episode of *The Perfect Home*: See how easy it is to assemble one of your very own from a kit? It has French double doors to match the house. They're made from plywood. Dawn likes the way our lot is wrapped in trees, like "a big bird's nest," our dappled woods cupping us and our future chickadees. But what if we have no chickadees? Our nest becomes a pile of sticks. Our French Colonial becomes five thousand square feet of drywall and HVAC.

Dawn goes to the bathroom, so I'm left in the absurdly large kitchen with my salad. I feel silly, oddly callow, sitting at the enormous U-shaped island.

We can afford this place, sure. But still. Our eyes were bigger than our stomachs.

I flip on the kitchen's TV for some distraction. Instead, I get more of us: a rerun of *The Perfect Home* as the credits roll. HLTV skips straight to the next episode, so here we are, Dawn and Wyatt, America's favorite fruitless couple, introducing ourselves yet again.

On-screen, I trudge up to the camera in slow motion, wearing the flannel I never wear in real life, a sledgehammer in my gloved hands.

I know renovation, I say.

And I know décor, Dawn adds, via voice-over. A scene shows her lifting a pedestal vase to a mantel of white-painted brick. I remember shooting that day. She complained she would never paint brick.

A montage follows: unveiling newly renovated ranch homes to families with strollers, moms cupping their mouths, and dads shooting silent *Wows* with their lips; Dawn using the stud finder over her considerable cleavage and laughing her perfect, throaty laugh; me bursting through wall paneling like the Kool-Aid man doing demo; our clients' happy toddlers jumping on their new race-car beds. Finally, a shot in front of a blurred-out house dollies away in slow motion as Dawn and I lean against each other. It strikes me—given all the houses we've upgraded for growing families—how lonely two childless people can look.

And together, we narrate, *we help you build your Perfect Home.*

The main title unfolds: *THE PERFECT HOME.*

Upbeat bumper music plays over an establishing shot of my Nashville office. Cut to me bursting down the hall with a mysterious package under my arm. I plop it down in front of Dawn. *Guess who we're renovating this week.*

Dawn pulls a pen out of her mouth, twists the package around. *Am I crazy if I say it's an urn?*

No. Well, yes, it's an urn, but what's inside? . . . It's a woman's ashes.

[Bleep], Dawn says, jumping like she's seen a spider.

The on-screen version of myself goes on to explain that we're renovating an undertaker's house that week. He wanted us to carry his mother's ashes around for a week so we'd get his vibe. Of course, none of this is exactly true. The ashes and the urn were props. But when I discovered the client was a part-time undertaker who handled the occasional cemetery lot, I knew the episode had its opening hook.

The segment is already well into demolition day by the first commercial break. In this episode, I accidentally sledgehammered through a copper pipe. The camera cuts to an interior POV from the wall as Dawn gives one of her eye-rolling talking heads.

If I wanted busted pipes, I could have stayed with my ex-boyfriend, she tells the camera. Oof. That joke did not age well. Then, showing the magic that Dawn adds to the show, her smile drops. *You can cut that part out, right?*

We didn't cut it out because that was Dawn at her best, a combination of self-conscious and unintentionally charming. As a drone shot shows the house from the exterior, the title card plays again: *THE PERFECT HOME.* Cue commercial. Buy this French onion dip; it's *perfect* for parties.

Yeah, I think, waking my phone. Everything in my life is perfect, perfect.

A website that ends in .*de* loads on my phone. *Kinderwun-schklinik* in Floranienburg, a suburb of Berlin. ASB, Angstrom Supplement-B, is illegal in most states.

I don't like doing illegal things if I don't have to. I won't even speed on an empty highway.

But now I'm wondering if I have to.

I always knew the problem was with me. That's why I spent the past few weeks on a private web browser, looking at sites most men shouldn't look at, the kind that make you clear your cookies. But the list of side effects was too long, the "friendly warnings" on un-friendly message boards too riddled with hard experience. I scrolled and rescrolled through the side effects until the words weren't so tart. High blood pressure. I've had that. I lived. But even so, why risk it? Our situation wasn't as dire as all that.

Not before today.

Footsteps clap down the marble and I quickly stuff my phone in my pocket. Dawn looks fresh after the bathroom, but judging by the way she plops her elbows on the island, she's been thinking too hard. "I know you don't want to have the adoption talk. . . ."

"That's because I don't want to adopt, period."

"Well, then, what *are* we talking about? A donor?"

I reel back. She might as well have slapped me. "A donor. Gosh, Dawn." Dawn's mother made me promise I would never curse around her daughter, and to make sure, I cut those words from my whole life.

"I'm sorry." Dawn sighs. "We just need to talk about our options if we can't have kids on our own."

"I wouldn't be so sure."

She blinks. "What does that mean?"

"Nothing. Nothing except—I don't know, sometimes doctors

get it wrong. The fertility doctor isn't God. And it's not like trying to have kids is a drag." I stifle a smile. "It's pretty fun."

"Yeah, but we're finding ways to suck all the fun out of it."

"Well, thanks."

"I mean, for you, too, right?"

"I'm a man, babycakes. I've never had bad sex." I become desperate to change the subject. "I want to try a treatment I found online."

Dawn dips her chin. "*I found online.* Famous last words."

"Indulge me. I can do a virtual visit with the clinic. They take my history—"

"Where is this clinic?"

"—they take my history, everything is aboveboard—"

"Wyatt. Where is this clinic?"

"Germany. Hey, it's still the Western world." Before thinking, I add, "We're desperate."

"*You're* desperate. I'm okay with adopting. We'll still love the baby, won't we? Modern people won't care whose baby cannon the kid shoots out of. They'll be too busy saying *aww.*"

For a second I consider debating the point, but I realize she means Modern People, the celebrity-feature website. Dawn has seen the vision board hanging in our exercise room. I had a staffer photoshop our spread from the cover of *HLTV Magazine* and digitally insert a baby into Dawn's arms, which Dawn found macabre despite my best intentions. And above our edited heads: M-O-D-E-R-N P-E-O-P-L-E. When I ride that exercise bike, I go to the highest setting, Mount Everest. Every morning, Modern People waits at the summit.

"It's my body," I protest. "I'm willing to take the risks. You heard the doctor—you're the healthy one. You have nothing to worry about. Zero side effects for you. Except possibly getting pregnant."

Dawn pouts. "You say that as if I shouldn't worry about you."

"You shouldn't! My life insurance is enormous."

Joke or not, one glance at her tells me this was the wrong thing to say. When her lips quiver, I hurry to the freezer, pull out the only tub of ice cream I see—butter brickle—and start layering it with whatever I can find: syrup, sprinkles, cherries. I even chop the cashews.

"Who *says* these things?" Dawn asks, facing away, like she's giving a talking-head segment to an invisible camera. "We're already rich. I want *you* here. For another fifty years. Aren't I enough of a family?"

I dip a spoon in the bowl, kiss the top of her head.

"Aw, hon," she says. "No. You've been doing so good on your diet."

"It's not for me."

She looks up. "I don't want that—"

I slide the carton in front of her so she can read *butter brickle*, then wrap her up in a hug.

"All right," I murmur. "If you don't want me to, I won't do it. I'm sorry. It was a careless thing to say. I want to live another fifty years if it means living with you. No matter what happens." Then, remembering what my mom always said when she hugged me as a child, *Tell me, a man has to say it,* I add, "I love you."

Peeling herself off me, Dawn has to wipe her snotty face to read the ice cream carton. "You got me butter brickle." And leaving the sundae alone, she hugs me again. "You remember every little thing."

We stay like that awhile, half in grief and half in relief, her heaving into my sweater, the echoes bouncing off our distant cathedral ceilings. We are two small birds in an enormous nest.

DAWN

Tuesday morning, the doorbell rings. No one is there. A small package lies on our novelty doormat: UNLESS YOU HAVE GIRL SCOUT

COOKIES OR MY AMAZON PACKAGES, GO AWAY. I picked that one out. I got tired of the minimalist-chic gray mats I always have to choose on the show.

This package looks like it's been through the wringer. It's been stamped a thousand times, and layers of packing tape choke it in the middle. I bring it inside. We get so many shipments, and 99 percent of them are Wyatt's: BCAA supplements, deco art prints for the basement he's refinishing, beard balm infused with lanolin, which he claims is what keeps merino sheep so soft. Normally, when we get a package, I don't even double-check the name. I just bring it in and add it to the overstuffed inbox of our lives.

But as I set it on the countertop (high-grade quartz, thank you HLTV), something compels me to read the return address.

Lackier Kinderwunschklinik
Postfach 10 01 08
32548-181 Floranienburg
Germany

The acid in my stomach churns. I don't speak German, but words like *Kinder* and *Klinik* are clear enough.

Instead of leaving the package on the countertop, I bring it upstairs with me. He won't know where it is; he'll think it hasn't come yet, and it's not like he'll be able to ask me, *Hey, babycakes, where is that experimental German medicine I ordered but promised I wouldn't?*

After I stuff the box underneath the nightstand, I dig out my gratitude journal and open to the most recent page.

I am grateful that my husband wants kids so much, he would risk his life. I think, then add, *He would do anything.*

CHAPTER 4

DAWN

I've always been too honest. It's the sort of honesty that leapfrogs God's truth into hyperbole and metaphors. So, when people ask how we met, I like to say our coworkers loaded me into a cannon and shot me straight at Wyatt's loins.

We met a little over five years ago. It was over cocktails at the penthouse of a downtown Nashville high-rise, a fumy, über-outré place smelling like a bar, all citrus and mint and sweat. Caterers had lacquered over Janie's living room with the odd combination of steam trays and fake Perma-Snow. It was technically an HLTV Christmas party. My intention was to show my face, shoplift a ginger ale or three, and then head out—until Janie made a beeline for me.

"Ya know, you're just Wyatt's type," she said.

"Oh. He likes vivacious, whip-smart blondes?"

The way infants learn to self-soothe against the coldness of the world, I've learned to self-flatter.

Janie shook her head, pinched the firmness of my arm—the cosmo in her other hand down to the parched lime—and said, "You're *twenty-five*. He's thirty. It's perfect."

I got a salivating butcher's vibe. *Take a gander at this plump heifer.* The way Janie pinched me, I half expected her to talk about my gorgeous marbling. I felt like all women feel like at some point: a broodmare. A pair of plump dimples. A date of birth on my driver's license. Inappropriate men have always told me I'd clean up well, that I'd practically be a supermodel with just *a little bit of makeup*, never understanding that I was already wearing foundation, mascara, and ten minutes' worth of concealer.

Still, the match seemed natural to everyone else: Wyatt Decker, newly divorced reality-TV star, the most dashing bachelor in the South since Rhett Butler; Dawn Fremont, line producer, single and looking, chipmunk cheeks with a neckline of the goddesses, though I wondered why Janie considered a five-year difference the *perfect* age.

"I thought he was married," I said.

Janie, caught mid-sip, smacked her lips. "Divorce ink just dried. Was a real messy thing. Terrible for each other. She was a real nut. Myra something."

Before I could ask what that meant, Wyatt walked in and Janie had to go play host. Taller in real life but not freakishly so, he wore a simple white button-down tucked in to show the V-shape of his torso. Glossy black hair. Lean, slightly off-kilter smile. He had these long, reedy forearms, handyman's forearms, where you could see every muscle dance whenever he moved his fingers. They had the cut-marble look of someone who'd spent a lifetime turning and squeezing things. He'd rolled up the button-down.

Show-off, I thought, steeling myself.

Later, he and I were filling plates at the buffet table when the crowd around us parted with the precision of synchronized swimmers. Wyatt was scooping helping after helping of mashed potatoes onto an enormous plate.

"It's a cheat meal," he said, blushing. He always blushes about food. "My trainer's letting me have whatever I can fill on one plate."

"Hey. I'm not judging." But I couldn't resist. "It looks good. Where'd you get that giant plate, though? Is there a manhole somewhere that needs a cover?"

He smiled, then wiped his hand with a cloth and stuck it out. "Wyatt Decker."

And I shook, enjoying how small my hand felt in his. "Dawn Decker."

"Oh?"

"*Fremont.* Dawn . . . Fremont. Sorry. I just—I know who you are. I had *Decker* on the brain. I love your show."

"Oh, fantastic. Lovely to finally meet half of my female audience. You don't happen to know the other woman who watches, do you?"

All modesty and jokes, Wyatt. By then, *The Perfect Home* was already the cornerstone of HLTV's Sunday-night lineup. Reruns played all week. God, with all he had going for him, he was even unassuming. I almost let out a groan as my desire to hate him dissolved.

I didn't reply, having nothing clever to say, imagining he'd forget me as soon as someone else demanded his attention. But after the momentum of the line carried us to the bar, Wyatt turned to me. "Can I buy you a drink?"

"Seltzer with a lime."

"You sure? It's Christmas."

I didn't want to make it a big deal. "Can't. I'm sorry. You can make it fun, though. See how many lime wedges you can fit into one glass."

His eyes went so bright, I could swear I saw flares. Years later, we would decide while bantering about paint colors on *The Perfect Home* that his famous shiny eyes are Byzantine Blue. Mine are brown. "Just brown," I said. When he tried to dress it up as "Gingerbread Brown," I looked at the camera and mouthed it again: *Just brown.*

"I'll tell them lime, with a splash of water," he said. I loved that this filled him up with so much happiness. "You know, like a joke."

"Sure." I grinned. "And like any good joke, you'll have to explain it."

We were still talking two hours later, mindlessly hogging the warm spot by the fireplace. As it turned out, in many ways we were the same person. We were both die-hard University of Tennessee Volunteers—which may not sound like much outside Vanderbilt territory, but it is here. Neither of us had siblings. I still had my mother left; his had died in a car accident when he was thirteen. Lung cancer had sent his father to heaven, and a love of slot machines and cocktail waitresses had sent mine to skid row. The last time I got a birthday card from him, I told Wyatt, it had a Vegas return address.

I changed subjects back to his show. "That stuff you said about your audience being all men . . ."

"Oh, I wasn't kidding. Our audience is seventy-thirty men-to-women. Ratings are good, but HLTV's bread and butter is women. They don't want beer commercials. They want Lowe's, Target, Bed Bath and Beyond."

"Well, your show is all men. You and the crew. The design tips are pretty good, but what women are still watching after five minutes? You're giving them three guys with beards. But I have at least two or three friends who swear by every design concept you post on Instagram."

"Yeah, and what are the names of these friends? Jim-Bob? Skeeter?"

"Victoria and Alice. My two closest friends. And I could never be friends with people who have horrible taste in TV."

He smiled. It was no longer off-kilter. "Maybe I'm making progress."

"Women are looking for an excuse to talk about this show, and you don't give it to them. Half of every episode focuses on your buddies, and all they do is prank each other. The show should be about you and the families you help. You think it's a show about houses. It should be about *you*." I made a circle motion in his direction. "With the total man-babe factor you got goin' on over there."

He mimed licking a pencil, writing this down. "Less pranks, more man-babe. Got it."

"*Fewer* pranks," I corrected. "And if you have a girlfriend, put her on."

I was just fishing, but Wyatt got a look like someone had just turned on the lights. He gave me his card and said to call his producer, not knowing I'd already met Janie, who was now singing karaoke in the corner and about one vodka tonic shy of wearing a lampshade.

Within a few weeks, Wyatt and Janie invited me on camera as a *consultant*. I already had a side gig refurbishing antiques on Etsy, so that became my thing on *The Perfect Home*: knickknacks and décor. The pranking friends lost their screen time and subsequently their interest in the show, while I brought my snark and grammar correcting.

Along with an instant boost in the eighteen-to-forty-five female demo.

Then came the comments on Instagram. Is she single? How does she not jump on that? How does *he* not jump on that? His followers doubled within months, most of them women. After a few dates (during which we did secretly *jump on that*) Wyatt went Instagram official with our relationship. He got his first mentions in the gossip blogs since his divorce. The ratings jumped overnight.

We lived half our courtship on-screen. The engagement episode: Wyatt redoing my childhood Murfreesboro home for my mother, who wasn't in long-term care yet. The wedding special: drama over who would walk me down the aisle, with my mom wheelchair-bound and my father presumably off spending his slot winnings on booze. Honeymoon: a special "travel" episode to the Keys, the first (and only) time I yelled at Janie after I found hidden cameras in our bedroom. Oh, and we updated a fisherman shack in Key West.

It only takes one conversation to change your entire life. Meeting Wyatt at Janie's party was mine. I thought line producer was a pretty good job, had my eyes set on an HLTV executive role twenty years down the line. All behind-the-camera stuff. Then, as if snatched away, Alice in Wonderland–style, I became a TV star. My name is everywhere next to his. On the *Perfect Home* antique shop. On the joint bank account with two commas. In the captions when the *Daily Mail* turns our coffee runs into lame real estate puns. (My favorite: "Curve Appeal! Dawn Decker Looks Snazzy in Sweats on a Nashville Coffee Run.")

Wyatt was born to be famous, but if I'm honest, I chafe against it. It feels like wearing glass clothes. I'm grateful for what it brought: a giant house in Belle Meade, satisfaction at work, money to help my mom. But the thousand cuts of fame ache after a while. Especially reading comments online with all their stinging compliments: *You're hope for all of us "regular" girls.* Though we registered the house under an LLC, strangers still somehow find out where we live and occasionally snap pictures. Once I even found a death threat in Wyatt's mail. He shrugged it off ("Maybe they meant to send it to Black and Decker, ha, ha"), but it took me several hours and about a gallon of matcha milk to fall asleep that night.

I don't want to sound ungrateful. Fame certainly has its charms. Right after my first episode aired, someone started an Instagram reply thread asking if Wyatt and I were dating. Down the chain the comments went, speculations galore, these middle-aged housewives practically picking out my wedding dress for me. And it ended with what I once thought was the greatest compliment of all.

Their babies are going to be so, so gorgeous.

Tonight, Wyatt is downtown for a business meeting, so I leave the Lackier Kinderwunschklinik package out on the kitchen counter. He'll find it when he comes home.

Even better, he'll know I saw it.

I do some laptop research in bed to pass the time. Search results for Angstrom Supplement-B are inconclusive. For a while, all I find is obscure medical data from Belgium and ads for penis pills. Searches like *male fertility ASB* are going to land me on some shady marketing lists. WebMD lists a couple of side effects—Wyatt would have to watch his thyroid and blood pressure—but the fertility forums have mostly rave reviews.

Great experience, one woman says. *After about a month or so of trying to conceive, I got pregnant!!!*

My favorite part was the increased libido, comes a reply. *We were like newlyweds. Same as you—pregnant in a month, due in September. Hurray for supersperm, lol.*

They should sell this over the counter, says Woman Number Three. *It's like beer goggles without the hangover.*

A dozen comments or so echo the same, celebrating revitalized sex lives and impending baby showers. I scroll past a few rows of eggplant emojis and double entendres until I find more text. One woman got a divorce after taking it, but vouched for ASB's impact on potency.

The last comment is a reply to her. *A divorce? Lucky, lucky. My scumbag brother-in-law took it, and my sister will never be the same.*

I look for a comment button to ask why, but there is none. The thread is from five years ago. It's a digital ghost town.

Even though it's a quarter after nine, I'm wired, wide-awake. A glance out the window shows no sign of Wyatt in the driveway. I grab my keys, head past the Kinderwunschklinik package still on the counter, and pop the door to my truck before I know where I'm going.

Mom, I think when the engine turns over. Always Mom.

It's only a five-minute drive, which was the appeal of putting her up in Long Grove Health and Retirement Care. It costs us two grand a month more than the next-best option, but the advantage is I can visit Mom whenever I want. And it's nicer. Just one story of brick and faux marble, it looks more like a country club than a nursing home.

Tonight, only a few cars are out back, which must belong to the night staff. That fills me with daughterly pride. No one gets as many visits as my mom.

Harlene Mae Fremont is big and round—always been round, she says, just like her mom—with a tanned complexion prone to freckles. Her rusty-blond curls are now gone and she has to paint her eyebrows, but her green eyes still have their gleam. When I come in, she's got a cream beauty mask on. I love her for that. In spite of everything, she still wants her skin to glow. She says she will never be stage five, the stage at which cancer metastasizes to the spirit.

As I walk through her door, I see she's wrapped up her legs in a flannel blanket, leaning back in a noisy leather chair, vegged out in front of *Friends* reruns. I know the episode on sight, "The One with the Worst Best Man Ever."

"Oh, baby," she says, which is her version of *hello*. No matter how routine, every visit shocks her like a surprise party. It's one reason everyone loves her. "You shoulda called. I look a mess."

"I was hopin' we could talk." I hear my voice slip back into Fremont mode, that Appalachian-foothill drawl.

She mutes the TV, even though I've told her a thousand times she can pause live TV now. It never takes. "Hit me with it, baby."

I tell her about the package and the ASB. My first instinct would usually be to tell Victoria—Vic—my former college roommate. No one knows you like your first wine buddy. But involving Vic would take our secret outside the family. Then there's Alice, the nurse, the absolute sweetheart, but she's so by the book she'd probably report us to the FDA. Momma Harlene, as we all call her, is a dead end of information. That's on purpose. She told me once that if you want people to tell you secrets, you should acquire a reputation for keeping them. By the end of my story, her eyes have gone bleary. She pinches the top of her nose.

"You all right, Mom?"

"Just this heat." She fans herself. "All right, I'm goin' to tell you how to deal with this. Be easy on Wyatt. He's already done so much for you. The big ol' house full of bedrooms. Cuttin' down all the trees in that backyard of yours. And didn't you say he didn't even wanna get tested at first? This'll be his worst fear come to life. A man finds out he's got bad sperm, or no sperm, whatever it was—there's gonna be a problem. How would you like finding out you got no eggs? I ain't had any for a long time and I'm still shook up about it.

Talk to him, make him feel like a man again, and maybe he never takes a single pill of that MSG."

"ASB." Acronyms aside, her mind seems sharp as ever. The diagnosis isn't technically terminal—immune therapy has kept her in a holding pattern for years—but I can tell by the way she wheezes between sentences that her body isn't the steamroller it once was.

She leans forward, making the leather in her chair scream, and gets that aiming-at-a-dartboard look in her eyes. "You know, there are options. Don't ever you think you can't adopt."

"I know," I say. But I don't know. I do know she *means* well, but I also know that on her sixtieth birthday I asked her what she wished for and she patted me over the womb with a wink. I know that before she moved into Long Grove Health, she kept an unassembled crib hidden in my old bedroom closet. I know that like me she was an only child. I know that if I mention any of this to her, she'll suck her teeth and say we should stop worrying and watch *Friends*, and somehow that will hurt more than any of it. I can't separate myself from the feeling of responsibility. What good are you to your parents if you don't make something of yourself before you die? Wyatt built a number one cable reality show. What did I build? All Momma Harlene ever asked for was a grandchild. If nothing else, I want to tell Mom, *Look, I made this, and you made me. Wasn't it all worth it? All those midnight feedings when I was an infant, all those fillings you paid for, all those boys you helped me cry over? Now the thing you made is making things.*

I draw a deep, speechmaking breath. "And if we did adopt—"

"This soon?" She frowns. "I meant down the line. Isn't that kind of early for the white flag, darlin'? You got plenty of good years left, and you can adopt anytime."

The envy in her voice—*plenty of good years left*—breaks my heart. "I just don't want to waste time trying for a baby if we know it's pointless."

"Doctors got all sorts of newfangled treatments, and it sounds like Wyatt's on top of all that. He's tryin' at least."

"Tryin', yeah. Without my permission. But if we adopt, you'd be able to meet your grandchild."

"Someone else's grandbaby."

"Mom, you *just* said you were okay with me adopting."

She whistles out a sigh. "Oh, listen to me. Of course you're right. Don't pay me no mind, baby. You could bring home a rhino from the Nashville Zoo and I'd love that grandbaby like it's my own."

"But if we can't . . ."

"It don't matter, baby, really. I've had a good life."

I've had a good life. She says it like adoption, not melanoma, is what will be the death of her. We lived with each other twenty years, Momma Harlene and me, both alone and together, dissolving the boundary between motherhood and sisterhood. That kind of intimacy means I can read her, too. She's going easy on me because I showed up at nine o'clock at night, later than usual. She senses I'm making an apology for what Wyatt can't do.

We watch TV together for a while, but I can't concentrate. By the time I leave, I decide this little retirement home kingdom of hers isn't nearly repayment enough for raising me.

I drive up to the house, the only car in the driveway. The package from Germany still sits on the kitchen counter. I start an angsty, melodramatic note: *blah blah trust between partners and blah blah thought we were in this together and blah blah thought you could tell*

*me anything and blah blah our wedding vows and blah blah you didn't
listen to me about adoption.*

I rip it up and toss it in the trash bin. I write a new note. One
sentence.

If we're doing this, we're doing it together.

Up in the bedroom, headlights roll through the window and wake
me from a dreamless sleep. Wyatt's truck rumbles, then shuts off. I
know the rest of his routine. Door opening. Kick, kicking the dirt
into the welcome mat, then the pat, pat of each shoe thumping off.
Keys clinking to the counter. But what's this? A pause. He's reading
my note.

The footsteps come slowly after that, measured, contemplating.
I sit up and tell Alexa to bring up the lights. Running my fingers
through my hair, I try to comb out the pillow poof that's appeared.

Wyatt opens the door slowly, just in case I'm asleep.

"I'm awake," I call.

Wyatt is six-four, but the crimped way he's standing makes him
look half a foot shorter. He's opened the package and is holding
just the bottle of pills now, but with both hands, like it's the hat of
Oliver Twist.

"How was downtown?"

He holds up the pills. "I swear I was going to tell you, babycakes."

Tears already. I wince and try to hide them by hugging my face into
my knees. "If you were going to tell me, you would have told me."

"I'm sorry." He sits at my feet, the mattress frowning into his
gravity. "I thought maybe if it just happened . . . naturally . . . then
it would be better. For you, I mean."

For me. He truly means that. He looks up at me, his wet eyes gone soft, a full basset-hound apology. And it softens me, too. I learned long ago that living with Wyatt means learning to swim comfortably in the wake of his whims. He means so well. I have a vision of him opening the bottle of ASB, practically panting and wagging his tail at the thought of how much it would please me.

I pinch my fingernails into my palms and steel myself. "But it's not *natural*, is it?"

"Tom Dale took it, and now they have three kids. No side effects."

Tom Dale. Wyatt says the name as though there's supposed to be such familiarity there. Tom Dale is a name from his college days, the *legend* famous for streaking in front of Aryes Hall who now makes his living as a plastic surgeon in Raleigh. "Then why isn't it legal here?"

"*Weed* isn't legal here, in half the states."

"Oh, is that next? A weed habit I don't know about?"

He finally turns to me, cupping my kneecaps in his big hands. "You're right, I'm sorry. I should have told you. Should have *asked* you before I went off and ordered it. But I thought maybe if you didn't know—it would be better, somehow. Like maybe I wasn't—" It takes him a while to find the appropriate word. "Malfunctioning."

Damn him for making me feel pity. I can still hear Mom: *How would you like finding out you got no eggs?* I take his hands. "Well, I'm not happy you tried to sneak it on me. But like I wrote, I'm with you. Let's try."

"Really?"

"If you promise never to hide anything like that from me again."

"Of course. I'm sorry. Have I said that yet?"

I giggle. "Three times now. Go ahead. Take one. If you get medical supervision. And if you promise to wean yourself off."

"I will."

I raise my eyebrows. "Promise?"

"Of course." He blinks, then hooks a finger and dabs me on the thigh. "Do I need to bring out the smile vise?"

I giggle. "No, no, it's okay." He opens my legs so he can swim up my body and kiss me. I put a finger between our lips. "No more secrets, okay?"

"No more secrets." He says it with his bedroom voice, that sleepy mumble. The fishhook shape in my spine goes slack as I feel myself give in. We'd dug such a groove of fertility-cycle sex that I forgot how good it can be. He has to stop a few times and change positions, just so he doesn't spend it all in one go. Silly as it is, I like how sexy that makes me in his eyes. We are newlyweds again. I feel new in his hands, that makeup-sex feeling of cheating on each other *with* each other. When we're done, I give one of his pecs a squeeze. Something about him feels new, too.

CHAPTER 5

DAWN

Usually, I'm the first one up, but one day I wake up at my usual six o'clock and see Wyatt's already gone. It's been a month now, and his morning habits have changed. The shower is still hot and dewy. Downstairs, there aren't any dishes in the sink, which means he skipped breakfast. I pull out a cranberry muffin, and as I toss out the wrapper, I see a full page of loose-leaf on top of the rest of the garbage. A note.

$50,000,000.

No elaboration.

I'm used to his random scribblings, his vision boards and positive thinking and goal setting. The only strange thing is that he threw it out.

No time to worry, though: like Wyatt, I am in a rush this morning. After breakfast, I throw on my favorite summer boho dress, the one with the chrysanthemum buds that make my eyes stand out. I have to stand out today. The Perfect Home—my antique store, not the show—has a signing event this morning. That means we have to be ready for the influx of foot traffic. I'm not a fan of book signings, but these are our high-margin days, when people come in for an anecdote and an Instagram snap and leave with a $500 nightstand. I know, pricey, pricey. In my defense, we refurbish the hell out of those nightstands.

Our store is in the cradle of 12 South, the kind of neighborhood where ordinary shops become, ahem, curated boutiques. The Perfect Home sits between two redbrick buildings, one a Draper James and the other a cutesy-hippie joint selling coffee/vintage clothes. We sell vintage décor, I suppose, though a sign in our storefront window blatantly screams AS SEEN ON HOME & LAWN TV.

Outside the entrance, Victoria Weatherly is waiting in sunglasses, holding coffee for two.

"Locked," she says. "When do I get my own key? I'm here often enough."

I take the cup she's extending my way. "You can have mine if you handle this signing for me."

"No deal." She grins. "Caffeine support only."

Victoria leans introvert like I do, which is why it took us a thousand glances before we met each other. We were seniors at Knoxville and living in the same apartment building on Clinch Avenue. One day we found ourselves in the laundry room hoping to score the last orange juice from the vending machine. She let me take it and wouldn't hear otherwise. We got to talking about postcollege life and found out we'd both had early-career breakthroughs; she'd had her first photo shoot with a national polo brand and I had just won a paid internship at HLTV. We'd both beaten out hundreds of people to get where we were. "We should hang out," Vic said while folding her tissue-thin bike shorts. "I think we might conquer the world."

I needed a friend at the time. My best friend in high school had gone to UCLA, and between the culture shock and time difference, our weekly check-ins had gone biannual. And I'd just lost my second roommate in a row. She had to move back home and take a semester off so she could "figure things out." If one roommate did that, it wouldn't be a big deal. Two was a pattern. We never argued, but I was such a homebody, my omnipresence in the living room must have itched them. My most recent roommate saw me watching HLTV one Saturday afternoon and said, "Don't you have, like, a hobby?"

But Victoria never asked those questions. When I told her I wanted to work in TV because half of my favorite memories were of sitting on the couch with my mom, she cooed and called it sweet.

Victoria and I walk in the store, which greets us with its hundred scents. I love how antique stores even smell ancient: lacquer, pine, dust, mahogany, damp soil for the houseplants, sweet marjoram growing in pots. The metallic bite of brass, the musk of old books. And I love all the little magic tricks of times forgotten. Sundials, aurora borealis glass, music from boxes. A row of mirrors lines the checkout counter, and when a customer walks up to it, the mirrors prism them into rainbows of humanity.

That's my favorite half of the store. The other half is all *Perfect Home*. T-shirts and coffee mugs and key chains and floral-vase pairings and essential oils with trademarked logos.

What can I say? Stores need money.

Kelly Maynard, the shop's official manager, laid out everything for me last night: a long table, space for a line, and an alarmingly lifelike cardboard cutout of yours truly. On the whole, I think the cutout looks good, if a little uncanny valley. Fake smile, linebacker shoulders (did that dress have shoulder pads?), and photoshopped skin, scraped of all pores.

We need another social media bump, so I hand Victoria my

phone and pose. I put a hand on my own beefy cardboard shoulder, buddy-buddy. She snaps the pic. My self-flattering caption: *Just met this babe at the Perfect Home book signing on 2303 12th Avenue South. She's so much nicer in person!*

"You got my good side," I say as I post it.

"You're full of good sides."

Sweet of her. A few years back, she ran for Miss Tennessee and placed fourth. I still remember running flash cards with her like we were in high school, except instead of quizzing her on words like *abstruse* and *recalcitrant*, I had to ask trick questions in search of humility: *What do you like most about yourself?* The experience left her sensitive to self-deprecation in others.

The door chimes and in walks Kelly: fifty-odd years old, antique lover, coffee bringer. My first hire for the store, and still my best. "Hey, y'all. You see that protest up the street?"

We all go to the window. Sure enough, there's a growing swarm of protesters at the intersection south of us. One of them even brought one of those drums you can sling over your chest. Not much of a police presence yet, though I make out one squad car in the distance. The officer leans over an open door and whispers something into the talkie on his cuff.

"Woulda texted you," Kelly says, "except I just heard. There's a protest like this in Memphis, too."

Victoria sucks her teeth. "I hope they're just passing through."

"Should we cancel?" I ask. "We don't want to be insensitive. What's it about?"

"I'm working on finding that out," Kelly says. "I was thinking we might cancel it anyway, just to be safe."

I snap my fingers. "Shoot. I just posted about it. With the cutout and everything. It's already out there."

"Maybe the protest will move on," Victoria says.

Wyatt doesn't answer his phone, so I place a call to Wyatt's PR woman—ostensibly my PR woman, too, though I never call her on my own—and the long groans I hear on the other end suggest she's already having a day full of these unpleasant coincidences. She makes me hold, and then by the time she picks up again and asks if there's a line out front of the antique store, I look, and there is.

"Then don't cancel," she tells me. "We can post later and make it clear you learned about the protests after the fact."

We take our spots, Kelly at the doors, me and Victoria behind the table with Sharpies of every color. Victoria's never turned down an opportunity to support me at these public events, and besides, between her Miss Chattanooga looks and the black sheath dresses she wears, people always assume she's some sort of high-powered publicist.

Maybe she's a version of that. From the day we first met, Victoria has been in my corner. She came from money and shared everything with a light touch. Back in college, when I couldn't find a new roommate in time to make rent, she was the first person to offer me a roof. A month later, my '98 Honda Civic finally lost its lifelong battle with the check-engine light, so she sold me her old BMW 3 Series at a discount. ("I was thinking of leveling up anyway.") She worked part-time at her dad's ad agency and the rest of her time building herself up as a model/influencer. Lots of gym time, lots of plain chicken-and-rice, lots of fretting over sodium content. She didn't have a traditional job, but she still had late, sigh-ridden days, always collapsing on the sofa at 8:00 p.m. for a good stare at the ceiling. That became our hangout time. One night, I told her how much her work ethic was rubbing off on me and her face went limp. I realized she might have thought I was making fun of her, but then her cheeks crinkled and she whispered that I was the only person in her life who saw how hard she was trying. We lived together for two years, until I was full-time at the network and finally had the pay stubs to get myself a condo. And in those two years, Victoria never once moved back home so she could "figure things out." We both cried heaps on moving day. They were all good tears. Maybe we hadn't yet conquered the world, but that felt like a victory.

"Door opening," Kelly announces, having learned to warn me when people are coming. "Look out below."

Nine o'clock sharp and we begin the parade of micro-interactions, which are supposed to feel authentic but sometimes feel too pre-packaged and bite-sized to be completely wholesome. But soon I relax, remembering that my fans—few as they are—aren't quite as rabid as Wyatt's. The kinds of people who go out of their way to meet Dawn Decker in an antique shop on a weekday morning are exactly the friendlies you'd hope they'd be. A grandma with her granddaughter who got a half day from school. A saucy lady who loves the way I "balance" Wyatt. A man getting a book autographed for his wife's birthday. A woman in a scrub cap who almost brings me to tears because bingeing *The Perfect Home* got her through che-motherapy. A woman's nearsighted daughter who's so nervous she can barely speak, but when she does, she says *please* and *thank-a-yew* in the sweetest Georgia-peach drawl I've ever heard.

Next up is a heavyset woman walking with a cane and work-ing her lips like she has ill-fitting dentures. Our chitchat starts well enough. As I'm signing the inside jacket of her book, she mutters, "You give me hope."

"Thank you," I say.

Victoria can't resist. "Hope? How so?"

"Regular ladies." The woman points a finger between herself and me, heart to heart. "That we can have it all, too."

I've been famous long enough to let this kind of comment slide. I'm kind of plain—big deal. Vanilla is a spice, too. And there's nothing I can do to ease the everlasting shock that I, one of the "regular ladies," snared a conventionally attractive man like Wyatt Decker. If Wyatt had married Victoria, at least the visuals would add up. But I'm comfortable with that. I can look in the mirror and smile at myself. I wish people like this woman could, too. I wish they knew how unkind they were being to both of us.

"What do you mean?" Victoria asks the woman.

"That women like us can have men out of our league."

"That's rude," Victoria says. I try to kick her, but my foot whiffs and knocks into a table leg. "What are you saying? Dawn Decker, TV star, isn't beautiful? Do you go around to book signings looking for celebrities to insult? She was nothing but nice to you."

The woman's froggy mouth pops open. She looks honestly taken aback. "I just meant—with Wyatt—I don't know—"

"Yeah, you don't know. You should think before you speak."

"I'm sorry," I tell the woman. "You know what? If you give me your address, I can have Wyatt sign it, too, and we'll mail it to you."

But this doesn't even register with her. Her face is darkening, locked on Victoria with a look in her eyes like she is looking at every beautiful woman who has ever told her off. "This is how y'all treat your fans?"

"You're not *my* fan," Victoria says.

"That's for damn sure."

I feel Kelly's presence at my side, spring-loaded and ready to pounce. I give her a tap on the wrist to let her know I'll handle it. "C'mon, Vic—I know what she was saying. It's not that bad. Ma'am, why don't I give you a gift card to enjoy the store?"

"Gift card?" Victoria scoffs. "*She* should apologize."

There is a beat of silence as I stare at the *regular lady* and she stares at me, perhaps because it's registering with each of us that Victoria is in the right.

"Y'all just trash TV anyway," the woman says. "Famous 'causa your husband." Then, clutching her book in one hand, she cane-waddles her way out the front door muttering something about "celebrities."

I know what she's going home to do. Despite my trying to fix everything, despite the promise of a gift certificate, I can't buy my way out of it. The woman will go online and tell the world what a bad experience she had meeting Dawn Decker. I can almost feel Wyatt's hand on my shoulder, reminding me how to deal with the inevitable bad apples that roll toward celebrities. *Patience,* he'd preach. *Infinite patience.*

A few shutter sounds snap. People are taking photos. There's a sharp pain in my jaw as I realize I've been grinding my teeth. With my luck, that's all the crowd will remember: sourpuss Dawn, the acid to Wyatt's base.

The line dwindles by lunchtime. Victoria and I take the helm behind the counter while Kelly goes out for her break. With the protests still noisy outside, our foot traffic has slowed to a trickle. I haven't made a sale in half an hour. Victoria finds an antique gondola chair and plants her face on her fist, scrolling through her phone.

I'm eyeing the protests down the street. The crowd has gotten rambunctious. Another drum set has joined in with the original, turning the heartbeat of the music irregular. On the far end, three new police cars have parked, and the officers have formed a nervous semicircle with each other, all of them shifting their weight.

"Maybe I'll text Kelly we're doing a half day," I say. "What if this becomes a riot? We don't have anything to board this place up."

"Wyatt's sure safe enough," Victoria says.

"What?"

"On Instagram. Look." She holds her phone out. I see Wyatt at the eighteenth green on some golf course, posing with three other khakied men. "I recognize two of them. But this old guy must not be on Insta, he's not tagged."

"Stop stalking Wyatt," I tease. "You follow him more closely than I do."

"Just checking he's not out with some . . . I don't know, hussy. Did he tell you he was out golfing?"

Squinting, I come around for another look. I can't tell if I recognize the untagged man. He's at least seventy years old, but there's a polish to him that shaves off a few years. He wears a fitted polo button-down showing his still-taut waist, and his thinning white hair is buzzed down to a cadet's cut. The wrist facing the camera has an oversized watch that could be worth as much as this store. I think of the note Wyatt left himself.

$50,000,000.

"I'll ask him about it," I say.

"He didn't tell you he was golfing?"

"No. He woke up before I did. He used to be such a drag to get out of bed." Not wanting to pull the conversational thread that leads to my husband's experimental medication, I turn away.

A loud crash sends a wave of screams from the crowd, and

Victoria jumps. I grab the keys from the counter. "That's it. We should lock up and get out of here."

"Good idea."

I wish I could board up the windows, but there's nothing here for that. The insurance value of the store is astronomical anyway, but somehow, as Victoria and I leave and lock the front door, it's not a reassuring thought.

The air is sweltering outside, gone thick with music and chanting. "Where'd you park?" I shout at Victoria.

"Down there."

But I can't see her car. She's pointing through the crowd.

"I'll walk you through," I say.

We huddle together like we're about to trudge through rain. There's a crack, then a sizzling. I hear people shout. "Tear gas!" someone screams, and I hear more calls of "Tear gas, tear gas" shuddering through before the crowd turns suddenly, like a startled school of fish, freezing Victoria and me in place as people run past. Sirens go off. Car engines kick to life. Police whistles sting the air. Someone stumbles into me, twisting me around, and I no longer have a sense of where I am, where Victoria is, where the grid of streets should point me.

"Dawn!" I hear, and it can only be Victoria's voice, but I can't see her. My eyes are already bleary from the gas that's wafted this way.

"I'm coming!"

"Dawn, move!"

My feet are kicking asphalt. Too late, I realize I'm in the street. Then there's a sound of thunder, or maybe an engine bearing down. I can't possibly know because I see nothing at all before it hits me.

CHAPTER 6

WYATT

"Mr. Decker." The woman's voice is jerky and robotic. "You are listed as Dawn Decker's emergency contact. This call is to inform you she's here at Vanderbilt University Medical Center."

"What? What's wrong?"

It cuts out. Hospitals don't place automated calls, do they? Maybe it's the service. I'm a Russian doll here: inside a stall inside a public bathroom inside a restroom area inside a clubhouse. I pull my pants up, buckle up, and race out of all four. I was the last one here, so there's no one to say goodbye to—I just load up the truck and set the GPS.

All sorts of possibilities swim through my head. They all feel equally possible, no matter how wild. Car accident. Brain aneurysm. Gunshot wound. Spontaneous combustion. I don't know—it could happen.

I blow through the lobby doors so fast I almost knock someone from their wheelchair. It's a labyrinth of lobby desks and elevators to the wrong floors until I find Dawn is stable and resting on the third floor. Victoria sees me first and leaves to get coffee. I'm grateful for the mercy of privacy.

"Babe," I say. I throw my arms around her, bury my head into her pillow.

"I'm okay."

She does look okay. Better than that—she's still dolled up from the book signing that morning, her cheeks red with blush, her eyes clear and gingerbread brown. It's such a startling sight I have to look her over twice, inspecting.

"My hip." Dawn turns over and pulls up the gown. It's less one bruise than a system of bruises, layered with yellows and purples and reds, and it runs from her thigh to the side of her stomach.

I groan and saddle myself at the edge of the bed. "What happened?"

"I texted you about that protest. It was chaos. Somehow, I ended up in the street, and I got caught in the crowd and someone ended up kicking me in the side. Good news is they said no internal bleeding."

"Did they catch the guy?"

"It was crowded. No one got a good look."

"So, what, is your hip broken? Did you have an X-ray?"

Her lips pull in, bracing for something important, or maybe waiting for the puzzle pieces to click into place. I can only stare.

"Yeah, about that," she says. "I'm pregnant."

"What?"

"We're going to have a baby."

It still doesn't register. "But . . . but your hip—"

"They make sure you're not pregnant before doing an X-ray. I said no, but they couldn't take my word for it, so they ran a test and . . . ding ding ding. I wasn't even that late yet. I've been later before." She pats her stomach with the monitor clip on her pinkie, which makes her hands look small and fragile. "Little Dawn Junior."

My chin shivers. I can barely speak. I always thought I'd be one of those perfect husbands who hugged his wife as soon as he heard the news, scooping her up like she told me she'd won the lottery. Turns out I'm a hot, blubbering mess. I can feel the veins seizing all over my face, that ugly-cry look men get when they don't want anyone to see. I can't help it. The sore hole in my manhood—the treadmill feeling of chasing the top page of Modern People every morning on the exercise bike—is filling up.

Dawn is pregnant. I have crossed the starting line.

I am no longer malfunctioning.

Dawn lowers her eyes at me. "Hey, honey. I was just kidding about Dawn Junior."

I finally hug her. It's almost a strangling grip, tight around her neck, because I don't want to lift her body from the pillow and send some shard of hip bone into my unborn child. I lean back and wipe my face off, finally able to speak. "The hospital's Vanderbilt University."

"I know." She cringes. "We'll make sure Modern People leaves that part out."

"Then your hip—is there any danger with the baby—"

"Bone bruise. I have to keep off it awhile, but I don't need surgery."

I pull up a piece of her gown again. Whatever hit her, it's left a sharp, wine-colored welt under her hip bone.

"What the hell happened at the store?"

She tells me about the protest and Victoria's car on the wrong side of the crowd and the tear gas that went up just as they were moving through.

"What was the protest about?" I ask.

"I texted you."

"I know. I'm sorry—I was on the golf course all day." She gives me a look, so I add, "Babycakes, you know it's bad form if I'm out with guys and I constantly look at my phone."

"Kelly was looking into it. I don't know anything yet. We'd been doing the signing all morning. But the police had their eyes on it, more people showed up, which meant more police—and it just got out of hand."

"Well, we'll need a story."

"A what?"

"We can't tell people you were injured during a protest," I say. Dawn looks taken aback, but it's true. "Our audience is fifty-five, forty-five. Republican-Democrat. Most people watch our show to get *away* from politics. We'd be cutting the audience in half overnight."

"But I wasn't even part of the protest. I was walking Vic to her car."

"We can figure it out later." Conscious of all the legitimate medical professionals in this building, I lower my voice. "The ASB only took a few weeks."

"I know. Potent. You'll have to wean off slowly now. Some people online said it's dangerous if you don't wean over several months."

"Of course. I'll take another pill tomorrow." Then a strange thought occurs to me, taboo and unutterable. For some reason, I utter it. "You know . . . you won't be able to drink for nine months."

"No different than the last eight years."

"You're right, you're right. Forget I mentioned it."

But she winces and turns away. The words haven't placated her. "Do you not think I'm going to be a good mom? God—what if I'm not?"

Me and my big dumb mouth—I've awakened her giant inner worrier. I turn her chin to me. "Only good parents worry about being bad parents."

"What do the bad parents do?"

"Hard drugs."

A chirpy sound sings out of her chest, that perfect laugh of hers, the one I haven't heard since we got the news about my sperm. I forgot what a good audience she is.

"Let's get me out of here," she says. "Before anyone finds out we ever had anything to do with Vanderbilt."

Later that day, I visit Long Grove Health to tell Momma Harlene we're pregnant, and she claps with her big chicken-wing arms. "Hoo, baby! Isn't this a moment? I should come. I should visit my baby. Oh—listen to me, calling Dawn my *baby*. Soon as you got yourself a baby, you aren't the baby anymore." She pushes herself forward. "New baby's comin' to visit, and so is Momma Harlene!"

Then she's wrestling with her La-Z-Boy, groaning to her feet, and I can tell by the way her legs are quaking it's a match she's going to lose.

"Dawn's got some resting to do." I press her down by the shoulders. "I'll tell her to FaceTime you."

Her mouth twists, the way Dawn's does when she hears something she doesn't like. "You mean I'm not gonna see her tonight?"

"You know Dawn. Her favorite thing in the world is takin' the night off." I bite down, conscious of dropping my *g*. Momma Harlene has a way of wringing every ounce of Tennessee out of people.

"Oh, I know it. She's prolly beat."

"I'm sorry. I'm going to get her to bed, then I gotta get to a meeting downtown, so there will be no one to take you home. Tomorrow morning, though. I'll drive you there and back."

"Her hip's that bad, huh?"

"Nothing's broken. But you should see it, all swollen up. Doctors say she has to rest quite a while. Plus, with the baby."

"Oh, course." The laugh lines at her eyes settle. "*The baby*. Listen to us! There's four of us now. Congrats, you big lug."

"Thanks, Momma. Is there anyone else we should tell? Maybe Dawn's dad?"

She blows a raspberry. "Sure. If y'all can find him, be my guest. Put out an APB on all the world's gutters."

"Aunts? Great-aunts?"

"Wyatt." Harlene tugs me by the shirt collar, and it's surprising how much of her big squishy body is muscle. I'm so close to her face I can smell the cinnamon of her Big Red. "Your heart's in the right place, but I always told y'all. There ain't nobody else worth tellin'. Growin' up, it was just Dawn and me in this world. She's all I had. With you and now this baby, that world's grown to four. You've given her a great life. You've been my perfect son-in-law, and that's not flattery, that's facts. You're kind to me. You gave me this place. But so help me, I will gut you like a tuna if you ever leave Dawn with this child like her dad did me. You hear?"

Her fingers are shaking under my collar and her breaths are staccato. It strikes me that I've never seen her cry. And looking at her with her spongy lips and the half-crackled makeup she worked so hard to apply, I'm certain I don't want to.

"Look at me, Momma." Pulling her hands down as gently as I can, I can feel the diesel drumbeat of her pulse. "I hear you. And I'm not going anywhere. You want to know what I was before Dawn?

Nothin'. A man out of a bad marriage who ate his dinners alone. Then I met her and everything changed. When we offered to pay for this place, do you remember you said no? You said you were putting your foot down."

"Y'all overruled me. You were the ones payin', and you overruled."

"Because I'll always do right by her. And by you."

"Oh, I'm sorry, Wyatt. Don't listen to me." Her leathery eyelids shut, sending her miles away. "You shaved your head when I got my first of them drips. I told you and Dawn not to, and Dawn listened 'cause that's how I raised her. But then you went off and did it anyway."

"I looked like Mr. Clean. HLTV was livid until they found out why I did it."

"Them corporate bastards. But I remember. I said to myself, 'Harlene, don't you ever forget what kind of boy your Wyatt is.'" She sniffs, chuckles, wipes a tear before it can bleed into the careful swoosh of her eyeliner. "All right now. Get. Keep Dawn comfy. When I'm not there, you're the one who's gonna have to take care of both my babies."

With *visit Momma Harlene* ticked off my checklist, I head outside and climb back into my F-150. My hands are hot with blood, the same rush I get when I meet fans. Momma Harlene: the nickname took some getting used to. But it grows on you as fast as she does. She's always been a good audience, which is my favorite trait in a person. There's something charming about being easy to charm.

At home, Dawn is conked out in bed. A pregnancy paperback that she bought ages ago lies spread-eagle on her breasts. I start disrobing and hear her take a heavy sniff, stirring. "Where's Mom?"

"I told her I'd drive her over tomorrow morning. Figured you'd be too tired."

"It's these pregnant-lady pain pills. They wipe me out."

"We're going to have to reschedule so many *Perfect Home* shoots. But it's going to be a great season."

She makes a dry groan, doesn't even open her eyes. "Yes. Good timing, ace. Let's talk about work."

"Don't mind me. Get some rest, babycakes."

By the time I'm down to a T-shirt and boxers, she's snoring again. I pull the book off her and replace it with the duvet. She takes it under her arms, rolling away into dreamland. I read the front cover. *The Pregnancy Encyclopedia.* The first half is marked up and dog-eared, with notes in the margins—*show this part to Wyatt,* she wrote, next to a section about how women should listen to all their eccentric pregnancy cravings. Did she do all this work just tonight? Of course. She was the straight A student at Tennessee. I'd been happy with my C average. Still, I envy how quickly Dawn can swallow a book, how she only needs to read a fact once to remember it forever.

As I set the book on the nightstand, I see her gratitude journal is still open. Sacred territory. At first I flip it shut, but there's a ribbon that keeps her place. I reopen it. It's a strange feeling running my fingertips down the white margins, the paper so thick it's almost fleshy. It reminds me of the first time my fingers ever felt the heat under a girl's skirt.

I'm grateful there is a healthy baby growing inside me, she started today's entry. *I'm grateful Wyatt can stop the ASB now.*

Then, in smaller letters, the bottom of the page reads:

Mostly, I'm grateful it's over.

I know right away what this means. I've been too rough. I'd gotten so used to Dawn's attacking me every time her fertility app went off that I'd pop half a chub every time her phone dinged, fertility app or not. A week into the ASB, she asked me how I felt. I told her the volume knob of my life had gone up. Second puberty. Morning wood every day. Hair growth in weird places—I've started shaving my shoulders. When we had sex, I didn't feel like the idle sperm donor anymore. I felt like a man, a real man, the man I was at Tennessee, hopped up with testosterone and yearning to fill the voids of the world.

Within a few weeks, I remembered what I'd found so attractive about Dawn. It was the young look in her eyes. Dawn lacks the poker face of older women, the hardness of skin that comes from lifetimes of cynicism and Botox. The last few weeks with Dawn have reminded me of a first date, that electric buzz of possibility hanging in the air. Maybe I bite too hard now—biting is new, but it feels right—but isn't it better than what we had the last few years?

If you're married, you'll know what I mean. It doesn't matter if a man marries Helen of Troy—eventually, it goes stale. The Spartans should have just waited out the Trojans. Helen's charm would have worn off on Paris. A few years of Helen yelling out reminders from the toilet: *Don't forget to wear the yellow tunic, I put it out for you.* A few years of Helen going *ahhhh* after every sip of wine. Mumbling in crowds. Leaving the front door open. Not drying off after the shower, leaving the bathroom floor a safety hazard.

Not that I have any regrets.

But whenever I bring any of this up with Janie or any of the thousand acquaintances from HLTV, I can feel them straining not to roll their eyes. You're not supposed to complain when you have a pretty wife, a giant house in Belle Meade, and make a seven-figure salary. *What's the big deal, Wyatt? Snap out of it. Some people get tongue cancer and have to eat through a straw. Your big struggle in life is Dawn chewing with her mouth open.* Fair enough.

We'd started out so well, Dawn and I. Walking Mallory Square on our honeymoon in Key West, I got to be the one who taught her about the Gulf Stream, and she got that freshman-student look, eyes narrowing, chin dipping, an eyebrow twitching. *Dawn.* Such an apt name. Everything was a bright new morning in her eyes. The memory might as well be a photograph: she wore her cherry sundress, which clung to her like water. Her flesh simmered in the pink lights, the shadows showing everything—pinpricks of sweat from the briny heat, the white tufts of body hair, the goose bumps from the breezes. She squeezed my hand and told me I was hot when talking geography. *You're* hot, I said dumbly. Another squeeze of the hand. Why don't we go back to the hotel? she asked. This was long before the pregnancy troubles, before I ever felt like a sperm donor. Her hands felt so small in mine. I liked my wife, then. I liked my wife a lot.

Now, with the pregnancy, life will return to how it was before the ASB. The volume knob of my world will slowly twist back into place. Something in me will mourn that.

My phone twitches in my pocket. Dawn stirs. "Who's that, babe?"

I look at the number flashing on my screen. "Tom Dale."

"Mmm. Tell him hi."

"He's in town. I think I need to go see him." I eye the text again and look back at Dawn to explain, but it doesn't matter. She's already out.

Good.

• • •

I throw on a decent chambray and rush down the stairs, feeling my blood pressure kick up, the humming in my veins. The address in my inbox brings me downtown and into the Gulch, the urban sinew connecting Nashville's business district with Music Row. Everything here sells the most expensive version of food—think "cacao shops" instead of chocolate—and the condos are nouveau riche, all sheer glass and square balconies. I pull into a covered garage and disappear into a douchebag sea of European cars.

Tom Dale. The number of times I've used Tom Dale's name this way—for impromptu Predators games, weekend trips in North Carolina—Dawn would hate him on sight.

The eighth floor is the penthouse here, so I press the number in the elevator and watch the digits ding each level. Something feels strange in my jeans. I rifle through a back pocket and pull out the bottle of ASB. Huh. I'd taken to carrying it on me, sure, but I'd forgotten I'd left it in these pants.

The doors open to the penthouse, hugging me with the scent of candle smoke. I buzz in through a second set of doors and find Victoria pouring wine in the kitchen.

I circle around her and mouth the nape of her neck until she hums and forgets about the wine. Fuck the wine. I get more drunk on her. I love how she smells—gardenias and the salt of skin.

Tom Dale is in North Carolina, just as he always is. At least I assume he is. To be honest, I haven't spoken to Tom Dale in about a year.

I have my hand halfway up Victoria's blouse when she surfaces and loosens my grip, gently, the way women slide out of nightgowns. "Tell me Dawn's all right," she says.

"Dawn's all right."

"No, I mean, really. How is she? And the baby?"

I draw a breath and hold it. It would be a mistake to sigh and let her see how hard it is to tap my brakes. "They're both good. Doctor said it's a bone bruise. Not as serious as a fracture. She'll have to stay off her feet a few days."

Victoria swallows, a light shake in her swanny neck. I've never seen her in her new apartment. The dusky light paints all the hollows of her face. She is headshot gorgeous, with a pouty bottom lip and thin, slicing eyes. She leans against the kitchen island and crosses her arms. I mirror the gesture against her countertop.

"You said a bone bruise?"

"Vic, she's fine. Really."

"And with a baby now—" She looks up at a skylight window. I follow her eyes. It's already dark outside, so there's nothing to see but our bright reflections, the bent angle of our figures from the waist down. Her feet have turned slightly away. I angle my toes to match.

"I know," I whisper. I'm guessing. I don't know. "It feels strange now, doesn't it?"

"You wanna go home, maybe? Make sure Dawn's okay?"

"What exactly happened this morning?"

Victoria recounts a story at the book signing: an old woman came in and called Dawn plain. Victoria never says it exactly, but she bends at the stomach when she feels guilty, cradling inward as if to warm the spot where her guts went cold. That's the pleasure of women like Victoria: defrosting the ice she shows the world. A woman like this could be anywhere right now, collecting $15 drinks from hopeless men who have no other idea how to win her over. Instead she's with me. No one else.

"I felt bad for Dawn," she says. "She looked so pretty, you know? And with one comment, that one woman took it all away." She chews her lip. "Kinda feels like I'm doing the same thing."

There it is. Gently, I clasp her wrist and pull it free, closing the distance between us and untangling the knot she's made of herself. "You're such a good person. You're not even thinking of yourself. But remember when I said we're not doing this *to* Dawn?"

A stiff nod.

"This stuff happens all the time," I say. "People marry the wrong people, they get divorced, they marry the right ones. I was married before Dawn. Think she feels any guilt about it?"

A slow headshake.

"Imagine if I'd met you before I met Dawn. You'd be the one on the show, doing the book signings. God knows you're meant for fame. It's just a timing thing—we'll sort it out. You'll be in the next season so our fans can get to know you, and we'll go from there. Dawn will probably be relieved you're her ticket out of this thing. You saw it today: she doesn't love being famous. Not like you would."

"But there's nothing I could have without stealing it from Dawn first. I still love Dawn."

"So do I. I love Dawn as a . . ." Concept? Friend? Both seem too cruel, so I trail off. "But I need you with me. These women wouldn't be insulting Dawn to her face if it had been you first. The public would eat you up."

"That's true." Her chest puffs.

That's what always wins me Victoria: reminding her she's been working her whole life for something Dawn can only half enjoy.

"Once you accept that you're doing her a favor," I say, "you'll see how loyal you've been." My hand slips into the silk curtain of her hair, cradling her neck as if her loyalty is what turns me on, her generosity of spirit. What I really like is the hot mint of her breath. She dizzies me, and dizzying me dizzies her. "We're not doing this *to* Dawn. We're doing it for . . ."

. . . and we're lost in each other again. Soon we're in the bedroom and I toss her, squealing and happy, and drape her long body with mine, smothering out the world.

Stuttering between our breaths, she says, "Do you have a condom—"

"No."

"You got—Dawn pregnant—"

"Fine."

I head to the bathroom and pull out an orange bottle. ANG-STROM SUPPLEMENT-B.

Once I'm sure Victoria is watching, I turn the bottle over the toilet, and the little white pips raindrop into the bowl. They fizzle slightly. Technically, I was supposed to wean off it, but a former Miss Chattanooga is waiting in bed. I need to make a show of my infertility.

"There," I announce. "I didn't take this morning's. I'm as good as sterile again."

"It's the same as a condom, right? Like, medically?"

I have no earthly idea, but the tone in her voice asks for only one response.

"Absolutely."

It's stupid, I know. It's a long rap sheet: Wyatt Decker is a cheater; a cheater with a pregnant wife; a cheater with his pregnant wife's best friend; a cheater who hates condoms; a cheater, cheater, cheater. My brand would go down in flames if word got out. But I can't help myself. There has always been something rudderless about me. Ask me about my career, and I'll list my exact goals: $50 million in net worth by the time I'm forty-five. But ask me about anything else and I might as well be a kid. My parents are dead. I don't have an older brother or sister to slap me over the head with wisdom. If I'm not at a book signing or on camera, I never know what to do with my hands. I wasn't sure whom to marry. I love Dawn, I do, but sometimes I watch her slurping ice cream and zoning out to *Love Is Blind* and hate the comatose routine of our off-camera lives. Most often I wish we were filming instead.

On our show, the electricians always lecture me about grounding. The electrons need somewhere to go, to disperse into equilibrium inside the house, and I remember thinking once, I get it. If we're not talking about *The Perfect Home*, I become a loose wire, all flailing energy. I need grounding, too.

"You coming?" Victoria calls. On the bed, resting on her elbows with her back arched, she leans to one side and unknots her hair with a finger twirl. A bolt of pleasure surges through me. Maybe that's all the grounding I need. She's ready for me again, despite the protests, despite her concern for Dawn—the ice queen has gone melted and wet. I did that. No one else.

"Yes," I say. I'm coming real soon.

Then I flush.

Part Two

EVIL COLORS

CHAPTER 7

DAWN

One year later

Twins!

Our reaction comes in three stages of punctuation. OhmyGodOhmyGodOhmyGod! Then: Oh, my God. And finally:

Oh. My God . . .

But, ready or not, there's no recorking this wine bottle. World, meet Wyatt Junior (*Junior* only, we decide early on, to avoid confusion) and Harlene Mae Decker. You'll know Junior for his pallid, fleshy cheeks, his chubby Popeye arms, the blue veins in his temples. Then there's Harlene and her strands of rosy-colored hair, so thick and twisty that in my postlabor delirium, I asked who had put a bow on her. Our house has two Harlenes now, so we always slap the middle name on the baby and dub her Harlene Mae.

After a false positive with Junior's cystic fibrosis screening, the hospital sent us home. With twins, it felt like nurses weren't sending us home so much as cutting bait. *Get the hell out of here. And good luck with all that ruckus.* Wyatt and I had no idea how to be parents, so we went overboard. A new security system. Drawer locks.

Enough diapers to stock a bomb shelter for three years. Wyatt has become half a prepper, loading the basement with canned food and toiletries. He's been going down YouTube rabbit holes lately, so he claimed he had a reason for everything. An envelope of $10,000 in cash: worried about bank runs. A Dopp kit full of wet wipes and floss: worried about bugging out of Nashville when the zombies come.

One day, he brings in his usual contractors and films a segment of *Perfect Home*, childproofing any corner in our house that isn't soft and round. The segment makes a joke out of it: look how much Wyatt loves his children, ha-ha, isn't he ca-raaaa-zeee?

Janie makes quick work of it all, then sweeps me up in it, tugging me by the sleeve and dragging our main camera operator to shoot a talking head segment in the kitchen. I can tell from the way he's framing me that the shot will reveal me down to my waist.

I groan. "Can you cut a different frame? I look awful."

"You're glowing," Janie says, though she says it into her phone screen without looking up. "We just need one of those classic Dawn Decker sassy-pants comments. Like maybe 'Wyatt is the type of guy to blow out birthday candles with a firehose.'"

"Can you just do my face?"

"Zoomed in? That'll look weird. Why? What's wrong?"

I'm already wearing a fisherman's sweater to hide the half-filled water balloons I'm packing underneath. Every book said the feeding would make me bigger and heavier there, and I suppose that's true, but gravity has just as much a say as Mother Nature. And we still haven't filmed me when I walk. My hip was supposed to be a bone bruise, but now they're not so sure, and giving birth to twins didn't help. Now I waddle around like one of my legs is longer than the other. So, so sexy.

I'm not going to get into the specifics with Janie. "I'm the Liberty Bell," I say. "Both size and shape."

"Perfect. Say that. Women love that. You'll make them feel better about themselves."

Really? I'm make-all-womankind-feel-better-about-their-weight big? A jolt of pride stiffens my spine. Quite the miraculous body I have. It can bear twins *and* the weight of Middle America's self-esteem.

So I say the line for the show, just to wrap filming, to get back to my family. Nothing will bring me down, not even Janie with her comments, not even the thought that Wyatt's five million followers on Instagram will be guessing my postpartum weight. No, Gladys_Goolsby17, the number does not start with a *two*. But even if it did, so what? I am a mother now. Better than that, I am a double mother. Sometimes I feather Harlene Mae's cheek with the back of a finger, just for the pleasure of knowing she is real. Momma Harlene used to tell me my father loved cash so much, she sometimes caught him in the kitchen just sitting there smelling dollar bills crisp from the bank. I do the same with my kids. I sniff them. Harlene is a delicious combination of talcum and sweat. Junior has notes of pine. Wyatt says I'm overthinking it, that babies smell like nothing, certainly not fresh wood, and he thinks I'm picking up the baby soap we use. But I know it comes from Junior. He is perfect and piney.

One perk to filming *Perfect Home* episodes in our real house is we get to keep the upgrades we make. It isn't always staged; Wyatt's contractors really did install a security system. It came with a new tablet so we can monitor the twins while we watch the new season of *Love Is Blind* on the living room sofa. Unfortunately, Wyatt is so nervous about newborns, he keeps making me pause it so he can go check on them.

"Then what was the point of the security camera?" I ask.

"Just one more time."

The third time he does this, I turn to Momma Harlene, still on her favorite La-Z-Boy, which we brought over from Long Grove Health when she moved in, and give her a grumble. "I'm a new parent, too, and even I know not to interrupt a sleeping baby."

She sucks in a tight breath. "Did the tall one end up dumpin' that guy? He's a mama's boy. All wrong for her."

"I paused it, Mom."

Her eyes are still closed. "Mmm. Don't start it back up without me."

"We won't. Go to sleep if you're tired."

This elicits no argument from Momma Harlene, who now sleeps most of the day. Her oncologist said that was good: the restorative power of sleep and all that. But now she dozes in big, heavy chunks. I know because I've been home on maternity leave, and it's been like old times, me and Momma Harlene in front of the TV. Except now instead of running out of steam at 9:00 p.m. sharp, she'll conk out any time there's been three minutes without an explosion. I used to shake her awake when it was Final Jeopardy! or Tribal Council. But since I brought the twins home and Momma Harlene first got to rub cheeks with her own grandbabies, she sleeps so happily I don't have the nerve to wake her up. Even for the best parts.

Wyatt's laptop gives a wake-up ping on the dining room table. I turn to see he's already sitting there with his glasses on. "You don't have to pause for me," he says. "I'm gonna do some work."

"Hon, it's the finale."

He doesn't look up. "You like that show more than I do."

Groaning, I walk to the dining table and rub a hand across the collar of his Vols sweatshirt, then let go. Lately, he's gotten sensitive about where I touch him, cringing out of back rubs and all my unconscious finger-dragging. I never knew how much I touched him until a few months back when he said he'd finished weaning off the ASB. It's made him so irritable, I don't push the issue. He has two laptops set up: one with the grayed night-vision feed of the twins' room. One with Twitter open, which takes all his attention.

More specifically, the profile of Kat Cameron.

Her Twitter icon is from a photo shoot of her autobiography cover. The crisp shirt is an island of white against a gray background, her cheek strategically placed in her palm for just the right level of empathy for the viewer. She looks good for sixty or so. Her dark skin is still smooth, her tawny eyes still bright and vital. If she's had work done, it hasn't left her with the taped-back, frozen-forehead look. *Journalist,* her bio reads. *Cohost of* Early Bird *on NBC, founder of Cameron Media. Mother.* The last part seems pasted on, almost an afterthought.

Cameron Media. I've learned through the osmosis of knowing Wyatt that Cameron Media is the primary name in a recent bid to buy out Modern People.

"Doing a little light stalking?" I ask.

Wyatt just gives me a token laugh, a burst of the nostrils.

"Seriously," I say. "Not Modern People again."

"Look at this. The top feature this month. Miguel Muñoz and Sara Raimes."

"Are they dating again? It's hard to imagine people still care."

"Exactly," he says. "So why can't it be us?"

"Because of the on-again, off-again thing. Because they're . . . I don't know. Spicy."

"We're spicy."

"Sure," I say. "Vanilla is a spice. Babe, we have the number one show on basic cable. You're worried about this random website? Do you worry about what they're saying on *Taste of Home*, too?"

He reels back, a sigh revealing his inner monologue: he's going to have to explain everything to his media-blind wife. "So obviously you know who Kat Cameron is. But I've already tried having our people blitz her people, and no dice. She probably gets a million requests a day. People like Kat Cameron, they have handlers who filter out the noise. And as of right now, we're noise. To her, basic-cable reality TV is a . . . backwater." He clicks to her Following page. "But this is different. It's right here in plain sight."

"What is?"

"The network effect. Her Twitter feed. The people she follows, listens to. If I can get one of *them* to talk about the twins—" He does a chef's kiss with his fingertips, giving them more affection than he's given me for the last several months. "Look at this. The offices of Modern People are at One World Trade. The features editor is *also* the social editor at the *New York Ledger*. The media types, they're all in New York. New York parties, New York Twitter accounts. Nashville is an afterthought. But she retweets the *New York Ledger* every week or so, when she sees it's something from this same editor. She must know him. Do you see that? That's how we get through the noise. We get the *Ledger*, we get Modern People, then we get Kat Cameron, too. Once Kat Cameron interviews us, we're not reality stars anymore. We're just stars." He clicks back to her profile. "Last month, she had that story about the Louisiana oystermen, right? Blah blah blah, dying industry, blah blah. Now look *two* months back. The reason Cameron caught wind of it was that the editor with the *Ledger* and Modern People retweeted something about it."

"But we're not oystermen," I object. "We're just reality-show stars with twins. There's nothing about us that ties in with climate change or—I don't know, dying coastlines."

Wyatt hands me his phone. It's a photo he took at the hospital. Junior's cystic fibrosis results before we found out it was a false positive.

"But he's fine," I say.

"I ran the stats. In the past five years, she's had nine couples on her show with newborn children. Eight out of those nine had some sort of issue. You remember that quarterback who has a kid with epilepsy? It's always something. You think we need something more than an infant with a lung thing?" He sags into the chair. "I can do more."

"I think we need to be honest. This is—I don't know. Manipulative. Creepy."

"As long as creepy works, hon."

Hon. Not *babycakes.* The question at my lips—what is *with* him lately?—feels better unasked.

I glance over at Momma Harlene. This wing of the house is an open concept, and however much she sleeps, her hearing has always been bat-sharp. When I was a teenager, she caught me sneaking past her bedroom door past curfew because a button fell out of my pocket and tapped on the hardwood floor. Really. A button. Despite how much she's been sleeping lately, an argument with Wyatt would be like dousing her with a bucket of cold water. It's better to leave her snoring in the living room, I figure—

My heart clenches in my throat.

She's not snoring.

I run to her La-Z-Boy. Momma Harlene's eyes are still closed. Her head's slinking into a shoulder and a thin streak of blood ribbons from the corner of her lips. I poke her, watch her chest. Not rising, not falling. I feel her wrist desperately. Nothing. Are pulses always so hard to find? I'm no nurse. I try again. Wrong spot. No pulse. Again. No pulse. It's my fault, I figure—I'm so bad at finding pulses.

I put my head on her chest, and when I hear nothing, I scream at Wyatt to call 911.

Later, when the paramedics are taking her out, I see the TV is still paused, so I turn it off and watch my matte reflection in the screen awhile. I leave it off. She said not to watch it without her.

I am grateful I got to experience Harlene Fremont for thirty-two beautiful years of my life, I write.

As our truck bounces down the highway to St. John's, I'm flooded with a thousand memories worth recording. When I was small enough, she could still take me to the park and swing me around and I'd laugh when she'd threaten to launch me into orbit. When she used to show me her sewing fingers, how she could prick at the callus with the needle and it wouldn't make a dent, I couldn't believe how strong she was. When she let a daddy longlegs crawl up her shin to show me they weren't scary, I couldn't believe how brave. When she saved, in secret, to buy me a dress for the prom because I would otherwise be the only one of my group of friends wearing her single mom's hand-me-down from the seventies. I suspected something was up when she stopped buying cigarettes. She struggled to quit for herself, but she had no problems quitting for me.

I turn to the car seats and pinch the little toe of Harlene Mae, then write the last bit.

And I am grateful she got to meet these two little beauties we made.

At least her life had gone with plenty of warning. When she first got her skin cancer diagnosis, I started hugging her every time I left her, telling her I loved her. That went on for years until it became habit. She thought it was morbid, but then she started getting used to it, and then, classic Momma Harlene, she started milking it, asking where her hug was, if I was going to bring chocolates next time. That was obviously a joke because of the diabetes, poor thing.

Officially, it had been cancer, or diabetes, or blood pressure, or one of a half dozen things. But I knew the real reason she went. She'd started fading right when she'd been able to hold her own grandkids.

Cause of death: *mission accomplished.*

We pull into the parking lot and find a line already formed outside St. John's for her wake. A line. A whole-ass line. It's as if a new Chick-fil-A is opening and giving away free sandwiches. Funny, I always thought it was Momma Harlene and me against the world, but it seems as though anyone who ever said two words to her has come.

I park myself by the casket with a fistful of tissues, fortifying myself for an assembly line of Momma Harlene stories. Everyone has one. Every story is a fresh reminder of how long even the most insignificant kindness will stick to the ribs. The woman from church raves about the pecan pies Momma Harlene would bring when her son died. The women from her Tuesday morning coffee club despair at the loss of their keystone conversationalist. A man whom I knew as a boy came to thank me for all the times Momma Harlene let him stay after school and pick at brownie batter while his parents fought in a living room two houses down. Everyone loves Harlene Fremont. Everyone is here. Everyone except my father.

Among the small heap of Momma Harlene's worldly posses-sions, there had been an address book. Inked inside the front cover was a P.O. box in Henderson, Nevada, no name. That could only be Dad's. I overnighted an invitation, just to let him know the lines are still open. But if he's here, he's disappeared into the crowd. I'm not even sure I would recognize him now. If he is here, he didn't come to hug his grieving daughter.

That leaves me to hug everyone else. I am the sole living repre-sentative of Harlene Fremont, and as the line of well-wishers wears on, I don't feel equal to the task. It's a wonder a woman that charm-ing could raise someone as stilted as me. People give me big, soggy hugs that feel too intimate, and when they pull away, it's always with a lingering pause, as if they're waiting for me to fill the silence the way my mother would. I can sense, with every hug that's a lit-tle too warm for me, that I am a disappointment next to Momma Harlene. Everyone will drive home with their spouses saying, "Boy, the apple fell far from *that* tree."

When everyone's seated, the minister declares an open session for eulogies. Anyone can come up. When I hear footsteps, I can't bear to look. I dip my head into my hands and imagine hearing his voice again. *Hi, everyone. My name is Tim Fremont.* But instead we get Momma Harlene's old work buddies, her Kentucky cousins, her pen pals. No Tim Fremont. When the minister declares the open eulogies over, I can't tell if I'm relieved or destroyed.

Since my primary public-speaking skill is the ability to drain the blood from my face on command, and since I can't think of anything more mortifying than limping my way up to the pulpit in front of everyone, Wyatt gives the longest scheduled eulogy. "You may know me from *The Perfect Home*," he says, by way of introduc-tion. "And if so, I'm sincerely sorry." Polite funeral laughter.

Then he is the old Wyatt for fifteen minutes: charming Wyatt, public relations Wyatt, carver of turkeys on Thanksgiving, the man who gives the toasts. Camera ready, his hair is freshly trimmed, his lean cheeks groomed to a buzz. He tells the story of how Momma Harlene once told him that she would "gut him like a tuna" if he ever mistreated me. I know it's true because Mom always said *tuna* when she needed a specific word for fish. I laugh through tears more times than I can count. Wyatt is all million-dollar smiles and pregnant pauses, polished charisma and occasion-appropriate swagger. He is the Wyatt I knew before the twins, before the pregnancy. Before the ASB.

When he sits down with me, I pat him on the wrist and whisper, "Great job, hon."

He pats me in return, then pulls his hand away.

"I'll take the twins home," he says later, just five minutes into the cafeteria lunch.

"What? Why? We're the main event for people."

And so we are. Our seats are near the door, right where the buffet table starts, where the hundred conversations of acquaintances and old friends seem to form, huddling close to us like we're giving off Momma Harlene's old warmth.

Wyatt blushes. "Look at their eyes. They're going to get crazy. I can tell."

The twins are next to me, each in a carry seat. Harlene Mae looks a little ornery, but Junior is—miraculously—fast asleep.

"People want to see her only grandchildren," I say. "Some are staying overnight in Nashville just to be here."

"We've been here for hours. It's tough on babies."

Now Harlene Mae is just smacking her lips, limp faced. But

one look at Wyatt tells me this is not an argument I can win—or even want to have in public. If there is any place on earth you *don't* yell at your husband and ask what's going on with him, it is at your mother's funeral. He takes my silence for acquiescence and hauls the twins away.

I whirl around, unsure of who's just seen that. The first friend to greet me is Alice Wright, who snaps me up in her tiny-armed hug. Her cheeks are red from an afternoon spent crying. I love her for that, even if I've seen her cry over thirty-second life insurance spots. I still remember her reactions to *The Perfect Home*'s wedding episode when it came out. Every two seconds, a new text: *DAWN. DAWN. DAWN!* Thirty emojis: roiling weepy-faces, teardrops, skulls. In Alice-speak that means our tearjerker wedding episode was dehydrating her to death. I wanted to reply, *You were a* bridesmaid, *Alice, you were there—you should remember all of this happening.* But that's Alice. Even in person, she's got coiling, hyper-expressive eyebrows and speaks in a language of half English and half emoji.

"You poor thing," she whispers. "Everyone loves your mom."

"'Loves,'" I echo. "Present tense. I like that."

"Oh, she's still here. Too stubborn not to be. She's a haunter for sure."

A little ghoulish, maybe, but I laugh at the way Alice flares an eyebrow like she can spy Momma Harlene in the room with us. I met Alice through Victoria, and as with a lot of secondhand friends, it took me a while to get used to the idea of our relationship existing independently, to figure out we weren't oil and vinegar, didn't need Victoria always around to shake us together. Over time, we've made a slurry all our own. I have Alice to thank for that. She can get along with anyone.

"You getting enough to eat?" Alice asks.

"I'm not really hungry."

"Don't believe your stomach. When my patients are grieving, their hunger signals never work right. C'mon. I'll fix you a plate."

We filter through the buffet line, Alice slapping mashed potatoes and corn bread and moussey cake on my plate. At the tables, we find Victoria nibbling on a plate of mixed berries, which she moves aside so that she can hug me with her free arm. I use the opportunity to whisper in her ear, "Does Wyatt seem off to you lately?"

"Hard to say." She shrugs. "You know him better than I do."

"I thought I did. You did just see that, right?"

"It's a tough time. Twins. Momma Harlene. I'm amazed you're holding up so well." Victoria squeezes my hand. "You sure you're not imagining things? Your mother did just pass. When my mom died, it was like I saw the world in evil colors for months."

Alice nods, her chipmunk cheeks muffled with corn bread. "I remember."

"Evil colors?"

"I hated everything," Victoria says. "Hated everyone who moved on quicker than I did. Hated some people just for being alive when my mom was dead. Bad thoughts." The quartered strawberry on her fork starts to bleed on her fingers, so she pops it into her mouth. "Evil colors."

It's evening when Alice gives me a ride home. Angel that she is, she offers to stay the night, but I have to swallow the *Yes, please* that comes bubbling up my throat. I can't admit how lonely I am. Evil colors, I decide. Victoria and Alice are right: like the hunger signals gone awry, I'm seeing the world wrong. I am postpartum and grieving and swollen with three fistfuls of funeral cake and I am seeing the world wrong.

"Anything you need," Alice calls through the window as she pulls out. "Phone call away."

But I wait under the portico until the sounds of her SUV are humming down the distant road. The trees are lush now, leaves thick in the steamy June evening. What I can see of the road only comes in trickles of headlights.

Inside, Wyatt left all the lights on. Mom's La-Z-Boy is still there, next to the couch. The smell of Momma Harlene stays with it, a brackish scent like grill smoke and coffee. Just sniffing her plaid blanket makes me heartsick again. She smells so close by. Conversation distance. It's a cruel tease to leave something so tangible behind. I've thought of keeping the chair as a reminder (empty chair, unfolded plaid blanket, like she's still watching her favorite shows with me), but Wyatt thinks I'm being macabre. I think he's being macabre.

"Wyatt?" I call.

No answer.

He left his laptop in the dining room again. Mindlessly, I snoop through the tabs—*Kat Cameron favorite TV show* in one search query, *grieving wife tips* in another. Maybe that was why he offered to take the twins: some blog told him to help with the kids. Wyatt wouldn't be the first dim husband who didn't know how to vocalize his empathy.

Maybe he's outside. I walk under the hot-gold floodlights of the back porch, looking out on our new lawn, our vestigial toolshed. It took half an episode of *The Perfect Home* to get the thing up because Wyatt had licensed the show's name to some premade plywood shed kits from some regional chain called Vesta Brands. I still remember the absurdly large fruit basket Vesta Brands sent us when they sold ten thousand kits that first week. It's been useful in that way, but Wyatt's never touched the thing. He wouldn't be out here.

So I head back inside, back to his laptop. The security feed shows big gray night-vision blocks of Junior's and Harlene Mae's cribs, the dim fuzz of sunset at the window. All's quiet. They're fast asleep. And finally I see Wyatt. His wide shoulders, his tiny ass. Standing there. He's changed out of his suit into a trucker hat and the plaid button-up he loves. There doesn't appear to be any movement, so I refresh the screen. Same. No movement.

I wish he would at least wipe his nose, or maybe put his hands in his pockets. My husband feels awkward when his hands have nothing to do, even on camera, so he's always leaning or fidgeting or rolling lint. Now he's dead armed, his hands at his side and his palms facing back. It's like he's anticipating falling onto an invisible railing behind him. I furrow my brow. Is this what he does when I'm not around? Stands there, staring at the wall?

I go upstairs, to the twins' room, and nudge the door open. The house is new and full of fresh hinges, so it doesn't make a sound. Neither does Wyatt. I kind of wish the doors would make one of those excruciating, horror-movie creaks, just so I don't have to be the one startling him with my voice. Is he sleepwalking? You're not supposed to wake up sleepwalkers.

The door is fully open now. Wyatt has his back to me, standing on the middle of the carpet, staring at the wall. His hands are in the same position. If it weren't for the slow bloating of his lungs, he wouldn't move at all.

"Wyatt," I whisper. "Babe. Are you okay?"

I drop my hand on his shoulder.

Then he starts, cringing away from my hand but smiling now. As if he realizes the mistake he made, he picks my hand out of the air and gives it a soppy kiss and drags me to the hall.

"Hey." He closes the door behind us. "Didn't hear you come in."

"I know. What were you doing? Daydreaming?"

His head twitches on his neck and he's gone all toothy, but I can't tell if he's suppressing a laugh or stalling for a lie. "Yeah, got lost in thought thinking about the twins' futures. Guess I ended up pulling a Myra."

"Their futures? What about?"

"Oh, I don't remember." He sniffs. "You should rest. Long day and all that. Why don't you watch some TV or something? Your hip must be screaming."

"I'll just check on the twins."

For some reason, I am grateful Wyatt doesn't follow me in. I want to see them myself, unadulterated, without his interpretation of how they slept or why they needed him to stand over them like a zombie.

Junior is sleeping better, his fists softly knocking his ears. Harlene Mae is almost sideways and snoring so loudly I'm surprised it doesn't wake her. I do my cheek-feathering motion with the back of my pinkie, to feel her realness again. A sobby thought bubbles up. Everything good about Momma Harlene might have skipped me, but it will go straight into you.

Then I, good wife that I am, head downstairs and try to forget what I just saw. I disappear into the pile of blankets and butter brickle. I'm not hungry, but the day has called for it. I watch trashy reality TV. Wyatt does some work at his computer before standing up and loudly declaring he's going to check on Junior because he hears him crying on the monitor.

After two episodes, I pause the TV and start to head upstairs, but I notice Wyatt has left his tablet on the dining room table. Out of curiosity, I pick up the tablet. Ever the digital minimalist: there are only two icons. A new file, I see—a written document, but when I try to open it, it's password protected. Years back, while creating a new joint email account for us, he suggested DAWNLOVR for the password and that became his go-to, his joke that he couldn't escape my prying and didn't want to. Anything new, anything we used together, our password would be DAWNLOVR or some variation. But the software only blinks and bounces, shaking its head at me. The other icon is the security camera feed. I loop back through the video, scrolling hours before I got home. The room was empty while we were at the funeral. No surprise there.

Then, about the time Wyatt drove home, it cuts to black.

VIDEO NOT AVAILABLE.

After buffering, the Play icon slides ahead a few hours. It picks up just after I woke Wyatt from his zombie daydreaming. I check the trash folder. Completely clean of everything. There isn't a single file left there. I restart the tablet, open the camera software again. No dice.

VIDEO, it repeats in all caps, as if insisting now, *NOT AVAILABLE.*

CHAPTER 8

DAWN

Wyatt is holding a nail gun when he says, "Jesus, Dawn, do you *want* me to hit you?"

I flinch. "Want you to *what?*"

"The recoil. You're crowding me. All right? You're crowding me. This thing is dangerous."

Two gas-cartridge blasts of nails go into the wood frame, *pop-pop.*

We're in a freshly demoed living room in Kingston Springs. The space is huge, open concept with vaulted lodge ceilings, and, thanks to the demo crew, empty of everything but sawdust and power cords. I back toward the hallway anyway. Wouldn't want to *crowd* him.

The first watery light of the day cuts through the bay window. We are early. Too early for filming, too early to do any real work on the wood, certainly too early if Janie and the cameraman aren't even here after their usual 6:00 a.m. bagel run. It's been years since I convinced Wyatt that it no longer makes sense to do any work off camera. It's a waste of sweat.

But he insisted on driving up a truckful of tools this morning, so we drove separate. I stayed with the new nanny a little too long. Did she know where the extra diapers were? The pre-pumped breast milk? Did she know how Harlene Mae likes it if you waltz around with her in your arms, humming the theme from *Sleeping Beauty*? The nanny (Hattie Wright, Alice's tiny, freckly, college-aged sister) just smiled. Whenever I threw more twin knowledge at her, she'd just say, "That's good, that's real good," like she was an old lady comforting her grandchild. I knew I sounded nuts, all hopped up on early-morning adrenaline and separation anxiety. Dawn the Worrier.

Yet as I drove off this morning, I felt something odd flood through me: relief. This was the first time the twins wouldn't have a parent around, and I knew I'd be texting Hattie every fifteen minutes for an update.

I drove into Kingston Springs and found Wyatt alone and already sweaty with work. I jotted down some notes for things I could say during the shoot, then picked my gratitude journal out of my purse. *I am grateful for Hattie Wright.* After trying to help him find a stud in the wall, he told me off, and now here I am, hip aching, cross-armed on a dusty floor, ostensibly here to find out how much dining room table I can fit into this space, wondering why I can't just be home with my twins instead.

"You hungry?" I ask. Yes, that'll fix him. It's just a blood sugar deficit. "I can text Janie to pick up something."

"You mean besides bagels? No."

"Something besides coffee, then. You're all sweaty already."

"I'm fine."

"Did you wash your hair this morning?"

"Why?" He sets the nail gun on a ledge and finds his reflection in his phone. "Oh, damn it. Look at me."

Through the front dining windows, I see Janie's SUV pull up to the curb. "Never mind. They're here."

"You could've warned me."

"Just did." There's tension in my jaw now. I can feel myself losing control of what I say. When I untether, I get snarky. "What? Worried Modern People will find out you have pores?"

Janie is coming up the walk now, so when Wyatt turns to me, it's with a whisper. Maybe it's the hungry morning light, but there are white burrows under his eyes now. "I liked you better when you were passed out in the hospital and not being such a cunt."

"What?"

Then he steamrolls through the front door and past Janie, who's left holding a bag of too many bagels.

"Nah, he's been fine," Janie chirps. "Good as ever. You sure we're talking about *our* Wyatt?"

"Absolutely sure. The other day, I caught him in the twins' bedroom, just staring. I think he was there for hours. Then today, I really thought he was going to hit me. He all but threatened to."

Janie stands there in the fuzzy diffusion of bay-window light, tonguing her bottom lip. "But—*our* Wyatt?"

Not sure what I expected. More empathy than confusion, maybe? I *am* the woman who just had two twins, and even at my postpartum weight, I'm about half Wyatt's size.

But this is Janie Baker I'm talking to. The same woman who pinched my arms when first setting me up with Wyatt, gauging, measuring. She told me she plucked Wyatt out for stardom the moment she saw the earliest iterations of *The Perfect Home* on YouTube. Six-four, high cheekbones, neon-bright eyes. If he could put a sentence together, she thought, he was a basic cable star waiting to happen. He could. So here we are.

When I came aboard *The Perfect Home*, the chemistry worked with me and Wyatt on camera, but off camera, I felt like the stepsister trying to butt her way into a family of established siblings, inserting myself into the intimacy of nonstop noogies and booger flicking. It made sense—I was the new girl and all. But when I started dating Wyatt, I couldn't help but feel some jealousy at the way Janie treated him. Licking her finger, wiping his eyebrows before shots. Picking specks off his shirts. The bagel runs, Wyatt said, only started happening when I arrived. After I became the female voice on the show and the ratings took off, bagels became the physical token of Janie's usefulness.

In the days Wyatt could still take a joke, I used to call her Wyatt's best friend. Even then, he would just look at me like I was speaking Spanish. She's just a lonely woman, he said, a widow, a career producer who'd achieved her greatest professional breakthrough late in life. The next time I saw her, she slipped me a tool belt she wanted Wyatt to sign for a cousin in Langport.

Janie's not a friend, I remember thinking. She's a fan.

Everyone is a fan of my husband.

Now it's the morning of a shoot and we don't have our star. The cameraman, sensing the tension in the room, complains about the shot and goes outside to erect some light-diffusing curtains. Janie has her arms crossed, the crimp in her forehead tight as ever. She circles the room, kicking up dust, rudderless without her captain.

"I'm serious," I say. "I've never seen him like this. It's starting to scare me. You saw him just now. Do you know what he said to me?"

She rolls her eyes. I can't tell if that's for Wyatt or for me. "I don't wanna know."

"You should know. Said he liked me better when I was in the hospital."

"That's not Wyatt."

"No," I agree. "So we have a problem. Back when I got pregnant, he was taking . . . some medication."

"What medication?"

"Just . . . well, not to get into any details, but has he seemed the same to you since then?"

"He's always been this Wyatt. You've known him almost as long as I have now."

"Not really," I say. But there is someone who knew him before either of us. "What do you know about Myra?"

The crimp in her forehead pulses tight. "There's not much to know. Not everyone is a love connection. Some people get married before they figure that out."

"There has to be something more than that."

"You didn't know Myra," Janie says. "She's strange. Probably in some LSD commune, off the grid, finding herself. She always talked about that, every time I saw her. Finding herself. I don't get people who say that. Look in the mirror, you're right there! Best guess, she doesn't even know how famous Wyatt is now."

All I can do is shrug.

"Listen." Janie pulls me in by a shoulder, sees a spot of sawdust on it, pecks it off. Somehow that comforts me. "I know it's going to be a tough time for Wyatt right now. Twins. They're gonna drive you nuts. Both of you. He's gonna say some things he never said before. You're going to look for something mean in everything he does. It's gonna be like that awhile. But you just weather this storm, you'll get through it, okay?"

Fighting back tears, I nod, taking her in for a hug before she can see how I look when I ugly-cry. Then something hits me. Tough time, she said, *for Wyatt*.

. . .

Wyatt won't respond to our calls or texts, so I drive home, *hospital* still whirring in my head. I keep working myself nauseous about it, fantasizing about the snappy and self-assured way I'll tell him off in the living room.

But he's not here. That makes it official: for the first time in the history of the show, he will miss a day of filming.

When I get back in, Hattie Wright is swiping her phone, legs draped over Mom's old chair. I don't say anything about it. If I do, I'll scream. My face is still hot. I can't take it out on this waifish, barely adult woman who doesn't know this was Momma Harlene's special chair.

She puts a freckly finger to her lips. "Just got them down. Everything okay? Thought you were filming all day."

"Calling an audible. Sorry. Of course I'll pay you for the full day. Did Wyatt come home?"

"No. Why?"

"No reason."

Hattie leaps up in the breezy, hollow-boned way only very young people can leap, then scratches her face. "If you're paying me for the full day, I can stick around and help you out? Otherwise, it's two against one."

"You're sweet, but thanks. Consider it a down payment. I'm buying your goodwill, for when the twins become too much."

"Sounds ominous," she says, then smiles a goodbye.

Once alone, I check on the twins, who are asleep as Hattie promised. That makes a tight window for me, so I rush back downstairs and dig out my laptop. Janie had nothing more about Wyatt's ex-wife. But apparently, Janie took pity in the desperate way I was crying and left Myra's last known email address in my inbox.

Not likely you'll get a response, Janie says. *But if you feel the need to try . . .*

After all these years of wondering who Myra was, and after all these years of never having any good answers, yes. I finally need to try.

"Oh, Hattie was great," I say into the tablet screen that night. "I got home and the twins were asleep. At the same time. It was her first try! You don't know what a big deal that is."

Alice's tight, dimply smile puckers from the screen. The red curls, the wan, spotty face. I never realized until today how much she looks like Hattie. "She'll be so glad to hear it. She really needs the extra money."

"Well, there's more where that came from." I have Harlene Mae in my arms, tucked like a burrito. She's not strictly asleep, but she's still in that newborn phase where unless she's hungry, it's too much effort to open her eyes. "I just need to find three more Hattie Wrights, then I'm golden."

"You can always call Vic. She's got that Instagram-influencer money. I don't think she ever works."

"Please. Victoria would have to call Uber Nannies or something whenever they start crying. What about you?"

"Sorry. Gotta work."

"Yeah, about that. Why do you have a job? Why can't you put your entire life aside and help *me?*"

That dimply smile again, lips half-open: happy-face emoji. Alice has the gift of the perfect smile—anything you say that remotely pleases her will get it out of her. It's no wonder men always think she's flirting with them. She's too good an audience. "Sure. Let me call my boss and tell her I quit. She loves *The Perfect Home*, you know."

"Really? Maybe she'd give you a few days off."

"Dawn. I was joking. Though she is a huge fan of Wyatt's."

Of course.

"Speaking of Mr. Verbally Abusive. Still not home?" Alice asks.

"No. Radio silence." I steal a glance at the front door, its empty windows, and outside, the slow-gradient dip of our lawn toward the road. Front doors are so ugly when you're alone. "Do I push people away, Alice?"

"Only when you're in line for coffee."

"Seriously."

Her chin juts forward. "No. Don't be so hard on yourself. It's not your fault. This is what abuse does to reasonable, good-hearted people. They start wondering if they deserve it. Don't become one of those."

"Thanks," I say, though I want to say much more. Thank you for reminding me of my sanity. Thank you for validating me. Thank you for being the one person in my life who realizes that not everything is as it looks on TV.

That's the problem with being a chronic worrier. When something real pops up, you're not sure how much worry is the appropriate amount. I worry so much that I begin to worry that my worry is ruining things for other people. "Dawn," Momma Harlene said, "you got the worryin' 'bout worryin'." Like it was a condition. My dad was like that, apparently: so overscrupulous about being pulled over by cops, he would check his brake lights once a week. He was a traffic cop himself, so he worried about traffic cop things. That might explain a lot. In half of my memories he was still in uniform, too tired to change before pouring a Scotch over rocks and sinking into the best TV chair. The Scotch—maybe I got that from him, too. I envy the people who look at the hats and the badges and the flashlights and see the time a friendly cop returned their lost dog or gave them a lift home or helped them change a tire. I don't. I see the first person who ever left me.

My mom had no such issues. She'd call the cops on a dog who barked too much, just to "give the poh-lice something to do."

Why couldn't I have gotten more of Mom in me?

I pick up Harlene Mae and hold her upright. "You wanna meet Aunt Alice again, baby?"

"Ohh, let me at her," Alice says. "Is there, like, an app that lets me pinch her Dawn Decker cheeks through the screen?"

Later that night, the sweep of Wyatt's headlights nudges me out of a nap. I push myself up, peel off the blankets. Harlene Mae coos in the baby rocking chair, mouth agape at my sudden movement. As if on cue, Junior starts crying over the intercom. I check the time. Nine fifteen. The night is still young. Yeah. I need another nanny.

The door opens with a sigh of damp summer wind. Wyatt seems more like himself. The old routine: kick, kicking the dirt into the welcome mat, the pat, pat of each shoe thumping off. Keys clinking. His dark hair is tousled, his shirt half-tucked, but at least he is fresh-faced. The burrows under his eyes are gone.

"Hey," he says.

I don't say anything.

"Fair." He picks up the keys, fiddles with them. "I have no excuse, Dawn."

"No. You don't."

Nestling next to me, he gives Harlene Mae one of his fingers. She doesn't squeeze. Wyatt shoots me a wounded look, but I'm not in the mood to tender any sympathy.

"Where were you all day?" I ask.

"Had a lot of thinking to do." He sighs. "You don't deserve that, Dawn. You're such a nice person."

"Nice?" I stop my hand from moving reflexively over my heart, where he's wounding me. I ball it into a fist instead. "I'm not just nice. I'm your wife."

"You're right. No one deserves it."

"And you didn't just say those horrible things to me. You left Janie and a whole TV production with a day of wasted budget."

"I know." Arm's length now, Wyatt rolls a lock of my hair in his fingers. I tilt my neck back and tug it away. He gets the message. "Listen. I don't know who that was this morning. But it wasn't me."

Static hums over the intercom feed. Junior is raging now.

"That's your son," I say.

"I'll take care of him. But—I'm sorry, Dawn. I really am. I know I'm in the doghouse. Hell, I'm beyond doghouses. I'm way the hell out there, out in the toolshed. And I deserve it. I mean it. I'll go to Home Depot right now and buy a cot so I can sleep in it tonight. If it makes you happy."

A laugh flares out of my nostrils. "You don't have to do that. But, Wyatt . . . this morning isn't just it. I'm worried about you. Did you wean off the ASB like you were supposed to?"

"Yeah. For months. I told you."

"I never saw you do it."

"Weaning isn't an easy thing to see."

I shrug. "I'm just saying. Staring at the wall. Saying cruel things. I can't forget that. I think you should see someone."

A flicker of his eyebrows: *That's a great idea.* "Yes. Yes, I will do that—I will call and make an appointment tomorrow. What's the normal amount? Once, twice a week?" Then he flashes me his pearlies.

After that, I can't help myself. I tug him around the neck, hugging, taking him in, all his musky sawdust scent, plus a perfumy afternote that reminds me of gardenias.

"Never again," I say.

"Never again. I'll do the bagel run tomorrow morning. I'll apologize to everyone before shooting. How's your hip?"

"Still weird."

"You should talk to the doctors. Maybe there's something they can do. For the pain, at least."

Though it's apparently been a long, tiring day of driving, he takes Harlene Mae off my hands and goes up to help Junior. There is something clean and pleasantly empty about the feeling he leaves in his wake. My appetite is back. And since it's too late for dinner, that makes it ice cream o'clock. With a spoon in a tub of butter brickle, I watch Wyatt through the security camera, rocking Junior as Harlene Mae fidgets in her crib. I think of making an entry into my gratitude journal.

On the tablet, I bring up the email client and refresh. Nothing new from Myra. I think better of leaving that in the Sent folder, so I delete it. Then it asks me to log in again, but the password autofills.

I pause.

One tap reveals the password, a random assortment of alphanumeric characters. A7f8af!e9eU. Another tap copies it to the clipboard.

I wonder.

Wyatt is still upstairs, holding Junior in the rocking chair now. He's not getting up anytime soon. It's just one more tap to open the document on Wyatt's tablet, the one he thought, for whatever reason, needed a password.

But I think better of it and head upstairs to finish the nap I'd started.

When I wake, the bedroom is almost pitch-black. A moonless night. Something startled me out of sleep, a desperate drowning noise, but I can't tell whether the gasp came out of me or Wyatt. He is sitting on the edge of the bed, staring at his hands.

"Bad dream?" I pat him on the back.

Slowly, he falls back to his spot on the bed. His neck is stiff. Usually he's a mouth breather, but heavy air swishes through his nostrils. I can almost hear the heat in it. Soon he relaxes, and it gives way to the *piff, piff* sound his lips make when he sleeps.

I go to the bathroom and close the door behind me, squinting through the harsh light. We have double vanities, so I shuffle to his side. There is no sign of ASB anywhere—not the pills, not even the empty bottle, though I can't remember what it stood for. Something *Supplement-B*? It's been so long.

An old comment on the internet, though—I seem to have no trouble remembering that. Every sentence of it.

A divorce? Lucky, lucky. My scumbag brother-in-law took it, and my sister will never be the same.

It's the *lucky, lucky* that sticks to my ribs.

Wyatt has always been a bit of a technophobe. When I met him, he still had a flip phone. He could rely on it, he said, and the battery lasted for days. It was something we played up on *The Perfect Home*: the irony of me (Mrs. Vintage Cutlery) introducing him (Mr. Hi-Def Security Camera) to the conveniences of a modern smartphone. Chuckle, chuckle. But he was really like that. One night, when I had to sneak into his old house to pick up some shoes

I'd forgotten, he texted me the four-digit security code. It was the same as his address.

Downstairs, I fire up Wyatt's tablet. The email client opens for me, and I do the double tap of copying and pasting. Even Mr. Hi-Def Security wouldn't be so dumb he'd use the same password twice, would he?

This document is password protected.

Tap-tap.

I'm in.

And once I am, my stomach sinks.

CHAPTER 9

Work backward: Modern People Modern People Modern People. Top link. MODERN PEOPLE, TOP LINK.

> *What gets me there?*
>
> *What is the photo?*
>
> *Me and Dawn. Sunset. Ranch setting. Sunset—autumn?* **Dawn weighs about 135-140.** *(Work on this). Big puffy sweater, vanilla. Her best color. Me—button-down and jeans. Big spooning. We are alone.*
>
> *TITLE:*
>
> *THE LONG ROAD FROM TRAGEDY.*
>
> *ON THE LONG ROAD FROM TRAGEDY.*
>
> *(Something like that)*
>
> *SUBTITLE:*
>
> *HOW TV'S FAVORITE COUPLE IS FINDING THE COURAGE TO MOVE ON.*
>
> *MOVING on?? How TV's favorite couple is moving on. simpler*
>
> *How TV's favorite couple is putting their grief past them.*
>
> *How TV's favorite couple is*
>
> *TV's favorite parents are parents no more*
>
> *INSERT: Nashville, TN.*
>
> *It has been a long road (cliché?) from* The Perfect Home. *Five*

months after the accidental drowning of their two twin children,
*Wyatt Jr. and Harlene Mae—something something **all of Nashville***
***turned up for the funeral**. Keith Urban? Why would he come. Wyatt*
and Dawn Decker are still searching for answers.

PUBLIC NEEDS SOMEONE TO BLAME. *PUBLIC NEEDS*
A VILLAIN.

Key: The nanny wasn't watching close enough.

Close friend. Hattie Wright, bath?

The NANNY. Remember this. Seemed so nice . . . going to
college . . . but incompetent . . . just nineteen years old . . .

Meanwhile Wyatt and Dawn filming The Perfect Home. ***Going***
***to need an angle:** it gutted them to be away from the twins yadda*
yadda. TOP PAGE OF MODERN PEOPLE

Nanny has a seizure or something—Hattie have a medical history?
If not we can give her one

*Hattie, passed out. Wakes up, children in **tub**, hands wet. 19 years*
old, perfect age, she'll think she did it.

*Forget all that. Maybe it's better if she's a **MURDERER**?*

***Hattie Wright**. Murderer. Sounds like a murderer name. Hattie*
Wright, crazy Hattie Wright.

Modern people could buy that.

Modern people modern people modern people.

Top page of Modern People. Start with the end.

*Get plenty on tape. Wyatt **loved** his kids. Loved, loved, loved, those*
kids. On tape. LOVED those kids. Put in hours. Singing, dancing,
perfect father.

One of those awful tragedies, everyone's talking about it.

***Baptize first** (go to Heaven)*

Destroy this after. Dropped tablet in the Tennessee River.

Oops.

Gloves—Hattie's gloves—are in the sock drawer.

Speech:

Infant newborns are not supposed to have personalities. And I know what you're thinking—of course I'm a grieving father, so I'm going to project personalities onto my newborns, even though they were just babies. But I'm being honest. I can tell you what each of my children was going to be like. My wife—my beautiful wife, Dawn—has this habit of hers that I've started to emulate. She keeps a gratitude journal. And I started writing something similar, just a few weeks ago, but with a little twist. I was writing letters to my son and my daughter, telling them who I knew they were going to grow up to be.

Wyatt Junior, you were going to be great at football.

You already have these wide shoulders, and if you grow up as tall as the old man, I'm thinking tight end, maybe even defensive end. You were going to be prom king, big man on campus. People always think it's the quarterbacks who get all the girls, but as a former tight end, let me tell you: they do. (Laughs, laughs). So don't listen to me. Start practicing those spirals. This is SEC country and competition's going to be rough. (Laughs, laughs).

Harlene Mae, you were going to be so beautiful, just like your mom. (Pause. Aw . . .)

And like your mom, you were going to capture the world's attention with your understated charm. See, people think it's me who's the star of The Perfect Home. *But I'm not. The show was just me for a long time, and for a few seasons, no one watched. It was your mom who changed everything. Your mom was responsible for all of it. She kept me in my place, she rolled her eyes along with the audience, she made the people at home feel like someone on-screen was representing them. Her dry wit, her sense of proportion, even the funny way she gets overanxious—that is who America fell in love with. And one day, America's going to fall in love with you.*

You might not see it now. Dawn didn't. She was a TV producer on her way up. She didn't even see herself on Home & Lawn permanently. She saw herself doing cooking shows and bake-offs. But there are some people who just can't help it—they've got something in them, something special, that you can't take your eyes off of.

You have that, Harlene Mae. I know it already. Most newborns come out of the womb looking like newborns. Not you. You came out with your hair in a swirl, and lips turned up like a smile. You came out looking like—I'm ready for my close-up, Mr. DeMille!

(Laughs, laughs. Sniff. Wipe away a tear. Look up from "notes.")

Wherever you both are now, I know it is a better place than I ever imagined for you. I know that we here on Earth are so inconsequential that something as perfect as God's wisdom doesn't always register with us. But I trust in Him, and I know that it's more important that you be with Jesus than it is you be with us. I know God forgives Hattie, just as I pray the world forgives Hattie. This isn't about her. This is about my two beautiful twins. And Wyatt, Harlene, wherever you are, know that Mom and Dad will always love you. I can't wait to meet you two again, and see how you grew up, then show you this journal, and say—see, your old man got one or two things right. I think as long as I had you, it's two things right.

(End, raucous applause, big hug with Dawn.)

Note to self. **Need plans for her.**

CHAPTER 10

DAWN

The tablet blinks to sleep. The hum of the kitchen becomes a roar—the mechanical roll of the refrigerator, the whisper of air-conditioning. After I exit out of Wyatt's insane document, a glance at the camera software shows me the twins are safe, at least. Safe and sleeping. There is no sign of Wyatt being with them. Good.

I stare again, my eyes going bleary, dual images of the tablet crisscrossing each other. If I stare long enough, maybe my eyes will shake something loose and make it unreal. I check again, just to be sure. Same password.

It's real.

Not just a document on a tablet. A real plan. A plan for our twins. *My* twins. Who even *conceives* of ideas like these, let alone types them out? One thing was familiar: Wyatt's writing style, words and fragments one at a time, when he vomits onto paper and circles the best ideas. But he couldn't use paper, could he? You can't password-protect paper. So instead, he put what he thinks are his best ideas in boldface. Baptize first. Hattie Wright. Tub.

And as I think of these things—as the words repeat somewhere in my head—I find myself lurching over the recycling bin. I vomit out a milky version of tonight's dinner.

I remember that comment that still rings inside me, screaming, like it metastasized to my eardrums:

A divorce? Lucky, lucky.

There is no more rationalization to do. No more worryin' 'bout worryin'. I wipe my mouth and grab a duffel bag. I carry it down to the basement. I'm determined never to be one of the unlucky ones.

Thank God Wyatt started prepping. Our basement shelves are full of incidentals I won't need, twenty-five-year meal replacements and cans of creamed spinach, but the rest of it is like Wyatt has done the packing for me. There are ready-made bags with phone chargers, diaper bags, infant formula. An envelope of $10,000 in cash: worried about bank runs. A Dopp kit full of wet wipes and floss: worried about bugging out of Nashville when the zombies come. Turns out he was right and I was wrong. Someone did need to bug out of Nashville.

Note, his journal said. *Need plans for her.*

The levee against the tears I have been fighting back finally breaks when I start packing the diapers. I am so stupid. So, so stupid. I was ready to forgive this monster. Alice's voice rattles in my head: that's what abuse does to you, it makes you feel like the small one, the wrong one. Wyatt has lost it. *Wyatt.* Today he basically threatened to put me in a hospital. Do good people do that? Do normal people do that? Do people who have properly weaned off ASB do that?

It's clear now: he never told his doctor about it. Whenever he stopped doing it, if he stopped, he didn't wean. I took him on his word. My husband was on an illegal, experimental drug and I took him on his word.

I stuff as much as I can into a duffel bag and then load another. The sun hasn't risen yet, but the sky is already dim blue, that rare time of day you usually only see through windows. Maybe I should heat the car up for the twins, but the engine would make too much noise. One of our bedroom windows hangs right over the driveway. I glance up at it, half expecting Wyatt to be standing there. Empty. If he wakes up at his usual time, I still have about forty-five minutes.

My Tahoe is packed. I leave the keys on the seat so they don't jingle when I move around inside the house. Car seats: already plugged in. Everything is ready except for the twins.

Mercifully, impossibly, they are both quiet in their room. Junior is practically comatose in his crib, mouth open in that slobbery remorselessness that gives baby sleep its name. Harlene Mae isn't in so deep, but at least her eyes are closed. If I know her, she will let me hold her for a few minutes without screaming bloody murder.

Wyatt Junior, I'm not so sure.

I scoop up Harlene Mae, then Junior, careful not to let his neck bend. *Yes, that's it, it's just another morning in your crib. Another hunky-dory day in the life of an infant.*

I'm in heavy shoes, but the hallway is carpeted and mutes each footfall. Thank God this is a new house. There are no creaks, no random woody groans. Harlene Mae gives a little coo, then scrunches her face like she's about to sneeze, but relents. Junior is still out cold. Then, at my bedroom door, I stop.

Was it halfway open when I came upstairs?

I lean into the open frame, hoping to hear Wyatt snoring.

There's nothing.

A drooling, sniffing sound cracks under my arm. Junior is awake.

I am standing outside my husband's door and Junior is awake. A smack of the lips, a shudder of the hands, and here it comes. The morning cry. The morning *wail*.

I get halfway downstairs before it starts. Then there's no more reason to sneak. I run as safely as a woman with two infants under her arms can run and get Junior in his car seat first, then Harlene Mae, who still hasn't opened her eyes. Then as I start up the car, I am in my head, sorting through potential destinations I can set on the GPS.

"Dawn," Wyatt calls. "What are you doing?"

He is standing at the front door, barefoot, hair tousled and puffy, his pajama pants still sleep-yanked and showing his ankles. I start the engine as he steps down, then freeze in the decision between blind-flooring it backward—what if I injure the twins?—and pretending everything is all right.

Wyatt approaches the window. I let it down, creating a sliver of air between us.

"I am . . . Well, I'm . . ."

I'm not nearly as good at bluffing as I pictured. There is too much to track. The gear is in reverse. My foot is on the brake. Is there anyone on the road? I don't know. Wyatt is approaching me now, and I always freeze when people eye me down. Something inside me is screaming: Lie to him. *Lie to him,* you hopeless, shy, people-pleasing nobody; tell him how you want to take the twins out for a drive around the block to see if it settles them. You'll be back in five minutes. *Lie.*

I hear myself say, "I'm just going for a drive."

Wyatt hooks his fingers over the lip of the window. It is an obscene, penetrating gesture: some small part of him is inside my truck. "At four thirty in the morning?"

A swallow sends needles down my throat. "They woke me up. Let go, Wyatt."

"Let go of what?"

His flinty eyes scan the Tahoe. Something about it looks unfamiliar to him, like he's seeing it for the first time at a dealership and wondering whether he likes the color, Alaskan Pine. God, I wish he would blink.

"Bring them in," he says. "Bring in the twins."

"Okay." Slow breaths, Dawn. Slow breaths. "Can you at least let go of my window so I can get out?"

Shrugging, he relents and takes a few steps back.

That's when I hit the gas.

"Vic? Hey, Vic?"

The intercom gives a staticky click like I'm about to hear her voice. Then it all gives way to silence. The door doesn't open.

"Vic, it's an emergency. I need a place to stay."

Nothing. I almost want to bang on the door. Scream her name. But the intercom stares at me, insect-like, looking out from its eye of a thousand holes, and I can't shake the feeling of having a camera on me. I wonder if I'm even ready to bring someone else into this.

Then I'm back on the road, just another SUV in a river of commuters. It's a burning-bright morning in the Gulch. Part of me hates that. The sky should be boiling, the roads should be slick, the windows should be quivering in thunder. Everyone should go inside and make room for me. But no. I have had to steal my children away from my insane husband, and it's a gorgeous crystal-blue day.

On the way to Victoria's, I kept rubbernecking the mirror, checking for Wyatt's F-150. But F-150s are so common around Nashville, they might as well be houseflies. And they're always, always blue like Wyatt's, so I feel myself pucker at every stoplight. What if Wyatt got out of one of the trucks and came up screaming behind me? What if he blamed everything on me? I could almost hear him. *Are you fucking nuts?* And then I could play dumb. *What, dear hubby? I'm just taking the twins to the park.* But Wyatt never came out, and I never saw his truck. Where is he? Is he chasing me? Calling the police? What?

Alice lives on the other side of town. I want to call the police on the way there, when I have a moment to dial my phone, but I get all green lights. Of course. If you want green lights, you, too, can work magic: it will happen when you desperately need a red. But I won't take my eyes off the road. Not with the twins in the car.

Then I remember my car has voice command.

"Nine," I say. "One."

I've never dialed 911 before. What will I say? *Well, you see, my husband's been kind of off lately, and I found his plans to murder our twins and possibly me on his tablet? Wyatt Decker. Yes, Wyatt Decker from HLTV. Hello?*

"Cancel," I say. "Call Alice."

Straight to voicemail.

As I merge onto the highway, where at least the driving will require less of my attention, I count down a list of people I can't call. Hattie won't have a place for me to stay. Kelly's been running the store for me while I'm on maternity leave, so she won't be home, and I can't go to the store because that might be the first place Wyatt goes. And I can't go to production. Janie is firmly on Team Wyatt.

One bad morning and I have officially run out of friends.

Long Grove Health might have worked, and my fingers flinch on the steering wheel just thinking about driving there, but Momma Harlene is no longer there to visit. God, how I need her now. I need her humor, her confidence, her penchant for knowing the next steps. She'd instantly take my side the same way she always did.

She'd wave a hand—*Say no more*—and say something like *Pack me up, darlin', I'm comin' with you. How's Atlantic City this time of year?*

And as my list of options runs low, my certainty dips with it.

"Call from," the Tahoe's sultry voice announces, "Wyatt."

The red button kills incoming calls. I give it a quick thumb and keep driving.

"Call from Janie Baker."

Janie. *Ugh—Janie.* This will be the second day of filming missed in a row. My heartbeat accelerates, matching the pound of tires on cracks in the road.

Still, I keep driving.

I have never called the police before. Once, when I was pulled over for speeding and I watched the officer walking up in the rearview as my engine idled, I was sure the flutters of the engine had been my own wavering heartbeat and that I was finally going to die of an excess of anxiety in the blood. The officer took one look at me hyperventilating into my sweatshirt and said, "Calm down, ma'am—it's just a routine traffic stop." I felt like a five-year-old at the dentist.

Even so, this call isn't for me. It's for the twins.

"Dial nine one one," I tell the car.

A sizzle, then a female voice on the line. "Nine one one, what's your emergency?"

I realize, too late, that this is the kind of call that they always release on the news several days after the fact. I am the five-year-old at the dentist again. It all comes spilling out in spits, stutters, sentence fragments. *My husband. A document—a letter to himself. He's going to kill my children. My children! Go to my home, make sure he's not following me. I'm leaving.*

Her voice is flat, the sound of someone checking off boxes. "What's your name, ma'am? And what address?"

"Dawn Decker. My husband's name is Wyatt." Thumbing the volume, I listen for a reaction, but there is none. Not even breathing. "Three thirteen Huckleberry Court, Belle Meade."

"All right. We'll send someone out there shortly to check on your children."

"No—they're with me. They're safe."

"Oh, they're safe?" Now I do hear her breathing, heavy and wet. It sounds like exasperation. "Well, we have to send someone over to check anyway."

"Check on *Wyatt*. There's a file on his tablet that spells everything out."

"We'll send someone over, ma'am, for a wellness check. Is there anything else?"

I kill the call with a jab of my middle finger to the screen. *Is there anything else?* This is an emergency, lady, not Chick-fil-A. She might as well have asked me if I wanted waffle fries with my Deluxe.

Junior hates the sudden absence of noise and screeches in his chair. It spreads to Harlene Mae, who can't stand the sound of a screaming infant, so she becomes a screaming infant, too. I suck in a long breath and, as a therapist once told me to do, mentally tick off a list of what I see. I am driving north on 65. A digital overhang tells me to tune in to 1100 AM for traffic updates. An exit sign wonders if I want to get off at Opryland. Maybe I do. Maybe I misread whatever Wyatt was writing on his tablet and he's not the threat I thought he was. Maybe I do need to talk to someone, because I feel like I'm losing my mind. But I hear Alice's voice in my head again: that is what gaslighting and verbal abuse does to people. It makes them doubt. And somewhere there's a comforting presence, like Momma Harlene is weighing in, too.

If she is, she's saying to keep my foot on the gas.

CHAPTER 11

DAWN

WELCOME TO INDIANA.

It has taken more than half the day to get here. Turns out newborn infants aren't ideal road trip buddies—it's better to bring people who *don't* poo their pants every fifteen minutes and cry when they're hungry—but it isn't until I put Kentucky and the Ohio River between me and Wyatt that I feel safe enough to get my bearings.

I pull over in a hotel parking lot on an empty section of highway, making sure to drive the long way around so the Tahoe and its Volunteer State license plate aren't visible from the road. I don't know where I'm going from here. I only know I've just started a new state and I can't take any more double twin screams.

The clerk in the lobby is a young, tomboyish woman with a buzz cut. Her eyes go wide when she sees me limping in, looking like a one-woman band: purse under my shoulder, twins in their carry seats under each arm, the weight of the world on my back.

"No—" she says, and I start apologizing, as if it's a crime to bring babies to a *hotel*, but she means something else. "That can't be you. Dawn *Decker?*"

Once I plunk down the caravan I've brought with me, I slap my ID to the counter. "Yep. Hi. Hello. I need a room, please."

"I love your hus—I love your show," the woman says, tapping away at the keyboard. The purple lipstick at her mouth quivers as she cycles through the various things she could say. I've heard them all. *You should take it easy on Wyatt! Why don't you ever stick to Wyatt's décor budget?* In the early days, I used to try to convince people that we were actors playing characters, but Janie warned me off that. *Reality* TV, she said. We have to sell the reality. I am forever Wyatt Decker's wry, ball-busting wife, not a frightened woman trying to save her twins. I am powerless to say it's just a TV show. No matter how much I spell it out, people give me dead-eyed looks. It Does Not Compute.

"I love what a bitch you are," she finally pipes up. "I'm sorry. I don't mean to be mean. Me and my boyfriend watch you all the time. What are you doing *here?*"

"Oh, you know," I say, but a good enough lie doesn't come.

She blinks. "And those are the famous twins?"

No, I just borrowed these babies. The twins will arrive in a horse-drawn carriage later. "Yep. Harlene Mae and the loud one there with the fists of rage is Wyatt Junior."

"Awwwww." She hands me my ID back. "Where's Daddy today?"

I swallow so hard, my tongue almost sucks down. "I don't mean to be rude," I say to the woman who just called me a bitch, "but I was wondering if maybe I could just get the room key? I'm sorry. The twins."

"Course." Her voice has gone staccato. "One one five."

"I'm sorry. Really. It's . . . extenuating circumstances. I can't say what. I hope you understand."

She tongues her teeth, leaving an impolite and open crook in her mouth, looking straight at her computer now. I have lost another fan.

I would be a much nicer person if I learned how to lie.

Room 115 is clean, but highway-hotel simple: two twin beds, a hardtop desk, a TV with a dozen channels. The back-window view shows nothing but my Tahoe waiting in the parking lot. Once I get Junior to take a nap, I check my phone. Three missed calls from Alice. I call her, but she must have gone in for another shift because I only hear her cutesy voicemail: "You've reached Wonderland. Alice can't come to the phone right now. . . ."

Dozens of text messages speckle my inbox. Janie wonders why I didn't show up for shooting today. Hattie Wright says, *Have a great spa day!* Clearly she spoke to Wyatt. And what was Wyatt doing all day? When I called the police, they promised a wellness check. Either they went to the house and found no one home, or Wyatt alone. I imagine two cops knocking on the door, standing around for half a minute, then moving on to the next call. Wyatt may already be driving up 65, too, halfway through Kentucky. I never did check my SUV for a GPS tracker, and now I can't put it past him.

As I'm scrolling through unread texts, the screen lights up. *VICTORIA WEATHERLY.*

"Vic," I say. "Thank God. Why didn't you pick up this morning?"

"I was sleeping. Why? Alice called me. She's super-worried about you."

"What did you hear?"

"Just that she got a call really early in the morning, and you wouldn't respond all day."

"I've been on the road."

"Where?"

The question snags under my skin like a splinter. Do I tell her? Do I tell *anyone*? I've crossed state lines, and everyone else thinks Wyatt can do no wrong. I'll probably sound crazy if I admit where I am.

"Dawn, talk to me. People are worrying about you."

Moving a pen across notepaper, I steal a glance at the hotel stationery. "RelaxInn. Helensville, Indiana."

"Indiana? What, are you filming there?"

I tell her everything, dating back to when we found out about Wyatt's sperm count. ASB. That weird day Wyatt was staring at the wall. The document on his laptop—to avoid turning into a blubbering mess, I only proffer the vaguest of details. When I finish, the phone sounds like it's gone dead. "Vic?"

"Sorry. I'm just . . . taking it all in. You haven't told me any of this before."

Which makes me sound even less credible. "I know. I'm sorry. It wasn't exactly the kind of thing we could talk about hanging out at the store, customers everywhere."

"Tell you what. I'll come to you. What room are you in?"

"Don't bother. I have money, my credit card. I'm just wondering what Wyatt's up to, if he's gone apeshit or what."

"You haven't called the police?"

"I did. Not that they've been any help."

A blip on my phone. *CALL FROM: ALICE.*

"Vic, can I let you go? Alice is finally calling me back."

"As long as you still pick up my calls."

"Always," I say, then swipe Alice's icon into place. "Alice. You got my voicemails?"

"All thirty. Did you talk to Wyatt?"

Guilt pulses through me. No—three missed calls from Wyatt so far. I declined them all. I could picture him talking me down some-how, charming me back to Nashville. I couldn't let that happen.

"I don't want to respond. What's he even going to say?"

"I don't know. But I say the next time he calls, take it. You need to figure this out, especially if the police are no help. What's your plan?"

"Take the twins as far away as possible." I bite my lip, like maybe if I bite hard enough it will squeeze some better words out. And it occurs to me, the reason I haven't been redialing the police, the reason I don't think I'll stand up to questioning. "I guess I'll need to prove what he planned on doing. Somehow."

"I assume you copied the document, took screenshots, some-thing?"

I bring the phone to the bathroom and find myself in the mir-ror. A drained and dreary woman looks back at me. I'm surprised the clerk recognized me as Dawn Decker. My skin is bumpy, my cheeks patched red with a flare-up of eczema, and my hair is flat from hours of driving through Kentucky with a Vols hat on. But that's not why I hate what I see.

"Shit," I say. "I didn't."

After a dinner of Chinese takeout and nursing the twins, Junior conks out on me, giving me ample time to rock Harlene Mae to sleep. It takes her a while. I watch dusk melt to night with her wrig-gling softly in my arms the whole time. Whenever I even think of putting her down, she murmurs a protest. She's trying to milk this one-on-one time for all it's worth. Me, too, darlin', I think, happy to hear Momma Harlene's voice burping up from somewhere inside me. I didn't take everything after my father.

My father. I know now why I haven't called the police until today. I was afraid the moment I called the police, it would be the second time a cop has disappointed me.

And here they are, disappointing me. The dispatch operator had called it a *wellness check*. Even if Wyatt was home when they got there, he'd just flash them the pearlies: *Gee, officers, my wife is at the store, you sure you got the right house?* And they'd say they loved *The Perfect Home*, they'd small talk about the Titans, and all would be forgotten.

There are no cribs here, so I set the twins in their carry seats near my bed. I can't sleep. I never slept well in hotels—the stiff sheets, the new ceilings, the TV with all the wrong channels. I get that from Momma Harlene, too. We were always natural nesters. Same chair for her, same spot by the couch arm for me. Only Dad had any love for the great world beyond.

So I get up and charge my phone, if only to make some use of the awake time. Through the front window, a street of highway traffic mumbles steadily, cars making swishing sounds on the road.

That's when I notice the squad car parked out front.

CHAPTER 12

DAWN

I see a fish-eye image of a police officer through the door, the peephole blowing his furrowed brow up to grave proportions. What are a citizen's rights in a hotel? I have no idea. It's not like I can demand to see a warrant if they've already let him in. It's not even my property. Has he seen me? Does he know I'm in here? I'd been standing at the front window, peeking through a curtain, only half-hidden.

"Ma'am, Helensville police." Another knuckle tap. "We've been asked to do a wellness check."

Yeah, I think. Those are going around.

Junior's awake, his fingers wringing imaginary sponges. I give us about a minute before he goes thermonuclear. That could work. I can open the door as if still squinty from sleep, tell the officer I'm fine, and then, when Junior goes off, use that as an excuse to end the conversation.

But then what? This officer called to a hotel room in the middle of the night is satisfied that this Tennessee woman who randomly packed up her twins and drove to Indiana is . . . totally sane?

"Ma'am. Helensville police. Are you all right in there?"

My hand instinctively shoots to the knob, but it doesn't turn. I've done nothing illegal. But does that always matter? I've done nothing illegal, no, but I am in the wrong state. I took my twins from my husband and my home. My driver's license is practically a lie—the photo is from before the twins and barely looks like me. What's to stop a wellness check from becoming *Ma'am, would you mind coming with me?* Especially without Wyatt's psychotic document to show them?

"Mrs. Decker." Pounds now, the back of his fist. "Dawn. Dawn Decker. If you don't respond, I can ask the clerk about getting the door open." After a little more pounding, I finally hear him sigh. His footsteps dwindle down the hall.

The view through the back window shows the empty side of the parking lot. My Tahoe's all alone. The only thing separating me from a quick escape are these windows and a screen I would have to punch through.

If I'm getting out of here with the twins, I'm adding *destruction of property* to the charges of *Ma'am, come with me.* But I am getting out of here.

The predawn highway is a relief, a hypnosis of mile markers and burger billboards. I play a baby-meditation track of ocean sounds to calm the twins. The rumble of semi engines rolling through the southbound lanes adds thunder to the waves.

It's a Friday. In an hour, commuters will probably clam up this highway on their way to Indianapolis, and for a while I think of getting off, taking side roads, and finding some Podunk motel where no one can send wellness checks after me. I can stay more than a night, if I'm lucky.

Aside from a broken hotel screen, I tell myself, I've done nothing wrong.

But after pulling off at a random exit, I feel self-conscious. My Tahoe is new and shiny; the newest truck I see on the side of the road is some beat-up Ford from the nineties. There is a barn that looks like a tornado got to it four decades ago. From the farmhouse porch, a woman in an ankle-length dress watches me like a portrait. HYDE OAKS, a sign announces. UNINCORPORATED. Wyatt's told me a million times our show does just okay in New York, but we're huge in the South and the Midwest. The Ohio River Valley is the cradle of our popularity.

If even one person has seen *The Perfect Home*, I will become the biggest story in the history of Hyde Oaks within an hour.

We'll be better hidden in a city. Louisville is behind us, but I've got nothing but time, so Indianapolis it is. And as I'm pulling back onto the highway, I feel better to have a plan of any sort: fingers tapping, neck loose, a June dawn hot on my skin. I don't know where I'll be tomorrow, but today, I have a place to go, a yellow-brick road to follow. Today, my children are safe. The rest is just details.

And as I'm starting to feel better, the Tahoe screen lights up and announces, "Call from Wyatt."

This time I take it.

"Dawn," he says. "Thank God. I've called you a thousand times."

"There's nothing to say."

"What do you mean? What's going on?" A pause. His voice is urgent and pitched up, making every word a question. "I swear, all day long, I was just driving. That's all I was doing."

With no camera to roll my eyes at, I shoot myself a frown in the rearview. "This isn't about yesterday."

"Then what's it about? Where are you?"

"Far away."

I can hear the heat in his breaths over the phone speakers. But it gives me goose bumps. The air conditioner spits it out cold. "Are the twins okay?"

"They are now."

"What do you mean?"

A swallow rolls down my stomach like a hot blade. He sounds just like he did when I first met him, all innocent, all cutely dumb. If I hadn't seen the plans for myself, I'd start to doubt. "You were planning on drowning our children."

Nothing on the end of the line now. No hot breaths, no goose bumps. When he speaks, his voice has dropped back to the low register I'm used to. "You have no evidence, Dawn."

"No? I read it in your own words. A *funeral* speech—" Junior riles up, a kick start of a moan at first, then a full wail. I don't care. I scream over him. "A funeral speech, Wyatt, about our drowned children, all blamed on Hattie Wright."

"I don't know what you think you found—"

"I have a copy with me," I lie.

A pause. "I was fear setting."

"Fear setting."

"You know—the book on Stoicism I've been reading. There's this thing called fear setting. I was thinking through the worst-case scenario to try and—I don't know, stop worrying. You know how nuts I've been with the kids. Childproofing everything. I was trying to rebuild my mental health. For you. For the kids."

The skin at my throat bursts up red so fast, I can watch my own blood pressure rise in the mirror. "Don't you fucking dare gaslight me. What *I'm* doing is for the kids."

"All right." The words are agreeable, but I know that tone. The charm hasn't worked and he knows it. He's not talking to me. He's only verbalizing some decision he's made in his head. And whatever it is, it satisfies him enough to hang up.

My instincts about the city turn out to be right. When I'm almost downtown, there's an entire diner full of people who don't know me from *The Perfect Home*. Or they don't care, which is just as good. Brittany, our ruddy-cheeked waitress, immediately coos over the twins—"These cheeks!"—and, after seeing how my hip is acting up, lets us have a corner booth all to ourselves. Bless her heart, she even soothes Wyatt Junior for a minute so I can book an Airbnb.

I'm already learning a few things. Airbnbs, not hotels. Punch in a code rather than hand a hotel clerk the ID that confirms you're a TV star. I use the diner Wi-Fi to set up a new account under a pseudonym and upload an AI-generated picture. World, meet Shailene Harper. The credit card: I can't do much about that. But I know that if someone is tracing me, they'll only find a generic Airbnb charge, not a location. Thanks to Midwestern prices, I book an entire guesthouse for $95 a night. The owner is a kind-faced elderly woman who sends me a private message with the code and well-wishes for a pleasant stay. She's leaving out a bottle of Pellegrino for me.

The guesthouse is lovely, if a little small, with barn-style ceilings and a second-level entry above the garage. To anyone looking in, it looks like a separate property. It's like I've lived in Indianapolis my entire life. The kind-faced elderly woman even set up a bassinet and a changing station because I told her I'm traveling with babies.

It's only once I have the twins safe inside this house that I find a moment to breathe. How long until Wyatt finds out I didn't take a copy of his document with me? In my panic, all I thought about was getting the babies away. Of course I can't blame myself for that, but now I feel stupid. I'd assumed one call to the cops would have cured everything. But Wyatt's up and about, so clearly they were no help.

I could call my attorney. Well, actually *our* attorney, as in mine and Wyatt's. When we met with her to help with Mom's estate, she spent the entire meeting laughing at Wyatt's jokes so hard I could see the fillings against the crisp white of her molars. She shook my hand but hugged Wyatt goodbye, sliding her hand down his wrist like a masseuse and asking when they were going to get nine holes in again. My mother had just died.

Still, there is no shortage of lawyers in the world. After disabling the location settings on my phone, I send out feelers to law firms all across Nashville without spelling out that I am in Indianapolis. The thought that a dozen lawyers may be looking me up makes me nervous. I had a DUI arrest when Victoria and I were roommates—technically expunged, but the whole experience left ink stains all over my memory. Everything about the law makes me nervous. But I decide that if even one legal expert tells me to go to the police again, I'll bite the bullet and do exactly that. Daddy issues or not.

While I wait for responses, I pass the time by trying normal things. Taking the twins to a park, shopping for groceries instead of takeout. My phone is abuzz all day—more Victoria, more Alice—but after the call with Wyatt, no one from HLTV. Not Wyatt, not Janie, not our publicist, not our attorney. Maybe I spooked him. Maybe now he's regrouping and awed at the backbone his postpartum wife is revealing. There is no way on earth he will call the police, not if he thinks I have a copy of his file.

At about eight o'clock, I finally get Junior down for a nap. Harlene Mae is not asleep, but at least she's less likely to scream until her throat bleeds, so she can stay with me while I watch *Married at First Sight* on the sofa. *Run,* I want to scream at the unfortunate phlebotomist whom the "experts" matched with a textbook narcissist. *Run!* It is the first time in my day that I don't feel I'm running from something myself.

I don't have my gratitude journal, but there's a pen and pad on the coffee table, and I write, *I'm grateful my twins are still alive.*

Then my phone buzzes. Alice.

Turn on CHN.

My stomach snags on a nerve. Something terrible has happened. Another mass shooting, a terrorist attack, a fire in downtown New York. Whenever Alice texts me to turn on the news, it's only when the scroll says BREAKING and there are about a hundred police sirens on-screen.

But when I turn it on, I don't see ambulances and cop cars and police tape. I just see Wyatt.

"Never," he says. "Not in a million years. Dawn . . . she is the woman you all see on TV."

On-screen, Wyatt looks five years younger. Forehead smoothly caked with fleshy makeup, beard trimmed down to handsome fuzz, blue eyes popping. I would never guess this is *my* Wyatt, drown-the-kids Wyatt, stare-at-the-wall-for-hours Wyatt. This Wyatt looks sane. Under him, a caption reads NASHVILLE, TN, and behind him, a green-screen version of downtown twinkles to match his eyes.

Trish Harrison, on the other side of the screen, nods oh so carefully, letting America know how she's processing what he's saying.

Plump-cheeked, helmet-haired, wearing her thirty years of crime journalism experience in the caverns under her eyes, she is American cable news's foremost legal expert and she's talking about me.

"Dawn, then, just to be clear," Harrison says, "was suffering from some sort of postpartum depression?"

"I don't know if it's fair of me to diagnose it," Wyatt says, fake straining. I can tell when he's fake straining. He gives a convincing twist to his face, but he leans forward in the chair slightly, like the lie is poking him in the ass. "But she hasn't been . . . *herself* lately."

An awful pain knifes me in the solar plexus. The absolute asshole. He's pinning it on me.

"Not herself—can you tell us what that means?"

"Oh, um. Moody. Verbally abusive, once or twice. And that's fine. I'm a man, I can take the occasional barb. I chalked it up to what her body was going through. It's not easy carrying twins. You'll get hungry and moody and angry, sometimes all at once. I always understood that. I was on board with it, to help her in any way I could. But after she had the kids—that's when she turned into someone I didn't recognize."

My phone buzzes, Alice again.

ARE YOU SEEING THIS? IS THIS TRUE?

NO, I text back, but it doesn't seem emphatic enough. There needs to be a button for a thousand red-cheeked angry faces. *NOT REMOTELY.*

On-screen, Harrison is asking my husband to elaborate on my psychosis.

"The other day, I saw her in the twins' room, just staring at the wall," Wyatt says.

I can't help it anymore. I stand up, scream at the TV, "That was *you,* you complete sociopath!" Harlene Mae starts crying. I have to start rocking her again, but there's no way she'll sleep while my heart's thumping under her like a kick drum.

"She's been verbally abusive," Wyatt says.

"If you don't mind being specific?" As Harrison leans in, I swear I can feel the weight of America leaning in with her.

"Oh, calling me a bunch of words I wouldn't repeat for your national audience. Sexual words."

"Okay—thank you," Harrison says. "And I—excuse me, but I'm just trying to digest this, like the rest of us, because I think we all know Dawn as someone who rarely curses without apologizing afterwards, much like yourself."

"Right," Wyatt says. "We just try to keep it clean, as a general rule. We're a Christian family."

The asshole has made me go to church alone throughout our entire marriage. I set Harlene Mae down in the bassinet because I'm afraid I'll squeeze her too tight.

"I think anyone who's seen *The Perfect Home* knows how important your Christian life is to you," Harrison says.

Wyatt swallows, nods. "And then yesterday, I woke up and went to the twins' cribs. And they were—" Now for the breakdown. I know it's coming and I can't wait to see how fake it looks. Wyatt and I used to watch these exact shows, and we always said the same thing to each other: real criers try *not* to cry. They're embarrassed by their crying. They fight it, suppressing their own bodies. And that's how he looks now. His breaths go staccato, his forehead crimps, the skin of his chin wriggles and seizes. His *chin wriggles*.

And that's when it occurs to me: I am now in a public relations battle with a man who knows how to cry on command. With a man who reads about dopamine and sales psychology to marionette a TV audience he will never see. With the same man who got up at my mother's funeral and held an entire church in the palm of his hand while his cold wife couldn't summon the courage to eulogize her own mother. I think of every time a fan scolded me for busting his balls, every time we were at a dinner party and I couldn't finish a story because I wasn't telling it right, so everyone looked at Wyatt to finish it. *Believed* Wyatt's version. His voice is so big and brassy, he can turn everyone in a room into an audience, bystanders watching a Dizzy Gillespie trumpet solo. Talking is his jazz, his real art. He's even shown me how easy it is to unleash his personality on people. *Watch,* he'd say. *I'll show 'em the pearlies.*

And me? I am Dawn Decker, wife prop, the stand-in for the audience. The one who gets to live out the fantasy that is *The Perfect Home.* The one batting out of her league while half of America's single women get to say, *If I were in Dawn's shoes, I would have done it differently.*

What are these women—what is *everyone*—going to think? That I kidnapped my own children and planned to murder them.

"They were gone," Wyatt finishes. "She took them. I don't know where she is."

"Mr. Decker, what happens now? Are you going to call the police?"

"Just before I went on air, I got off the phone with the Nashville Police Department. We believe there's a possibility that she's crossed state lines. With how long it's been. So now, we think the only thing is to let the country know."

Again, his chin wriggles. Trying so, so hard not to cry. "I never meant for it to come to this. I thought it was just a normal pregnancy thing, that she was going through something I could never understand, being a man. I didn't want to say anything to anybody because of that. But now I know the danger my children are in."

After another long swallow, like he is trying to fortify himself for what's next, his voice clears. "This is something I never wanted to tell the world. Dawn has a problem with alcohol. Apparently it started long before I met her, when she had come out of rehab and gotten her life and career together. But it was always something that hung over our marriage. She can't have a drink without it becoming ten drinks. She's a tense person, Dawn, a worrier, and alcohol was always one of the few things that calmed her down."

Asshole. God, can he lie. Like all good lies, it's flavored with enough truth that people will believe it. Even Alice and Victoria know I refuse all drinks.

"Thank you for sharing this," Harrison says. As if it's difficult for *him*, somehow, and he's doing *her* the favor.

Wyatt nods. The camera has zoomed in close, a honeycomb of pores and stubble filling the screen.

No. It's not the camera that's zoomed in. It's me, kneeling right in front of the TV.

"There were a lot of tough years," Wyatt says. "For a long time, she tried hard. Very hard. But I think the bigger the show got, the more scrutiny she received, the easier it got to come home and shake up the occasional cocktail. You know, one or two at first. To prove she could handle it. And by the time she started drinking more, I'd research rehab clinics, but she would just scream at me and say that I didn't have a problem when she was drinking one or two, and I should have stopped her then. And you know what? I should have."

Placing the blame on himself. I can imagine America reaching out its collective hand, patting him on the shoulder. There there, dear Wyatt. It's not your fault.

"And then her mother died," Wyatt says. "And that was it. She was off the deep end. She and her mother were so close, and I didn't know how to comfort her."

"How did her mother die?" Harrison asks.

"Momma Harlene, everyone called her that."

"Momma Harlene."

A shock moves through me, hearing her name come out of Harrison's mouth. Momma Harlene would have passed out. She used to watch Trish Harrison every night at the home. Right after *Wheel of Fortune*, right before *Friends*. "Seeing what the animals are up to," she called it. "Trish always finds 'em."

Look, Mom. We're on TV.

"Momma Harlene was struggling with cancer and diabetes." As soon as Wyatt says it, my stomach starts burning. "She moved in with us. And I think she found out how much Dawn was really drinking. It strained their relationship. If you want to know the truth, I think Momma Harlene couldn't take seeing her daughter like that. But I didn't know what to do. She didn't know what to do. I should have gotten help. If I hadn't waited, maybe Momma Harlene would still be alive today."

Whatever glass still left in me shatters. It's good there's a couch to catch me, because I fall apart, muscles mushy, all my strings snipped. My eyes well up and go cloudy. There is a faint ringing in my ears while Wyatt keeps talking on the screen, Dawn this and Dawn that, but none of it matters anymore. The world thinks I'm off the wagon and that the grief of it killed Momma Harlene.

I already know Wyatt's painting me as the monster so he can keep his image up for any future shows he has in mind. *The Perfect Divorce. The Perfect Bachelor. The Perfect Home 2: Even Perfecter.* As long as he can escape this with his brand intact, he'll say anything.

My stomach is still heavy with aftershock when the ringing fades from my ears.

"You don't mean to suggest she . . ." Harrison trails off.

"Of course not," Wyatt says. "Momma Harlene was an ill woman. I thought we were helping her by having her live with us. Now I see it was a mistake."

"And what do you think happens from here? What do you most hope happens next?"

"I just hope that when she comes back, when the twins are in my arms, safe and sound, we can finally get Dawn the help she needs."

The screen cuts out, gone peachy white, zooming out from someone's headshot. With burgeoning horror I realize it is me. The shot is from our honeymoon. Deep-sea fishing, with me leaning over the edge of a boat while our guide helped me hold an ugly red snapper. Its mouth was agape, still shocked to have lost the game of life to this goofy woman. Look at me: sandy hair, sunburned cheeks, hungry brown eyes squinting in the salt, a life jacket giving my prenatal body a sexy squeeze. It is easily my favorite picture of myself. Not only because it's so flattering, but because I looked so thrilled.

God, my life was so good then.

"Mr. Decker, you can't see the screen," Harrison says, "but we're showing a picture of your wife, Dawn Decker, your wife and costar on *The Perfect Home*, just for anyone who's not a viewer."

If the suggestion that some people haven't seen our show bugs Wyatt, he doesn't show it. "Yes. She's put on a little weight since then, though I always told her she's never been more beautiful to me. She has a hip injury that makes her walk with a limp. Her right hip. And, of course, I hope to God she still has our twins with her. Anyone who sees her, who has any information on her, please contact the authorities immediately."

A pause follows, an anguish of dead air. Harrison clears the quiver out of her throat. I've seen at least a dozen episodes; she is always dry. Thirty years of interviewing sad-sack spouses with tales of kidnappings and *she just went jogging and never came home*, and it's my husband and his fake story that finally make a dent in her. She must be a fan. Everyone is a fan of my husband.

"Mr. Decker, if you could say anything to Dawn—if she was watching right now—what would you tell her?"

And he leans in as if talking to me. Only I know that he's talking to everyone. When Wyatt is in front of a camera, he is only capable of speaking to the entire world. It's the way one side of his mouth twitches. He so desperately wants to show America the pearlies.

"Dawn, I love you. I love our children. Come home. Please, whatever you're planning on doing, don't do it. If our twins are still okay—there is still time to fix this. There is time to get you the help that you need. You don't have to suffer anymore. But please. Turn yourself in. We lost Momma Harlene. There's still a chance you can save our kids. Please. I love you, babycakes."

Again my photo flashes on the screen. Ugly red snapper, bright gummy smile. This time, a phone number blinks under it.

"There is a tip line that we're displaying on the bottom of the screen," Harrison says. "This is in case anyone has seen Dawn Decker, especially in case anyone doesn't recognize her from her work on your popular show, a photo Mr. Decker has provided us."

Of course Wyatt provided it. Wyatt. The asshole could have chosen a more recent one, but he knows perfectly well it's my favorite solo picture.

Now it's my mug shot.

Part Three

DOUBLE NEGATIVES

CHAPTER 13

WYATT

Okay, I admit it. I've made a few mistakes. But hand over heart, I had no other choice.

Let me explain.

First, let's get the bad news out of the way. I never told my doctor. *Illegal pills from Europe* didn't sound like anything I'd ever want on my medical records. And there were no side effects, I swear. Well—at first. I never hallucinated. I never wandered into traffic. That time Dawn found me in the twins' room, staring at the wall? Maybe time got away from me, but I can tell you exactly what I was thinking when I came to. I was thinking how I hated having twins. The wet and greasy diapers, the constant shrieks pinballing in your ears, the feeling of life becoming some Vegas act, juggling balls, spinning plates on sticks.

So there's your honesty: I hate having twins. I don't *hate the twins*. There's a difference.

I promise. I'm thinking clearly. It's me.

Here's another promise: I don't remember writing that document.

It took a lot of mistakes to bring us to this point, I admit. The stuff with Victoria—yeah, mea culpa, and, yeah, I'm going to end it, but you'll understand if I don't publicly admit to the affair in the middle of a crisis. Dawn has the twins. While I will poke and prod her out into the open, I'm not going to risk upsetting her on that level. Victoria's on the back burner. I will resolve it as peacefully as I can, when we are all sane, clearheaded, and calm. Whatever I've done—or supposedly planned on doing—it's clear I have to be the sober one now.

I should never have flushed the pills. That was another mistake. I was weak and horny, which amount to the same thing. The mix of ASB and Miss Chattanooga might as well have been cocaine and heroin. Isn't that the paradox? ASB did its job. It turned me into a firm cartridge full of bullets, chest up, chin high. It made me virile and powerful and fertile. It didn't just make me capable of impregnating women, it made me *want* to impregnate women. Women. Plural.

So I admit it: in a hot moment, I wanted to be infertile again so I didn't have to wear a condom when I committed adultery with Victoria Weatherly. I wasn't thinking; I was making a show of it for her sake.

That's the whole story.

Dawn fancies herself a truth teller—authentic with her audience to the core. But to me, that's a mistake. When I was new to TV, I believed in the basic intelligence and goodness of my audience. I believed the cliché advice people gave me. "Be yourself." So I tried it. *Myself* was interested in home care, so I ended every episode with maintenance tips. Stain most natural woods. Drain your water heater once a year. Pressure wash your siding to boost curb appeal. *Myself* bored people to tears. Only three hundred thousand of you watched the average episode.

We only got a second season because HLTV had new ownership and wanted to try me in a new slot. "He looks like a young

Charlton Heston," someone told me the new president said. "That deserves at least one renewal."

A new slot, I decided, would come with a new Wyatt Decker. No more *Myself*. *Myself* disappointed you. *Myself* got low ratings. No more home-care tips, no more end-of-episode bullet points about preventing mold in exhaust fans. I read an article on how phone apps trigger addictive behavior by using reward chimes and moving targets to trigger dopamine escalation. On the spot, I knew I would rather give people what they want than fail another season as *Myself*. What do people want? Whatever the brain wants, and the brain wants nothing more than being tickled, marionetted, finger fucked. The rest is secondary. In the twenty-first century, we are so tied to our amusement that YouTube algorithms ding your videos if you don't deliver a punch line in the first three seconds. We tap our phones like addicts tap the insides of their elbows, popping up veins, demanding ecstasy at bloodstream speed. We drift through our worlds, sleepy eyed, anesthetized, letting technology dangle carrots from point to point. Every reality show understands you never go to a commercial break without a twist—uh-oh, is this a *load-bearing* wall? The dopamine spikes and the carrot dangles. For season two, I ditched the helpful tips, switching to comedy and cliff-hangers. The audience doubled. You started noticing. Then I ditched the comedy and added Dawn, who became our target audience's perfect avatar: a plain-Jane mold so female viewers could insert themselves into our little American Dream fantasy. I now consider us a form of pornography. There is very little information on home renovation because people are happier as idiots. We are happier with the tricks. There is a place inside every human being, somewhere hidden and primeval, that is disappointed when the magician reveals the invisible thread at his thumb.

We get three million viewers an episode now.

I am finally *Myself.*

The ASB, though. That wasn't *Myself.* At the time, I didn't know that I couldn't order another batch to properly wean myself. Problem one: waiting for the new shipment of pills would have meant a week of going cold turkey anyway. Problem two: I'd have to explain to Dawn why I threw out the pills in the first place.

I ran a thousand excuses in my head. They all sounded worse than the awful reality: *I threw them out in a moment of horniness.* How would *that* go over? *C'mon, babe, you know how much I hate condoms. And if I'm going to cheat on you, isn't it more responsible if I try not to get your best friend pregnant?*

For a while, it went smoothly. We got through the pregnancy, had the twins. I got a little ornery from time to time. Yelled at Dawn when she used the recycling bags to line the trash bin. (I even put *labels* on them.) But nothing you couldn't chalk up to stress and pregnancy and twins. Then, I admit, weird stuff started happening. Daydreaming in the kids' room and only coming to when Dawn touched my shoulder. It felt like I was there for a minute or two. I checked the video footage, saw it was a few hours, and deleted it out of sheer horror.

And then another moment of weakness. I lobbied my PR woman for the top feature of Modern People, only to hear they found nothing interesting about fertility struggles.

"It's been done," an editor said. "Try the *Huffington Post.*"

I started daydreaming again. Apparently, one day, I opened a document on my tablet and let the dreams go a little too far. I wrote about drowning the twins, about buying a small pair of gloves so I could pin it on Hattie Wright. And sure enough, I found two small gloves in my sock drawer. Somehow I bought a pair of gloves without remembering. I don't know how I got them. I don't have a receipt.

Dawn taking the twins was the wake-up call I needed, a splash of cold water to the face. I went to my tablet and read what I'd written. It horrified me. I splashed my face with real cold water and looked at my dripping mug in the mirror for at least ten minutes. But I didn't lose track of time, like that one time in the twins' room. I remember every one of those ten minutes. The pain peeled across me like the world's slowest Band-Aid.

If I was to get out of this, I needed to be sober again. No more staring at walls, no more mysterious gloves. I went to Dr. Pete Mendoza's office and confessed to the ASB and going cold turkey. He looked at me under his big caterpillar eyebrows and said I was lucky I didn't hurt anybody. But what could he do? I left the clinic with a B-vitamin shot and a prescription for the namby-pamby American ASB equivalent. It wouldn't make me as fertile, Mendoza said, but at least it would give me another chance at weaning, like methadone for heroin addicts. Just wean as directed, he warned me.

And I will. This time I really will.

Getting out of this—what do I call it? Crisis? Emergency? Jam?—is not going to be easy. So bear with me on that. I am going to have to lie. White lies, bald-faced lies, they're all coming. I see no way out of that. Wouldn't *you* lie? With $5 million a year and the career you've been building up your whole adult life hanging by a thread? Your whole *family* hanging by a thread? You'd lie. I'd lie. The greater good makes liars of us all.

After I called Dawn and it was clear she thought I really did mean to murder the children, I didn't see any other choice but to get ahead of the story. I grabbed my attorney and went to the police. They directed me to a portly lieutenant named Guzman who said she'd gotten her kitchen remodeled just like the Deckers'. I shot her the pearlies and told her that if we got my twins back, I'd help her spring for the cathedral ceilings. Cathartic laughs all around. Guzman believed every word I said and recommended I use my platform as a basic cable celebrity to make a plea to Dawn. The lawyer loved the idea. It made me look so innocent, which, in her mind, I was. Besides, we had an offer from Trish Harrison: her entire A block in exchange for the exclusive.

After years of the public getting used to the Deckers, after years of unrequited overtures to Modern People, I relished the feeling of being chased again.

As for using Dawn's favorite picture and telling everyone her history with alcohol, I'm sorry. Really, I am. But I have to squeeze her out. I need her to make the first mistake. The police have a report from a hotel in southern Indiana, but that's all we have. Even if I did think of killing the children at some point—and I refuse to believe it was ever a serious threat—the best thing I can do is get Dawn to come back. From here on out, it's a public relations battle between us. And I am undefeated on that field.

Thank God Dawn took the twins because that woke me up. After I get them back, I can ask forgiveness for everything I've done. Everything I'm doing. But I'm finally on the right track. After Dr. Mendoza's shot and the new pills, I feel well. I have sprung up from the abyss. I am alert. I am sober. I am the old Wyatt.

And I am no longer making mistakes.

Trish Harrison leaves me with a staticky "Thank you and good luck" in my earpiece and the segment ends. Behind the camera, my team of cheerleaders awaits. At the head of them is the PR coordinator, a woman whose slick face looks like it's held together with two hundred grand in plastic surgery and a hefty amount of butcher's twine. She holds her hands together by her nose, prayerlike. "That was perfect, Wyatt. We're going to have the entire country looking for your babies."

A producer helps me peel off the microphone pack. Nothing is as it looks on TV. To see me on *Developing with Trish Harrison*, you would think I was a Concerned Husband, fresh-faced and broadcasting live from a high-rise in downtown Nashville. The face is all bronzer. "Downtown Nashville" is a green curtain hanging in a dank TV studio. The Concerned Husband wants to see his twins, yes, but he's just as concerned about what Dawn is up to. What Dawn has on him.

"Just as long as we get them back," I say.

The producer, a fortysomething woman with the thick legs of someone who spends most of her day sitting—my exact audience— shoots me a sympathetic look.

I am winning the PR battle already.

My publicist drives me and our makeshift support team to the police station where my car's parked. Lieutenant Eliza Guzman has been waiting for me in the lobby. It has to be her: bronze hair in a fat ponytail, all over a smooth, featureless neck. When she sees us pull in, she shoulders her thumby body through the doors and gives a finger whistle that startles me. It's good that it startles me. A husband in my situation should look frazzled and jumpy.

"Heard anything?" I ask as Guzman walks up.

"We're in touch with dispatches across Indiana, gave a bunch of people her license plate and photo, mentioned the bad hip. Nothing yet. Obviously she knows she has a recognizable face. Probably lying low."

"What about the credit card charges?"

"If they were in your name, sure. But we need a judge to sign a warrant if we want to see hers. We're working on that, too."

"She could last awhile, then. She's got a million cards. And I mentioned the missing cash, right—"

"Wyatt—"

"There was at least ten grand there—"

"Mr. Decker. Wyatt." Guzman can't be much taller than five feet, which forces her to stretch almost comically to meet my eyeline. Despite the ten years she has on me, despite the police uniform, I can only think of her tippy-toe posture and wide eyes as cute. "We're on it. You just let us do our jobs."

"Isn't there anything else I can do?"

"Rest. You've done enough tonight. More than enough. It's not every case we have the option to send the husband on national TV and get everyone looking for the fugitive." Guzman's look falls away and she nods at my truck. "Who's that?"

"Who's who?"

"The very attractive woman who just let herself in the passenger's side of your vehicle."

I don't even have to look to know. "Oh. Dawn's friend. She was with us at the studio tonight in case Trish Harrison had time. But then they just gave us one segment. I promised I'd drive her home."

Guzman's gaze lingers. She tongues the inside of her cheek. I can't tell if she's straining for a conclusion to make or if she's already reached one. "Oh."

I turn in the direction of Guzman's stare. Victoria is fiddling with her phone, still rouged and TV-ready in her strapless dress. I wish she'd worn a sweatshirt. She looks like we have dinner reservations.

"After I drop her off," I say, "I'm hitting the hay. I'm beat."

"We'll call if there are any updates."

Her words are nice enough. But the way Guzman looks at me—mouth half-open, scratching her jaw—is no longer cute.

Inside my truck, I throw a wave at our PR consultant, who looks relieved to finally pull out of a police garage. Victoria doesn't say anything. After I start the car, I feel her bony fingers crawling up my thigh. I lift her hand off and drive out into the hot night, hoping I'm wearing the bland expression of a husband with nothing to hide.

"I'm glad they cut me off the end of the show."

"Why?" I ask.

Vic shrugs. "Second thoughts. If they didn't cut me off, I would have told Trish all about Dawn coming over and the bleach. And when you think about it, I don't really know anything except what you told me."

Victoria and I are standing in my kitchen, under the cathedral ceilings Dawn and I had picked out. The island lights dice us into shards and shadows. With the rest of the house dark, there is something sterile and medical about it, about the way it spotlights Victoria's face, shows the phlegmy texture of the bronzer on her cheeks. I look up at her, my eyes flitting, searching the memory of what I told her this morning. Hopefully I don't look as empty-headed as I feel.

"You told me Dawn came to your place, acting crazy," I say.

"But bleach?" Victoria's tone turns it into a question. "That stuff about 'going to be with the twins forever.' It doesn't read like Dawn. She was more worried than anything."

"Right." I open my phone and flip through the text thread. *Fair warning. Dawn is being weird. Stole cash and I think a bottle of bleach. Drove off saying something ominous about being with the twins forever. I think she might be headed your way.*

And Victoria: *Does she know about us?* Then: *Is "bleach" a typo?*

Know what? That's me being careful, committing nothing to writing. *And no. Bleach is bleach.*

There's nothing else until a few hours later, 1:13 p.m., when I asked Victoria if she'd like to be on TV. Her yes came within seconds. *But when you said I could be on TV one day, this isn't what I had in mind.*

It's for my kids, I replied. *So people know the danger.*

Victoria heads to the fridge, pulls out a mini-Pellegrino, sips without asking. Then she leaves it hissing on the counter. It's as if the point is to show how little she needs my permission. "You never answered, Wyatt. Does she know about us?"

"No."

"So why did she come to my place?"

"She's completely unhinged. I can't explain anything she does."

"And the crazy thing is, I talked to her today. On the phone. Did I tell you that?"

My cheeks flush as the seed of a migraine sprouts between my eyes. No, she didn't tell me. "How was she?"

"Worried, but herself. She seemed okay, given everything." Victoria's eyes pinch. "Not crazy like you said."

The light flitters above us. It lasts as long as a skipped heartbeat—an entire lifetime between blinks. It takes everything I have to pucker myself so I don't flinch.

"It goes in and out," I say. "Postpartum depression can be ugly and unfair."

"In and out? I don't think it works that way."

"Maybe not."

"So what is it, then?"

"Me," I whisper with a long vowel, the word slow-slipping out of me like a hot glaze. "I wasn't paying enough attention to her. Wasn't seeing the signs. After she took the twins, I saw the drawer—" I point right where Victoria's standing. "There was a mess, some things were gone. I didn't see bleach, but why else rummage under the sink?"

Victoria's lips part, her fingers tickle-guarding her throat. Almost there.

The instinct is to argue and contradict, to throw your weight into the deep end of the lie. That's wrong. People will believe anything if it sounds like a confession.

"Blame me," I say. "It's my fault. Maybe I *should* have admitted to the affair months ago. Maybe I should have ripped off this Band-Aid before the kids."

"Oh." Victoria puffs out her stuck breath. "But in her state now . . . ?"

"No. It'd be too embarrassing for her. It's embarrassing for me. I probably should have told Trish Harrison, too, but I'm worried about my children." My voice bounces off the high ceilings: *dren, dren, ren*. I like that I can hear the anxiety of my delivery. It's not half-bad.

"I'm sorry. Of course you are. Maybe I could reach out to her again—tell her how much I love her—"

"I wouldn't. What if you let something slip? We can't make any mistakes—no revelations to the press. At least until Dawn is back safe with the twins."

"All right." She caps the Pellegrino and slides her purse up her arm, then pulls up a rideshare app on her phone. "There's a car in the neighborhood. Maybe it's best if I go home."

"I think so."

And I do. If she's asking this many questions, it's better she gets her story from the Trish Harrisons of the world.

Vic closes her sleeveless arms, bending slightly at the waist, looking both worried and achy cold. I walk over and rub her on the shoulders so she can feel the hot blood in my hands. "Let's get her back, safe and happy. As happy as she can be. For Dawn's sake. After a while, when people see the problems I've had with her, no one will blame us for getting a divorce. Then, when the public's ready for it, it's you and me. You won't be taking anything from Dawn she's not willingly throwing away."

She nods. "All right."

I slip my arms around her shoulders for a hug, and she pours herself into it. The way her body slots into mine is instant pleasure. It reminds me of plugging into an old-fashioned outlet; I can practically hear the sharp click of the spark. Her head right under my cheekbone, the softness of her breasts against my solar plexus. I pull back and let her look up at my eyes, but she doesn't dip in for the kiss. If anything, she pulls away.

An arc of headlights swings through the windows by the portico: her ride is already here. So I let her go. Our hands slide off each other's arms, but slowly.

"I can wait," she whispers in my ear, "if you can."

I can't, but I'll have to.

I'm in the dining room sucking my way to the bottom of a glass of Jack Daniel's when my tablet blinks awake. I almost forgot it was there. My mind has been knotting up all day, thumbing between the threads of what I told people had happened and what really had. Jack Daniel's is a good cure for that. It licks like a massage from the inside. If the tablet blinking is just another notification of a press request, they can wait another glass or two.

The notification turns out to be nothing—some spam email from an axe-throwing place I went to once. But at least it has me looking at the tablet again. The file is still there. Tap-tap, copy/paste the password, and I'm back in.

It's startling. Beyond startling. All the talk of *tragedy* and *baptize first* and *Hattie's gloves* and I remember writing none of it. The weird language, the sentence fragments, the random caps—they might as well be a foreign language. But even more startling is the speech. The speech sounds like me. I even wrote in little cues, when to wait to let the audience stop laughing, or crying.

How close was I to really doing it?

The gloves are still upstairs, and those are easy enough to get rid of. I can see myself shrugging at Guzman: *What gloves? I throw away stuff all the time. Oh, you mean that was* evidence? *Shucks, shucks, shucks.* If Dawn somehow turns things around on me, at least there won't be a pair of Hattie-sized gloves in the sock drawer. I'm not that stupid.

But that doesn't mean I'm not stupid, period. Smart people don't end up where I am. I know enough to avoid googling *how to destroy a tablet* or *how to wipe a tablet.* I know enough that taking a hammer to this thing or deleting old files—files the FBI can probably restore anyway—is only going to make me look guilty. I stare at the tablet awhile. Dawn left it. I don't know why. She says she copied the file. I can just say she invented the file entirely.

If she wanted to prove her story, she should have taken the whole tablet.

Now, with the gloves and that tablet in hand, I walk to the backyard. It's pockmarked with the clumps and craters of removed tree stumps. A quarter moon stains the clouds. It's a tangy summer night in suburban Nashville. This is the life I wanted for my twins, a childhood completely unlike mine. And what was my childhood like? I can pinpoint the exact sound. A steel guitar in my headphones, distorted to a tinny twang, cutting through my parents' fights about what makes a steak medium rare. For a few minutes, at least, every song rephrased my life in red ink. "I paid six dollars a pound for the sirloin you just ruined" *(Well our house in Sugar Hill wasn't much to see)* / "Good, that's only an hour of work for you down at the shop" *(But my mama had a knack for findin' deals for three)* / "I gotta leave, because if I don't, I know I'll put this steak knife right through your Goddamn eye" *(And my daddy was a map for how a man should be)*.

There's always the toolshed, out on the lip where our yard meets the trees. It stands there in the far corner of our lot, 150 square feet of sore thumb. Yet we never really *see* it. It's the kind of thing that hides in plain sight. Everything about it is prepackaged, down to the digital lock on the double doors, password VESTABRANDS1. I punch it in and it gives a soft, welcoming beep. Still works. The air inside is musty, smelling of Styrofoam and cardboard. The automatic light we installed doesn't flicker on. We never tested it. Vesta Brands provided a corkboard wall's worth of tools, a thirty-piece wrench set still hanging in perfect ascending order, short to long. I feel slightly guilty about that. The corkboard should be an unfinished jigsaw puzzle, the whole shed grassy and muddy with use. Oh, well. The shed can still have its uses.

I find a Phillips head and unscrew a corner of the corkboard so I can pull a piece of it away long enough to slip the tablet inside. The toolshed, the combination lock, the corkboard. Three reasons no guest will ever find it. Three is a good number.

Outside, I watch the lock of the double doors kiss into place, hum with a green light that says the shed's closed properly. I take a happy sniff. The cicadas are out, trilling. Looking out at the flattened, football-field yard we'd carved into the trees, I'm a little jealous of my twins. They would have grown up with a father who had a toolshed. They would have grown up in Belle Meade. The whistling forest, the chorus of cicadas, all the busy silence of nature. And inside, they would have grown up to the sound of laughing, happy parents.

Maybe they still can. One happy parent, at least.

CHAPTER 14

DAWN

"You know, she was just, like, really rude to me. Then I saw what Wyatt said on the news and it all made sense."

I'm filling up the Tahoe on pump eleven when a familiar face flashes on the news-and-weather screen. There she is: scowling lips, hair trimmed to peach fuzz. The tomboy clerk from the RelaxInn. The one I'd apologized to.

The screen rolls stock footage of Chevy Tahoes as a reporter's voice-over cuts through. " . . . the Decker twins were still alive as of a few days ago. However, it's not clear how long that will last."

Before they cut to a live shot of the reporter, the TV blinks and I see a flash of my resting bitch face reflecting on-screen. Is this how the world sees me? If *The Perfect Home* is a sitcom, then I play the role of naggy wife, perpetually waiting at home in curling irons, telling America to pick up its dirty clothes. It works, Wyatt used to say, because I was the first person to poke holes in his Teflon façade. But that left no other role for me than the foot-dragging spouse. Janie always encouraged us to use our real personalities, so out came Dawn the Worrier. I remember watching the dailies from my first shoot and searching for myself in the background, then wondering why I always wore a scowl. "No, hon," Janie had said. "You just look like that. You'll get used to it." Apparently, so did the country. No matter how much I try to smile, how pleasant I try to be to the clerks of the world, the cake of my personality is already set in America's mind.

I grab the gas receipt, check the twins' car seats, and pull away into the morning commute.

Filling up feels silly now, an unnecessary risk. I've watched those missing-persons movies where the heroine just *has* to come out of hiding for one reason or another. Reaching out to her mother, agreeing to meet an ex-lover in a very public place. I always want to scream at them, *Stay put! Someone will see you!* But we forget how much we are all Blanche DuBois, always relying on the kindness of strangers for basic needs. Coffee, breakfast, gas, cash. I try to stick to automatic services: gas station pumps and self-checkout aisles. ATMs, I figure, are too hot.

To become invisible, I have to change some very obvious facts about myself. The most obvious would be the two tiny humans I lug everywhere. I couldn't be any more conspicuous in public with two heaping piles of dynamite under my arms. I'm not the only woman in America with infant twins, but I am the only famous runaway with them. It's not like I can swing by Alice's all the way from Indiana and drop them off. And if I leave them in a hot car in late June, someone is going to notice and ask questions. I think about leaving them home, but that would make me a bad mother, and besides, what if the police show up when I'm out?

No. If I must get "caught," I will be caught being a good mother.

The second problem is the limp. I don't know if it's the stress, or all the sitting around and driving, but it's getting worse. There's not much I can do about that. Even without the pain, it would feel like someone had slapped one of those police tire boots on my hip bone. I literally can't walk straight if I try. So I don't. I lean into it. I buy myself an old-man cane at a Walgreens.

Last is my appearance. There is no changing this body. There are no self-serve breast-reduction clinics, no drive-through teeth straighteners. And I'm five-ten, even if I don't look it standing next to Wyatt on TV. No heels with this bum hip, so I'm not getting any shorter than I already am in my flats. Petite women have always complained to me about how invisible they feel to the world. Count me jealous.

At least I can change my hair color. I buy a dye-at-home kit while out for supplies. Junior gave a particularly anus-clenching scream as I dyed myself in the Airbnb bathroom, like he knew how bad it was going to be. He was right. My hair is brunette now, yes, but blotchy and badly in need of another woman's touch. I have never not been blonde. I hate it. I look like if Jackie Kennedy discovered camping and fast food.

After a couple of rehearsals of my walk in the mirror, I sigh and fall into a chair. I am trying to become *less* conspicuous. Instead it's costumey. I have turned myself into an obvious thirty-two-year-old cosplaying as a limpy hobo. All I'm missing are the Groucho Marx glasses and fake mustache.

I pick Junior out of his seat and try to shush him, but he can only sense the world in whiffs of primary colors. To him, this brunette blob holding him is a stranger. He screams bloody murder and none of my bouncing or patting soothes him. The ruckus wakes Harlene Mae, who takes her older brother's harmonic cues and starts screaming alto.

I am not cut out for this.

• • •

The second time I send a message to Judy, the Airbnb owner, to see if the house is available for an extra day, her replies seem hesitant:

I have a cleaning crew who comes through, and someone's booked it for Monday. I'd really like the cleaning crew to have a full shift with it. Sorry. I get bad reviews if it's not clean.

Are you sure? I ask. *I could pay extra.*

I'm so sorry, Shailene.

She's polite but firm—as though she suspects I might be Dawn Decker, but not enough to risk losing Shailene's five-star review. Am I growing too paranoid? I don't know. But I can read a tinge of doubt in the way she writes *Shailene*. It's the first time she's called me by my fake name.

Now it's Sunday morning and my checkout time has officially passed. My Tahoe sits inside a first-floor garage, off the street for the moment. But how long until I *have* to drive it again? If anyone notices that obvious Volunteer State license plate, the next time I drive it could be my last. I open a duffel bag and start packing the twins' things, if only for the reassuring sound of zipping up luggage, but I don't know where I'm going next. Technically, I am a trespasser. And I don't know when the cleaning crew gets in.

The main house, a navy-blue Craftsman on a busy intersection, has been quiet. I haven't seen the owner once. From the puckered old smile she gives in her online avatar, Judy Rutledge is at least seventy-five. Her backyard's raised lattice has gone mossy and wild, at least a month overdue for trimming.

I wonder if that means she does nothing on her weekends but watch the news.

Whatever she's watching, it's time for me to go.

I cinch Harlene Mae into her car seat, then Junior. A horseshoe of hair has filled in above his ears. The blue veins in his forehead make him look like a forty-year-old in an infant's body. Maybe I'm one of those crazy mothers who sees things in her children that aren't there, but there is something ancient and perma-conscious about him, like a carving of an infant in Egyptian limestone. With his eyes half-shut, he tips his head at me. *You have no idea what you're doing. Do you, Mom?*

No, Mom does not.

And as I'm meditating on an imaginary conversation with my infant son, the code key at the door beeps.

The shades are drawn, but two distinct shadows hover in the window above the lock. I run to the door and hold my end in place. Silence. Then a second round of beeps.

The lock groans, trying to turn over, but I stifle the doorknob with my hands.

"Cleaning," a woman's voice announces in a vaguely Eastern European accent. "Cleaning crew."

My eyes are closed, but I can imagine the two of them outside and I know they are looking at each other.

"Go see downstairs," one says.

Downstairs. As in the garage holding my Tahoe. The only way I can get down there is through the same stairs they're blocking now.

Both twins are still awake in their car seats on the floor. Harlene Mae smacks her lips, flirting with a doze. Junior's fists are bunched up and his eyes are closed like always, but there's a dim feeling in the air like rain clouds scudding up on a sunny day. Five minutes, buddy. Just give me five minutes, and we're out of here as soon as they are.

A jolt pulses through the house. The garage door is opening. There's nothing I can do—they're going to see the Tahoe. What if I run for it? I'll look like a crazy woman, running down the street holding the handles of two car seats, legs swaying unevenly, but the intersection is busy enough. Maybe a yellow cab will take pity on me.

"Still here," the other woman says about a minute later, climbing the stairs.

"They suppose to be check out."

"Call the woman."

But through the other window, I can see Judy is already shuffling on her back porch. I recognize her from her photo, but in real life she wears a pissy grimace, all pretzeled with scoliosis and leaning on a walker and its feet of halved tennis balls. She takes the steps like someone defusing a bomb. One wrong step, and kaboom.

At least that gives me time. I let go of the door, grab my purse, and lug the car seats outside. Two moon-faced women with heavy cheeks and white lips glare back at me, agog.

"I'm so sorry." I thread the needle between them and limp down the stairs. "Lost track of the time. I'll be out of your hair."

"Why you lock us out?"

"Lost track of the time," I repeat.

"Wait for Missus Judy," the other one says. "We call her."

"Gotta go!"

"You're limping," a new voice says. I turn the corner at the bottom of the stairs and hear who said it: *Missus Judy.* Funny, her spine straightens when she looks at me, though she wears the same look on her face that the ornery get when they have to get up off the couch.

"Oh." The cane is under my arm. I wasn't using it. I don't have that as an excuse. "Had a hip replaced. Just recently. Recovering well, though, as you can see."

"Been watching the news." Judy's voice sounds like a smoker's, buzzy and masculine. "There's this woman who they say took her baby twins. Young woman, said to be walking with a limp."

"Oh? Right side or left side? Mine's the left."

This seems to throw her off, but she crinkles a brow, and I can watch in real time as her resolve reasserts itself. "Can't say. Shailene, I'm a little disappointed. You don't look like you do in your picture."

"Neither do you, Judy."

"I'm just old. But you're a whole other woman."

I set Harlene Mae down and tug on a lock of my newly brunette hair. "I change things up a lot. But I understand you have to clear this place out, so I will be out of your way, just as soon as—" I move, but Judy shuffles to block me. "Just as soon as you'll let me into my car."

"I don't think so." Judy calls up to the cleaning women. "Don't touch anything in there yet. Leave it all as she left it."

"Listen. Judy, I'm not who you seem to think I am, whoever this is—"

She leans to pull her phone from her pocket. "I'm calling the police."

Junior has heard the commotion, and now the rainstorm that has been on his horizon all day has arrived. He starts the fist-shaking shrieks.

"No," I say. "Please don't."

But Judy's already on the line. "This is Judy Rutledge, I'm at one oh nine Tavern Boulevard. I have a woman here who fits the description—"

"You can tell them whatever you want. But I'm leaving."

"—yes, I believe it's her. She's trying to leave. She's in a green Chevy Tahoe. . . . Yes, thank you." She angles herself between the car and the sidewalk, still the human traffic cone. "Young woman, the police say they'll be here any minute."

My chin seizes. Junior is shrieking in his seat and both of them are getting heavy. Even if I do get them away in time, I'm spotted.

Green Chevy Tahoe, southern Indianapolis, big ol' thirty-two-year-old with a limp and two twins.

I throw the seats in the back as safely as I can and go around the front—through Judy's Weedwackers and garden gnomes—as I hit the locks. Once in, I rev the engine. The backup camera shows Judy's hunched figure standing between me and the road.

"Out of the way," I shout. "I'll do it."

But she doesn't move. I rev—once, twice, and then a screaming third—before giving up. I am not adding *attempted murder* to whatever this will be. I am not that kind of woman. I pull the twins' seats out of the car, one by one, and start jogging off.

It's too late. A dark SUV with a siren light on the roof pulls up to the curb, and a man in a blue jacket steps out. Even in my panic, I'm surprised how old he is. He has a neatly trimmed gray beard, close-cropped hair around a lonely patch of scalp, and a notch on his nose like someone once broke it.

"Detective Sipowicz," he says, flipping open a wallet with a badge inside, then flipping it closed in the same movement, a quick flick he must have done a thousand times. "We got your call. I happened to be in the area."

"This is Dawn Decker. The woman from TV."

I set my twins down. There is nothing more I can do. At least Junior and Harlene Mae are safe.

"I can see that. The woman who's been all over the news." There is something warm and tranquil about his gaze. He seems to fast-forward through the Miranda rights. "Ma'am, you have the right to remain silent—anything you say can and will be—you have the right to an attorney." Wasting no time, he opens the doors to his truck. "Your twins are welcome to come along. I don't have car seats. But you can carry them in, and we'll accommodate them later."

I oblige, pulling my two crying twins into the damp backseat of the Suburban. Sipowicz moves a few of my bags from the Tahoe into his trunk. I don't know why. The windows are so soundproof I can only catch the back end of his conversation with Judy.

"Thank you, Ms. Rutledge," he's saying as he gets in. "One of my colleagues will be along shortly to collect a statement."

Ms. Rutledge. So he knows her. She's the kind of woman whom the cops would know, the kind who calls them up whenever she doesn't like boys skateboarding on the sidewalks. She watches me, standing upright with her fists on her hips. All she's missing is the superhero cape. I've made her day. Her month. Her entire lifetime. She will always be the Woman Who Spotted Dawn Decker.

And me? Who will I always be? In the eyes of America, I am Wyatt's psycho ex-wife, and soon, news will come over the wire that I was done in by an eighty-year-old woman who can barely walk. No, I'm not cut out for this. I never was. Wyatt Decker is still the world's hero, and here I am, in the back of some detective's car, under arrest for kidnapping the children I was trying to save. Somehow it feels like destiny. When you aren't good with people, when you're uncomfortable telling them stories, they will fill the vacuum of your silence with stories of their own.

That story will be simple enough for the media to put together now. New mom. Postpartum depression. The pressure of a hit TV show. Everything else after that will probably be up to Wyatt. He's never had any problem telling people where to look, pointing at one palm while the other slides out an ace. I don't know who my lawyer will be, or if they'll be any good, or if I'll end up in prison for ten years, or what will happen to *The Perfect Home*, or whether I'll die a bitter old maid like Ms. Rutledge, or what the twins will think of me when they've grown up, whether they'll buy what the rest of the world bought.

All I know is I'm giving Judy Rutledge one star.

"I didn't kidnap my children," I tell Sipowicz.

"Of course not." Sipowicz's cupped eyes glance at me in the rearview mirror. They're half-open and dozy, betraying nothing. Why is he familiar? I've never been to Indianapolis, yet I'm certain that he must have been to Tennessee before. Maybe someone who came to a signing once? Thanks to *The Perfect Home*, I've met enough people to fill a lifetime. People look familiar to me all the time, and I always have to apologize for my face blindness. This man could be anyone. Still, the feeling cuts down to my marrow.

"You never took my ID," I say slowly. "Or cuffed me."

"No. I didn't."

The light goes yellow and he slows to make the stop. I hear sirens somewhere. "I know you're familiar. Have you ever been to Nashville?"

"Oh, once or twice," he says, too calm. Like we are on our way to pick up gas or firewood or beer. Nothing about this feels like an arrest. "I only started wearing a beard in my old age. I did try it once, but when you were—oh, yay high—you stopped recognizing me then, too. I didn't like that. So back when you knew me, I made sure dear old Dad was always clean-shaven."

I stare at him.

"There's my girl." The light goes green. "What do you say we go for a drive, darlin'?"

CHAPTER 15

DAWN

Tim Fremont hands me two styrofoam containers smelling of fish and burned batter. "There y'are. Road food is good for nerves. Get something fried in you."

He rummages through the rest of the bag and pulls out bowl after styrofoam bowl. "I didn't know what to get the twins, so I got a little bit of everything."

"They've been breastfeeding. And I have formula in my bag."

"Right." He scratches his head on the crown, where it's all empty scalp. "Never was great with kids. Your mom, she was the all-star."

We are in a Louisville motel room. Though the curtains are drawn, I can hear cars outside thumping over potholes. It's the kind of place where if you tilt one of the paintings of fruit bowls, you'll discover a slice of rusty stain that might be either Coke or blood. I hope it's Coke. We are sitting in a foggy silence, just like the one that followed us as he drove through Greenwood, through Scottsburg, through southern Indiana. It felt like there was nothing good we could say. Not while driving.

We. As in me, my two children, and the father I haven't seen in over twenty years.

Tim stands with his hands in his khaki pockets, clicking his tongue, making a song out of it. The fish isn't half-bad, but there's so much vinegar in the coleslaw it almost tastes boozy. Looking at my dad—at Tim Fremont—makes me feel full of vinegar already. I slap a knob of butter onto the bread.

"I've rehearsed this speech a thousand times." His voice is a cello, ringing and full of bass. It hasn't aged at all. The sound of it gnaws right through me, resonating in the parts of me that are still three years old, the parts that still hear Dad as the voice of God. "But, boy, I'm forgettin' every word right now."

"How'd you find me? Your timing was good, I'll give you that. 'Detective Sipowicz'?"

"*NYPD Blue*. Loved that show, but no one remembers it. Anyways, you can probably gather I didn't just happen upon you. Been tailin' you since Kentucky, and I've had the Indianapolis PD scanner on for a few days now. I'm used to spendin' a lotta time in cars. But when your address came up on the police radio, I didn't see another way. I had to step in."

"Why didn't you tell me that it was you?"

He cringes. "I've seen your show. You're—I'm sorry—you're not a great actress, darlin'. And there wasn't much time."

"Don't call me that."

"What?"

"I'm not your darlin'."

"Sorry. Habit."

Habit. What habit? Do the grooves in his brain that label me *darlin'* really keep after twenty years? My hand raises to my throat, guarding. "How long have you been following me?"

"I've been around. Looking in. I saw what was going on and wanted to make sure you were safe."

"I didn't know I was that easy to find. The police haven't even found me."

His smile squeezes a flurry of new wrinkles around his ears. "Well, there's a lot I can do that the cops can't."

"Why not?"

"Because it's illegal."

Junior starts a mild cry—mild for him, at least—so I pick him out of his seat and start rocking. "What, like going through my trash?"

"They need a warrant to go through some of your financial records. I don't."

"That's a blatant invasion of my privacy."

"You were in trouble. So, yeah, I won't deny it."

"*Won't deny.* That's a double negative."

"Double negative makes a positive." He snaps a finger. "I forgot. Owe you a quarter, don't I?"

An old running joke between us. So old, in fact, I'd forgotten it and would have gone on forgetting it if he weren't in the room with me now. When I was a kid, he said he wanted to raise me to "speak proper," so anytime I'd drop a phrase like "wouldn't do nothing," he'd cry out, "Double negative! Makes a positive!," and make me say it right. I remember being a brat and making up the most egregious double negatives I could think of. One time, before he left, I even remember dropping a quintuple his way. "I'm not not not not going to miss school," I said once right before summer vacation.

Most people remember only a handful of actual conversations from when they were ten. My memory's even worse. Most of my recollections of Tim Fremont are just sensations. The sandpaper feeling of his cheeks when he hadn't shaved. The smell when he'd been drinking, the juniper in his gin, the piney mouthwash he'd use to hide it. But I do remember his rules about double negatives. *I won't not stay up late, ha-ha. Makes a positive, Dad, you said!*

"What?" he asks.

I realize I've been staring at him. "You're not how I pictured."

"Yeah? How's that?"

"I don't know. The clean haircut, for one. Your clothes fit." I scan him. Momma Harlene said the last time she saw him, he'd put on twenty pounds since the most recent photo we had. It's a fuzzy Polaroid, him wearing a baggy Nike polo, a comb-over dangling on his scalp like a loose tooth. But now he wears a Harrington jacket, a button-down, dark khakis that show a tauter waist.

"I guess I always had this image of you as a man with a permanent beer stain on his shirt," I say.

A snicker comes out of him, high-pitched and surprising. I haven't heard that laugh in twenty years.

"You're not too far off," he says. "Maybe fifteen years ago, at least. I wasn't good. I'd always been like that, always a shirt size too fat. I was in the Henderson PD awhile. One night I was so drunk at work I tried flirting with a woman whose son just died in a car crash. Mind you, flirting is the nice-people word. I was hittin' on her. That was my bottom. Take a sabbatical, they said, but what they really mean by that is you're fired, and maybe reapply for your job if you come back cleaned up. So I did. Went cold turkey. Had the shakes and everything. Haven't had a drop of booze since. I tried to quit a thousand times before, you know, and God knows why it took this time.

"Anyways, no one was hiring an alcoholic still technically on sabbatical, so I got my private investigator license. There's a lot of PI work in the Vegas area, I'm sure you can imagine. It's not a bad living. Just a little sad, watching husbands cheat on their wives, wives cheat on their husbands. It's decent enough money that I never did come back from that sabbatical. Most of my coworkers assumed I'd fallen into the part of the gutter there's no getting out from."

"I thought the same thing," I say.

He takes a sip of bottled water, cringing like it burns as hard as gin. "Yeah."

"You're a private investigator. Figures. I could have used you so much the past few weeks." Junior's little hand gives a squeeze at my neck. My voice cracks with it. "Past few years."

"I'm sorry. It's how your mom wanted it."

I raise my eyebrows. "That's not what she said."

"Harlene was—" He shakes his head. "No one knows this better than you. She was a great woman, but bullheaded. She made me promise not to contact you."

I close my eyes because if I don't, he'll see them rolling.

"I'm tellin' the truth," he insists.

"You left us." My pulse quickening, I set Junior back in his seat so he can sleep. "That much I know. You left us because you liked that other life better. That's the only explanation. What kind of father are you?"

"Well, now, that's the thing." He sighs and sits down on the other bed, clasping his hands. "I'm not."

Here we go. *I didn't sign up for a daughter*, or some other bullshit excuse that would make it okay not to send so much as a birthday card.

"You don't believe me," he says.

"It's always something with you."

"No, darlin', listen to what I'm sayin' to you." He looks up, his eyes gone veiny. "I married your mother. I helped raise you for a while. But you're not my biological child."

My head goes light, untethered. I sit down slowly on the bed opposite him. My mouth is open and smacking a little.

"This is why I didn't want to have this conversation in the car." He sighs. "I met your mother when you were two. Of course you can't remember. I was going door-to-door then, selling these dumbass coupon books to pay my way until I could become a cop. One day I walked in your mom's office and she told me off right on the spot. I can hear her voice now: 'This is a place of business, now git!'"

In spite of myself, I can't help but smile at how spot-on his impression is. Momma Harlene definitely said that.

Tim seems encouraged and continues a little louder. "I was a bit of a dick back then, so I saw something flirty in it. Gave her my card. She didn't call, so I showed up the next week with apology flowers. You shoulda seen the look on her face when she realized it wasn't a delivery for someone else in the office—someone brought *her* flowers. It was a whirlwind from there. Everything with your mother was a whirlwind. Well, turns out she didn't have much to her name, and she came with one condition."

"Me."

"Yeah. Rather than having me raise you as a stepfather, Harlene said she'd take my name and we'd tell you I was the genuine article. We both thought it was better. For you."

A thousand memories slip through my fingers. Momma Harlene was an only child, just like me, and her parents both died young, but she did have an aunt and a distant cousin in La Vergne with the last name Mintz. Once we visited a single mom who lived in a manufactured home that smelled like propane and skunk spray. "Aren'tya glad our name ain't *Mintz*?" Mom asked me on the long drive home. I always assumed she was talking about living in that house.

"But I don't understand," I say. "Who's my father? She said you were the only man she'd ever dated." Momma Harlene's voice cracks through me, as loud as if it's in the room: *Only man I ever dated, and that experience is more than enough for me, darlin'.*

"Don't know. She was too ashamed to talk about your real father. Eventually I just stopped askin'. Should have kept pushin', though. Should have told you from the start. But that woman. When we had our last fight, she said she finally did tell you who I really was, and that you wanted nothing to do with me. I wrote to her for years asking if I could come back, and she always said the same thing. You didn't want me around. Well, I admit I was a drunk, and I was no good for the two of you, and I was a grade-A screwup who wanted to leave. So when she made me promise I'd never talk to you, it seemed like the best thing I could do for you was just step back and . . . oblige."

"I was *ten*. You should have overruled me."

"Not by then, you weren't. You were fifteen, then you were twenty, then you were twenty-five. Then you were famous and livin' in this whole other world. I know it's a coward's excuse, but it got harder every year that slipped by. I thought it was too late, that you'd only hate me, and the longer it got, the more you'd hate me for letting it go so long. It's not easy asking forgiveness for all the dumb things you did while drinkin'. It's like turning over rocks and not knowin' what bugs will crawl out."

"Her funeral. You never came."

"The lawyer sent me the wrong address. It was in her will to do that. She knew I'd come lookin' for you." He shakes his head. "I took the bait and ended up on the other side of Nashville."

"She's not as vindictive as that."

"We all got our sore spots," he says gently. "Even Harlene. But even after all these years, I wasn't *not* going to come to Harlene's funeral."

"Double negative."

He gives a wan smile. "Fifty cents I owe you now."

I shake my head, trying to process it all. "So . . . you were in Nashville? And you didn't . . . ?"

"Come to see you? I wanted to, real bad. I was gonna turn up and tell you the truth. But I don't know—it felt like pickin' a scab. And with you in pain, what was I gonna do—say, 'Hey, your fake father is back'? I ain't happy to say it, but I went back to Nevada." He takes a long sip. "Honestly? The longer I waited, the harder it got. Even when I was just a short drive away. I hope you know, I have always loved you. I watched you on that show and I felt guilty, but a lot more proud than guilty, so I kept watchin'. Thinking about how you loved me back then."

"I loved you, sure. A long time ago. I remember I used to send you birthday cards. Me, eleven years old, sending my dad birthday cards. And what did I get back? I don't even remember. I just remember when I grew up, I would tell people your love always had a 'return to sender' stamp on it."

He shakes his head. "I never got any cards."

"Still. I sent them." A wave of heat simmers up my neck. The same thing happens whenever my blood pressure rises, which is usually when I'm at a book signing and see the line goes out for at least an hour's worth of awkward conversations. Or when I read a comment on social media about how someone met Wyatt and me, and how Wyatt was warm and funny but talking to Dawn was like pulling teeth. It's an old feeling. A feeling I recognize as I sit here with him. It is the same twist in my stomach every time Momma Harlene told me that, no, there was nothing in the mail for me that day. No brown package, no letter, not even a postcard.

"You're why I'm no good with people," I say, just as much realization as accusation.

"I'm sorry." Now when he sips the bottled water, his hands shake. "Well, then what happened happened. You were on the news, and you can put the rest together. Just the thought of you alone in the world with these twins. I finally had something I could give you that would make a difference."

"I'm grateful for your help getting out of Indianapolis. But I don't know how you being here helps me."

"Well, for starters, you'd be under arrest right now if it wasn't for me."

"So what am I—fleeing the real police? I don't see how that's better. Dawn Decker, resisting arrest."

"You have to be under arrest to resist it. And we got you out of that Tahoe. Even if they do get a warrant for your financial records, there's not going to be any charges for them to track you. It's my dime now, if you'll have me."

Harlene Mae stirs from her nap, and, immediately lonely, she starts crying. I lift her up, the way I wish someone could have lifted me up when I was ten, and hold her over my shoulder, tapping the loneliness out of her. What a wonderful age. To Harlene Mae, one hug from Mom fills up the entire universe.

Tim smiles at us. "You named her Harlene."

"Certainly wasn't going to name her *Tim*."

"Your mom would have said not to name her Harlene, but secretly she would have loved it. Even back then, she talked about wanting grandkids. How happy was she to meet these two?"

There is nothing I can say that won't make me keel over sobbing, so I only get out one word. "Happy."

He stands from the bed, his hands hanging awkwardly in the air. "May I?"

Reluctantly, I hand her over. But Harlene Mae doesn't make a sound. She leans on his shoulder like she was leaning on mine, her neck too weary for her heavy head. Tim gives her the same finger taps on the back.

"I know I'm not their grandpa," Tim says. "I didn't figure I'd love 'em this much."

Turning away so he can't see the tear in my eyes, I hear the sound of something tapping on plastic. Drops. A leak, probably—it's the kind of motel where the air conditioner sweats for some reason. But when I find the plastic bag, it's with the takeout Tim brought in. One of the bags is slick with cream.

"What's this?" I ask.

"I forgot. It's all melted. I got you your favorite."

"My favorite what?" I tip it over the garbage can and something like milk comes out. "Is this ice cream?"

"You once told me there was no ice cream worth eating but butter brickle. Hope you haven't outgrown that?"

I smile when I see the tub. "I wouldn't say no."

"Double negative," he says, rocking Harlene Mae to a state of bliss. "Makes a positive."

CHAPTER 16

DAWN

I spend hours trying to sleep, but it's summer in Kentucky and the air conditioner only spits out hot sweat. Junior coos a little bit. I've learned these are the first waves of his rising tide. After pushing myself out of bed and picking him up, I go to the window and rock him while I street-watch.

I've never stayed in motels as an adult. It's a naked feeling to have a door open to the street. No driveway, no lobby—nothing between you and the world. This isn't a friendly neighborhood. There's a check-cashing place on the corner with bars on its windows. A no-brand sandwich shop is still open, awash in crackling light. I see a car slide in the drive-through every so often, but otherwise, it's empty.

It occurs to me that this must be how Tim Fremont's life has felt since he cleaned himself up. Street-watching. Observing the undercarriage of the world. All those bad marriages, suspicious husbands and wives who always turn out to be right. And what's the best-case scenario for a private investigator? That there's *nothing* to see? You collect $50 an hour watching a middle-aged housewife go grocery shopping and drop the dog at the groomer's? Even the best days have to be so lonely. There is nothing more lonely than being silent in a sea of people.

At least Tim's taken care of himself. Though he's lost more of it, his hair is better now than it was twenty years ago—he's cropped it like someone who's accepted the limits of his hairline. And he tucks in his shirts now. When I pictured him, I'd always conjure up images of that same slob from the photos, just with graying hair and a few extra wrinkles. The way Momma Harlene talked, he was more likely dead in a gutter than trim and flourishing.

Mom, I think. Is it true, then? You didn't want him to come back because you didn't want me knowing your secret?

Junior handles the heat better than I do and soon he's dozing on my shoulder. I set him down next to Harlene Mae. The two angels. I still can't get over how twins look together, cupped in their little chairs. They're fraternal, but at this stage, every newborn looks alike. They look like some two-for-one deal I got from heaven.

I'm usually a good sleeper (straight through the night, no naps required), but if I can't get down before 1:00 a.m., I know the night is going to be useless. So I open my phone and check Wyatt's Instagram page.

The motel's crappy Wi-Fi makes slow agony of every tap, but I've got nothing else to do, so I wait until his most recent post loads. It's a wall of text, white on black. *Thank you to everyone for your incredible support. Though I know there will be a lot of interest, I ask you to respect the authorities and my family's privacy at this time. The only way we can get through this is with Dawn back with the twins, safe and sound.*

Dawn, if you're reading this, I know you won't hurt the twins.

My heart quickens, thumping in my throat. The asshole. Of course I won't hurt them. But I've learned enough from Wyatt to know what this will make every person think. They will only take three words out of it.

Dawn. Hurt. Twins.

I know a lot has changed between us recently, but, Dawn, that doesn't have to be the end of things.

Dawn. End. Things.

The man is seeding the public. And it's working. The comments underneath the post are as they always are: 95 percent supportive, 5 percent nutjob. I scroll past every *Praying for you* and *Our thoughts are with your family at this difficult time* to find what people really think. Skybunny9231 says, *I always knew Dawn was going to do something super fucked up. She has it out for him, and she can't bear that she's going to be the fourth-most-famous person in that family. She's got those shifty eyes.* I think my eyes are nice.

That starts a comment thread where everyone agrees. *Post-partum madness. It happens, especially to women like her.* What does *that* mean? Someone says he can trace my whereabouts to the Atlanta area—he has an inside source, y'all! Everyone is a doctor, a psychologist, a crime scene investigator, a sociologist, an obstetrician, all equally as confident as they are wrong.

There isn't one comment that exhorts the others to wait to hear Dawn's side. I scroll through twice, just to make sure. Not one.

Tim's all I've got.

By the time I'm done, it's 2:00 a.m. and I'm more awake than I was an hour ago. I hook my phone into the wall and decide to go tap on Tim's door and see if he's as awake as I am. But I don't have to knock. He's already outside at the Coca-Cola vending machine. He doesn't hear me yet, so I watch his finger spin above an orange soda, tempted and struggling, but he opts for a bottle of water instead. *Ker-plunk.* Sipping, he turns around.

"Whoa!" He taps his heart. "Don't do that to an old man."

"Sorry." I must look ghoulish under the fluorescent light, wearing a crinkly Carrie Underwood tee and workout pants for pajamas.

"Couldn't sleep." Tim tips back the bottle and gives a painful belch, thumping his fist into his solar plexus. "Figured it wasn't worth fighting it."

"Same." I can only look at him. The cheap lighting shows his age, all sagging frown lines and crinkling around his nose, wrinkles sinking into the halved onions of his eye sockets.

"You're still wonderin' about me." He eyes me cautiously. "About all this."

I shrug.

"I know, it's askin' a lot. Forgiveness, I mean. So if you want me to go away, I'll let you take my car and you can go wherever you need. If you get pulled over and they ask for registration, you have my permission for the car. I can get myself a plane ticket home. I don't have to be in your life if you don't want me. I just want to help. Really. And if I can't do that, just let you know that I'm okay, and that I know you'd never do anything bad to those babies."

The smile he offers looks like it pains him, like the muscles are sore from rehearsing it and he can't bear to try it again. The smile of twenty years. The smile he's always wanted to give me.

I drape my arms around him and squeeze.

"No," I say. "Stay."

The next morning, I want to go out for breakfast, but Tim warns against it. From now on, he says, the only place I go in public is behind a windshield. So he brings in eggs and sausage from

McDonald's and closes the blinds while we eat, somewhat pathetically, in the curtained dark.

Sometimes I watch Tim as he chews, wondering if I've really forgiven him. But knowing what I know now makes twenty years of resentment feel as useless as punching in a dream. There isn't a father here for me to hate. There is just this man, Tim Fremont. He isn't wearing a wedding ring. The emotion I feel is closest to pity, imagining all those years he spent in empty apartments agonizing over the secondhand daughter he thought hated him. Maybe that's for the best. He's good with the twins, he runs errands, and money isn't a problem. He can stay in my debt for a little while.

The TV is set to the news, just in case someone talks about us, but we leave it on mute. It's one of the few times both twins have been asleep at the same time.

"I can't hide forever," I say.

"No, that's true. But here's the thing. You're a legal guardian to these children. They haven't been mistreated, I can testify to that. This isn't any kidnappin', no matter what your husband says."

"So why are we hiding? Can't I go back now, tell the world?"

"Because the police have no reason to know your side of the story. Because what's happening is, you're up against one of the most media-savvy people I've ever come across."

"Wyatt," I say aloud, if only to shatter the feeling of He Who Must Not Be Named that's been congealing in the room. "But that means he also has the police convinced—"

"Let the police be convinced. Let them arrest you, even, at some point. But charges? A trial? You really think Wyatt wants you in a public trial, knowing what you know about him?"

"And what do I know?"

He finishes eating first, pinching the grease from his hands with a napkin. "I was hopin' you'd tell me."

So I tell him about what I found, all the way back to the package from Germany. I tell him about the gloves to frame Hattie, the notes on Wyatt's tablet, quote from what I can remember of his prewritten funeral speech for the twins. Tim watches me with his arms crossed and a look in his eyes like he's rereading a book he memorized.

"And you don't have any of this proof with you," he says, more statement than question.

"I didn't know I'd need it. I just wanted the twins out of that house."

"Well, I don't blame you. But if Wyatt has half the world convinced you're kidnapping his children, you're going to need something that verifies your side of the story. There's no jury more unfair or more cruel than the court of public opinion. All it takes is one judge who's a fan of Wyatt and *The Perfect Home* and you'll be lucky if you can see those kids once a month on visits. That's if they don't convict you just because a jury likes Wyatt more."

"They wouldn't do that, would they? A jury?"

"A jury of your peers in the state of Tennessee? More like Wyatt's peers."

Point taken. "I told him I made a copy of the file, if it helps. Maybe he didn't destroy it."

"Is there anything in that house that might help us?"

I try to form a mental picture of the house. The enormous foyer, the unused rooms upstairs, the kitchen and its cathedral ceilings. (I almost laugh now to think how important cathedral ceilings were to me.) The gloves in Wyatt's sock drawer, according to his note. The dining room where he kept his tablet. He'll have deleted everything by now. And thrown away the gloves. Hell, he could have had a full evidence-burning ritual in the backyard and no one would have known. I think about going back there, but there's the security system, the cameras we installed—

The cameras we installed.

"There could be footage," I say. "There's cameras all over. Even if he deleted anything incriminating, I could find myself the morning I left and testify that's what I saw. Is that enough?"

"It's not nothin'."

"Double negative."

But Tim doesn't hear me because he's staring at the TV screen now. The scroll at the bottom punches me in the gut. DAWN DECKER SPOTTED IN INDIANAPOLIS.

"Turn it up," he says, but I've already grabbed the remote.

On-screen, a freshly coiffed reporter is standing on a familiar roadside, Tavern Boulevard, Indianapolis. "—seen yesterday here at this Airbnb owned by a woman named Judy Rutledge. Now, Rutledge claims she rented out the guesthouse to Dawn Decker for consecutive days, though at the time, she didn't know it was her. Decker was apparently using a fake name."

It cuts to an interview. There is Judy Rutledge, standing in the same place I saw her last. Her voice is warbly, nothing like it was when she spoke to me, and she leans over her walker as if trying to make a point of it. She's playing up her age. Of course she is.

"It was time for her to check out," Rutledge says. "And I saw there was some trouble with the cleaning crew, so I came outside. She dyed her hair brunette, but I knew right away it was her. Twins and limp and all, just like they said on the news. Certainly wasn't the woman from her profile picture. I called the police and this man claiming to be a Detective Sipowicz came in and, I thought, arrested her."

"Detective Sipowicz," the reporter fills in off-screen, "a possible reference to the popular Dennis Franz character from *NYPD Blue*. But only a few short minutes later, when the real police turned up, Judy Rutledge realized her mistake. Police recovered a Chevy Tahoe with a license plate registered to Dawn Decker in the state of Tennessee, confirming Judy's story. And according to her, the twins are safe, for the time being."

"For the time bein'." Tim spits the words back at the TV. "Listen to the media. They've already decided."

The camera cuts back to Judy Rutledge. "I made out a Nevada license plate when the car left. Not sure what kind of car it was, but it was big, like something the FBI might drive."

"Thank God," Tim says. "No make or model."

Then back to the reporter's live shot just off Tavern Boulevard. "Janet, police aren't sure just who came to take Dawn Decker while falsely passing themselves off as an officer, but—"

Tim grabs the remote and mutes it. "We should go to Nevada."

"Nevada? Why?"

"Well, let's see. For starters, it's the only state full of Nevada plates."

"Funny. So that's it? Go to Nevada and . . . what, exactly? We'll be just as stuck there as we are here. This isn't a storm I can ride out. Maybe it is for you—"

"Now, just hold on," Tim says. "Nevada license plate, no make or model. But how long before Wyatt puts two and two together and tells the police about Dawn's long-lost father figure? I'm in this just as much as you are now. Besides, I have contacts. Other PIs,

people who can help us. We get some of *them* to find what evidence
we can—"

"And then they go to our house in Nashville and immediately
know they're part of the Dawn Decker story. How long until they
find out that *TMZ* pays more for that story than Tim Fremont does?"

"I see your point."

Junior makes a hungry grumbling sound and I go to see if he'll
take formula, but instead he shakes me off like he's been dreaming
and wants to stay there. I can sympathize.

"We'll go to Nashville," I say.

"Nashville." Tim chuckles. "You were making fun of me for my
Nevada idea, just sayin'. And you want to go where everyone will
know you?"

"Nothing is going to matter until I change how people see me,
right? Hearts and minds and all that. And if I show up in front of a
camera without any evidence, there's nothing I can say that doesn't
make me sound crazy. If there is any evidence left, there's only one
place on earth it will be. We have to go back to my house."

Tim drives us down Highway 65 and we finally cross the Cumber-
land River as the sun sets. It's almost July now, which means the
days are as long as days get, staining pinks and reds into the glassy
Nashville skyline. Junior is resting on my collarbone, screaming that
he's ready for formula, or fresh air, or whatever infants scream for.
We've stopped trying to decipher him. Taking breaks for the twins
has already turned a three-hour drive into six.

We needed the rest, Tim says as we circle our way to North
Nashville. But now he seems fixed on finishing the drive. He drops
a window to muffle the sound of Junior crying. It works. A waft of

humid air rolls in, Junior goes silent, and I swear I can taste Nashville go dewy under my tongue. There's live music bouncing off the buildings. Bass thumping, drum kit beating, blues guitar licking the tang off the evening sky. That's what I love about Nashville. It has so much going on, it forgets all about you.

"The address again?" Tim asks.

"Six oh six Hope Gardens."

"Hope Gardens? I'll take that as a good sign."

It's not long before we reach a hazel-blue town house in North Nashville. Tim helps me with the twins, taking Harlene Mae, who's fast asleep in her car seat, and thankfully Junior is still calm. It's a quiet neighborhood with wide yards, so thick with brush and country you wouldn't think downtown was just a hop away.

I ring the bell and soon a woman with tight, dimply cheeks smiles back at me. "Your *hair*!" Alice chirps. "Is it really you? Come inside, before anyone sees."

While Tim drove us down, I sent texts back and forth with Kelly and Alice, two of the three women I trusted and the ones more likely to be home. I kept the details vague with Kelly, but Alice jumped at the chance. And of course she did. I drove out of Tennessee so fast I'd forgotten what a guardian angel she could be.

Her house is brassy and dim with all the antique lighting she bought from my store. The crisp scent of basil hangs in the air. Alice takes Junior off me, cooing at his cuteness, then waves us in past the staircase and into a living room built for one. On the show, Wyatt and I used to call this "closed concept" or "a tad cramped." When we were being polite.

"You must be the famous Tim Fremont," Alice says. I filled her in on that little development, too. "I just want you to know, I think it's great you're helping Dawn like this."

"Least I could do." Tim smiles as best he can. He sets Harlene Mae's car seat beside the couch and sags into the cushions. "May I?"

"Of course. I'm so sorry—do you want something to drink?"

"Yes," we both say.

Alice goes and returns with two glasses of lukewarm Nashville tap. It goes down sweeter than soda.

"We wouldn't have asked you to do this if you were technically abetting a criminal," Tim says, rubbing that notch in his nose. "Right now, it's a missing person's case, but if Wyatt does something and the police decide they need to bring charges, you could be liable down the road. Just so you know. For now, at least, I think you're good."

Alice nods. "You wouldn't know it to read Twitter. There's whole threads of people trying to put together Dawn's whole life history to figure out where your mystery car took her."

"Yeah?" I ask, stomach sour. "Where am I?"

"The biggest thread I saw concluded you'd gone on to Chicago. I guess you have a second cousin there, or something?"

"I mean, it's possible." How many people know their second cousins? I certainly don't. Yet on the internet, even faint connections can sound like truth.

"Some people even took to the streets," Alice says, bouncing Junior. "One person took a picture of a woman with brunette hair because she was wearing sunglasses. Of course it's fuzzy, and she looks nothing like you, but you know how Twitter is. I'm glad you're back in town. What's your plan?"

I lie back on the lounge chair by the TV. Oh, right—that's what comfort is. It's strange having neither of my arms occupied with a meaty, squirming infant.

"First, getting my car and its Nevada plates off your street," Tim says. "Then I go find Wyatt while he's still out."

"You know he's out?" Alice asks. "How is that possible? The only thing he's posted on social media since you left is a thank-you message to his fans."

"Let's put it this way," Tim says. "I can't not know where he is."

I smile, biting my lip.

Alice squints. "Why does he need to be out?"

"Thank you for the hospitality," Tim says, groaning as he pushes himself up by the knees. "You're very kind to help Dawn in a moment like this. Keep your phones on, and charged. I'll let you know what I find."

When the door closes, Alice turns to me. "What's going on?"

"I can't show up to the press empty-handed. If it's going to be she said, he said, then Wyatt's going to win that argument. I need proof that he was really planning on killing the twins."

"So why does Tim need to go find him?"

Not *find* him, I think, but keep him wherever he is. I need a good hour with the house alone.

"You've been through hell," Alice says, as if just realizing it.

"Yesterday morning, I was in an Airbnb in Indianapolis. And yesterday morning, I was still convinced Tim Fremont was really my father and had forgotten about me. A week ago, I was only famous for a TV show. I had a house in Belle Meade and a family and a perfect life."

"Was it? Clearly something wasn't right. You don't have to tell me what went down between you and Wyatt, but . . ."

I've already texted her about the ASB, about how Wyatt changed as the pregnancy wore on, how there was no way he could have properly weaned. I didn't tell her how close it got to Hattie. It feels wrong letting someone as innocent as Hattie get caught up if she didn't have to.

"But what?" I ask.

"I don't know. When it rains, I guess." Alice sits down and cups Junior by her shoulder. "You know I'll take care of your babies as long as you want. This afternoon I got everything you said, diapers, the formula brand you asked for."

"It's just for tonight. I'll be back as soon as I can, but I don't know exactly when that will be."

"You poor thing."

I wave her off. "It's funny the things I used to care about. Like the shelving in my kitchen or how wide our yard is. Did you know I used to bug Wyatt asking about when the show could go into syndication and we could sit around on our asses collecting royalties? Of course he thought it would be insane to retire. But, God, I would have loved it. My favorite memories of my mom aren't from trips or park visits or anything all Kodak-y like that. I like having someone on the weeknights, talking over the commercials. Momma Harlene used to make fun of all the side effects to allergy medicine. She started making up her own. 'May cause delusions of grandeur. Auditory diarrhea. Bloody belches.' God, I loved that woman."

I stroke my cheek, loosening the knot forming in my face. "But you don't need all the trappings to have a family. I can go from hotel to hotel, and it doesn't matter how shitty or run-down the place is. As long as they're okay. As long as their mom's with them."

"They'll be okay here. You can be sure of that."

"You texted that I can borrow your car. Is that offer still on the table?"

"Yeah. Of course. Keys are by the door. As long as you promise not to do anything illegal."

"Who, me?"

I grab the keys and jangle them in my hands. Then I turn. Harlene Mae is flicking her fingers in her car seat, her brain off somewhere else. It relieves me that she won't remember nights like these. Both twins are beautifully untouched by it all. Harlene Mae with her hair in a swirl, her fat cheeks. Junior with his veiny forehead, the pinched eyelids. I tap my cheek to his, and, yes, there is the piney smell of his I love.

Wyatt always said it was soap, and eventually I realized that it's the wipes I use. But I don't care. It is the clean, innocent smell of a person still unchanged by the world. I jangle the keys again, stalling. I know I'm a hormonal mother who just spent a few days straight with these god-awful, beautiful, mind-numbingly frustrating jewels. But why does it feel so final to say goodbye?

"Wave bye-bye, Juney-Juney," Alice whispers, puppeting his hand. "Mama's gonna go fix things."

Yes, I think, she is. She's going to fix things so Mama never has to say bye-bye again.

Alice's Honda Accord is parked out on the street, and of course it is clean and vacuumed and as piney-smelling as Junior, and of course Alice was thoughtful enough to fill the tank. Real friends are worth their weight in gold.

I hesitate before turning it over and roll down the window. The first few stars are out. The air has started to go cool and crisp. I don't have my Tahoe, but I still have my home keys, and for the first time since we bought the place, the thought of walking through that front door makes me nervous.

WYATT

The Sevens Country Club. I am uncomfortable here. There's a club soda in my hands, but even that—lime wedge, fizzy drink, ice cubes—seems too indulgent for a husband who should be home and worried sick about his kids. The only way I agreed to this meeting was if I didn't have to be in a public bar, so I'm in something of a private skybox that overlooks the ninth green.

That's not comfortable, either. There is something blasphemous about golf courses at night.

Drake Jennings doesn't seem to notice. About two drinks in, he yammers on about how cable TV works, the attrition rate for reality shows in syndication, or some such—all things I've heard before. He's a wiry seventy-year-old, the skinny kind where only the sag in his neck shows his age.

"Then my stake hasn't changed," I say, trying to sum up so we can start saying goodbye.

"No. This is one of those all-news-is-good-news situations. If anything, there's more interest in Wyatt Decker than ever."

"Shouldn't have told me that. Now I'm going to ask for more."

He leans in, his breath minty with julep. "Between you and me, if you ask for it, you might get it. There is no deal without someone from *The Perfect Home*. Ask for twenty-five. And don't say ol' Drake never did you a favor."

Twenty-five percent. I do the napkin math in my head. Another twelve million or so, just for asking, just because he's a little tipsy and I'm not.

God bless America.

I try to smile. "You know, this could have been a Zoom."

Jennings shoots me a hurt look. "Thought you could use the air. I'm sorry. I know how stressful this situation must be on ya. Some air, some good news, thought it could do you good."

"You're right. I apologize."

"Nothing to apologize for." His hand lingers on my shoulder too long. I meet his eyeline. Is he staring me down? "You're in a tough spot. Don't know what I would do if my wife took my kids halfway across the country."

"It's not easy."

"No?" The stare down again. "You make it look so easy."

"That comes from half a lifetime spent on camera."

"Ha—touché. That's why you're the star and I just smile at meetings." After one last sip, he sets the glass down. "Next time I'll have my people email you. Go home, would ya? Rest up and focus on getting those twins back, safe and sound."

Once he's gone, I set my glass down, too. For all I know, there's a sniper photographer out on the ninth green and tomorrow I'll lead the *Daily Mail*: WYATT DECKER SECRET MEETING WITH MEDIA MOGUL. I should have turned down his invite. But Drake Jennings is worth several billion dollars and has a way of turning the word *no* into an act of self-mutilation.

Now the bar has filled up downstairs. I give myself a look in the bathroom mirror: button-down and jeans, sensible silver belt buckle. Business casual made sense when I put it on, but it's made me too recognizable. All I'm missing from an episode of *The Perfect Home* are the safety goggles and tool belt.

So I take the safety stairs instead of the elevator and walk out to the ninth green, hands in my pockets, making myself small. A few golfers are still rolling in from the night. One or two couples make the long journey from their Mercedes to the bar, but it's dark enough that most people don't give me a second look.

"Hey—excuse me. Wyatt Decker, right?"

Shit.

A man steps from under the parking lights and extends a hand. "Yeah! *The Perfect Home.* My wife watches your show all the time, man."

So tempted to lie—*Yeah, I get that all the time, we're doppel-gängers, I even met him after winning a look-alike contest.*

Wouldn't *you* lie if you could get away with it? I don't think I can. My pearlies come out—ancient instinct by now—but I remember I am supposed to be a man worn down by worry and potential family tragedy. "Pleasure to meet you . . ."

"Rockford," the man fills in.

For a moment, I worry I have a stalker. Usually my obsessive fans tend to be fortysomething women, though, nothing at all like the bare-scalped old fart in front of me. The most obvious thing is the notch in his nose, which has clearly been broken once or twice—under the parking light, it's like the thing has two tips. He's wearing a dark Harrington jacket that couldn't have been meant for a country club, and something in the way his hips turn toward me makes me feel like I was his destination, not the bar.

"James Rockford," he says. "Sorry, didn't mean to throw you. I know what you're going through right now. But imagine my surprise. It's like you leapt right out of the TV."

"I was just heading home."

"Of course, of course. But I don't think I could let my one chance go by without at least offering. Let me buy you a drink, or a hot meal. Don't act like you can't use it—the whole world knows you can use it."

"To be honest, I haven't been very hungry these past few days."

"A drink, then. A Seven and Seven at the Sevens. Good for the nerves."

Dammit, he has me. I've already been spotted at the Sevens, and now if I don't get a drink with him, he can go on Twitter and complain to the world. I can already see it: *Hey, y'all—guess who was just*

rude to me while coming out of the bar of a hoity-toity country club?
Mr. Concerned Husband, Wyatt Decker.

So we go inside and have that drink, me slinking into a table by
the corner so I can turn my back to the rest of the room. The man
brings back a cranberry juice for himself and a Seven and Seven for
me. I only touch the drink to my lips, sipping as much as politeness
requires. He goes on and on with a story about how *The Perfect*
Home is becoming a big hit out West, but he keeps looking at his
watch like he's on some sort of timer.

"So, your twins," he says. The guy fancies himself an old pal.
"Hell of a situation. You been throwing up a lot?"

He catches me mid-sip, so I pretend it goes down rough. "Sure,
yeah. More like haven't eaten, though." White lie. I had wings for
dinner.

"Big guy like you? You have to eat. Remember to eat, that's what
my mom always said." He pats his gut. "Like a fella could ever forget."

"All moms say that," I agree. Not all moms.

"Your mom was the same, huh?"

No, not quite. Carolyn Marie Decker was a dipper and a chain-
smoker who never had an appetite for anything except strange
men, so if *she* never wanted dinner, why should little Wyatt whine
about not having his? There were plenty of cornflakes in the cup-
board. I remember asking why I couldn't have a regular cake for my
birthday, like Dottie Carlson down the street—just asking, that's
all—only for Carolyn to pick out the single candle, snuff it in her
calloused fingers, and throw the whole gas-station cupcake down
the sink. "Because," she said, "Dottie Carlson is in the St. Mark's
choir and you set off fireworks in the church parking lot last week."

Just remembering that makes me take a double swallow of the Seven and Seven, forget where I am and who might see me. I want to forget a lot of things about myself.

My phone vibrates. "Sorry. It could be—"

"Of course, of course. Anytime there's a buzz on your phone, you must be on edge." Rockford's lips are juicy red from the cranberry. I feel a bit cheated by that. "For what it's worth, I happen to know a private investigator or two in the Indiana area."

"The police tell me they have it well in hand." Last I heard from Guzman, the police had a look at Dawn's Tahoe and found nothing but burger wrappers and diapers. She could be anywhere, they told me. I drop a twenty and stand up. "I'm sorry—James, was it?—but I really have to go. Thanks for the drink, but it's on me."

"Well, you've barely started it."

"I have to drive home." If only to get away from you.

"Okay, no sense beating around the bush. I think I may know where Dawn is."

A day ago, I might have jumped at this and made myself look antsy to find Dawn, but after a thousand emails each putting Dawn in a different state, I've numbed to it.

"Look, James, I've been patient here, but if you have a legitimate tip on Dawn"—I say this in a tone that lets him know just how much I believe him—"then you should take it to the FBI tip line."

"Hear me out. I have it on good authority that she may have gone to Chicago—"

"Heard that one."

"Just ten minutes, Mr. Decker. Ten minutes of your time."

"Thanks for the drink."

Then I'm out the door. God, I can't wait to be home.

CHAPTER 17

DAWN

Even with my key sliding in, being inside my own home feels like breaking and entering. Everything feels wrong. The lights automatically come on, for starters. Those were Wyatt's idea and I have no idea how to shut them off. After some convincing, our smart speaker handles it for me, but now if Wyatt checks the speaker's app, he'll see someone was in the house at roughly nine o'clock. One minute in, and I'm already past the point of no return.

The house is impeccably clean and tropical sweet, sprayed down with the Bora Bora Febreze that means Wyatt's done the cleaning. He's been hard at it. Cushions are tucked in, books are put away, and there is a hanger for every coat. A Roomba nods carelessly into a corner. Momma Harlene's old chenille blankets are tucked on her La-Z-Boy, even though I left them ruffled like she always did, and the chair's retracted back into place. On the fridge, there are twice as many pictures of the twins as when I'd left.

Everything is police-inspection-ready.

I head upstairs first. A pair of gloves is pinched in the sock drawer. *The* gloves, the tiny ones he'd bought to pass off as Hattie Wright's? I pull them halfway out and sure enough, their little leather fingers are too small for his hands. These wouldn't even fit on me. I almost pocket them before thinking better of it. What's to stop him from claiming I bought these gloves myself? And he's in the sock drawer every day. He'll know if someone's been here.

The nightstands aren't like we left them. Mine is cleared of everything but a lamp. A ring of water stain where I always kept my cups is all that marks it as mine. There's an open jewelry box on his, a loose collection of knickknacks I don't recognize. Lip balm, safe keys, some of my old earrings.

Unconsciously, I pull open the drawer, and there is my old gratitude journal. Wyatt even tucked the magnetic pen to the side. I open it, if only to scan the highlight reel of the months that have gotten us here.

I'm grateful we don't need any biopsies.

I am grateful that my husband wants kids so much, he would risk his life. He would do anything.

I am grateful that people who think we're trash TV still show up to autograph signings. I am grateful for the grateful fans of our show. I am grateful I have a show. Some people don't even have jobs. And I'm grateful for my friends.

I'm grateful there is a healthy baby growing inside me. I'm grateful Wyatt can stop the ASB now. Mostly, I'm grateful it's over.

A thousand years ago. Look at me gratituding my way to rationalization, thinking every step backward is progress, never once imagining how every step only brought us closer to the ledge.

Tim would think it's imprudent, but I'd wager Wyatt hasn't looked at this journal—or inside this nightstand at all—since whenever he tucked it away. I'm taking it with me.

I give a quick sweep of the other rooms, just in case he's left the tablet in the open, but this place is still newish and the second floor is mostly big, empty, white-carpeted rooms meant to fill over time. There's more house here than home. Wyatt's first-floor office is pristine, his desk spotless, even dusted. He never dusts. My heart leaps when I see a tablet sitting on a stack of files, but when it asks for me to create a new user profile, I realize it's the wrong one.

My phone buzzes. Tim.

Held him up as long as I could. Headed your way—ETA ten minutes. Assume seven.

Sent thirty seconds ago. Six and a half minutes, then.

Alice's car is parked blocks away, so I don't have to worry about Wyatt finding that. All I have to do is be out of this house by the time Wyatt is back. I can walk the long way around and cut through the woods. How many of our neighbors really see what's happening on their property at nine at night? Unless you're outdoors under the floodlights, it's like looking out into empty ocean.

The last thing I can think of is the security footage, which works on Wyatt's computer in his office. I peek outside the front door and into the driveway, grateful to see it's still empty.

Wyatt didn't change the log-in info. That's a good sign, along with the gun safe: he never even considered that *I* might be the first one searching the house. He didn't want to look like he had anything to hide. I open the program and it gives me the hourglass, and I pound my fists into the desk like maybe that will help (*Damn you, open up*) and finally I'm in. What day was it when Wyatt was staring at the wall? Doesn't matter. He deleted that. Maybe he deleted other footage, too. There's nothing I can do but air-drop it onto my phone, but that gives me another hourglass. I check my phone. Two minutes. One minute. The screen says ten seconds left. It says that for at least another minute.

I am debating whether to cut the airdrop early and hope something incriminating has already transferred to my phone when a set of white lights splashes into the room. Wyatt's F-150 burls up the drive with that janky style of his, always hard on his brakes. The door opens and shuts.

I run to the living room. The backyard deck is right outside, just a doorknob away, but I nearly trip on the stupid vacuum and it sends me flailing into the couch. All I can do is pull a blanket over me.

Then his keys chime and the door opens and I hear Wyatt, kick-kicking the dirt into the welcome mat. He's wearing dress shoes that tap out exactly where he is, and like always, he beelines for the kitchen and pours himself tap water from the filter.

"Yeah," he says suddenly. "You texted? I'm here."

I didn't hear his phone ring. Clearly he's talking into it because there's a voice on the other end. It's feminine and nasally, but that's all I can make out.

"No." Wyatt stretches out the word like he's not sure. "Driveway was empty."

Garble, garble on the other end. It's a notch too quiet to hear, but something is familiar in it.

"Nothing. Looks fine. Are you sure?" Garble, garble. "Well, I'll check."

He keeps talking, his voice fading down the hall in the direction of his office. In the silence I can hear my breath go dewy against the blanket. My heart beats so loudly I'm worried it will shake the blanket off. There is only so quiet a human being can make herself.

Wyatt comes clop-clopping back up the hardwood, still talking to whoever is on the other end. "All right, well, thanks." He sounds skeptical. "No. I'm looking right at everything. I'm good. Maybe something else happened. Yep. Keep texting, we'll figure it out. Thanks. Bye."

A soft *plop* on one of the chairs. That can only be his phone. No more clop-clop. He is standing there. Doing what? I don't know. When it was just him and me, the sofa was my domain. How often does he really look this way? He'd rather be in the office or the dining room or the bedroom—anything that's not in front of the TV. Still, I feel the hair in my nostrils go tight when I imagine him jumping mindlessly onto the sofa, his ass meeting a rubbery postpartum woman with a bum hip.

What will I say? *Oh, hey, babe. Didn't know you wanted the sofa.*

Something buzzes. It sounds distant and muffled. Wyatt's phone? He didn't toss it on *this* couch.

I feel for it. No. It's in my pocket. It's mine.

I forgot to turn off my phone.

WYATT

Buzz.

Funny. I *just* tossed my phone down, and there it goes again. One thing I hate about being famous: your text inbox becomes public domain. Anyone who's even remotely an acquaintance will send you their two cents because maybe they saw some tweet they want you to debunk, or they have a worthless bit of their personal family gossip to share so they can lube their way into *your* secrets— either way, they know you're already getting a thousand texts, so they figure there's no harm in being another drop in the ocean.

When I check my phone again, there's nothing there.

Huh.

After that phone call, I figure I might as well lock the doors. The driveway is still empty, save for my truck. I'm so used to the sight of Dawn's Tahoe that I wonder, briefly, whether she went to the grocery store or to visit Momma Harlene. But it's just a pulse, an old routine feeling. Of course, neither can be true. Life can change so quickly that you'll still feel the old pull of habits. The Greeks used to imagine Fates holding the strings of life—one snap, and yours is irrevocably changed. That's all it takes.

Water isn't enough, so I go to the kitchen and pour myself about a half shot of Jack. Rockford, or whatever his name was, teased me with those few sips of booze, and now I've got a taste for it. I wonder about him. How often is it that I can't just shake off a fan when I want to shake them off? Show them the pearlies, smile for a selfie, and poof—transaction complete. This guy didn't ask for a selfie. And it's like he only wanted me to go where I absolutely didn't want to go— somewhere public, somewhere I had to spend a minute being seen. This is not the time to be seen. I should be invisible except when I'm on CHN or talking to my publicist or talking to the police.

The Jack tastes pungent, so I throw in a splash of Dr Pepper. I sip without saying *ahhhh*, thinking of Dawn. There's some rustling out by the back porch. Raccoons again. Maybe I'll throw on the lights, grab a broomstick. But by the time I hear them, it's usually too late. No, I'm too tired to defend the castle. The obligations of my day are over. It might be the time to check CHN and see what they're saying, so for once, I'll allow myself some TV.

I take my Jack and Pepper to the living room and plop my ass down on the sofa.

DAWN

My breath catches in my throat.

Ten seconds earlier, Wyatt would have jumped right on me. But he lingered by that front door so long, it was clear he was getting lost in some daydream. That was my chance. The only noise the back door to the deck made was a little slide of the lock, too small to hear, so I ran to it and closed it as quietly as I could. Wyatt was already walking back while I was standing out on the deck, plain to see, but how often do you look outside *every* window in your home? His eyes were elsewhere, on that glass of Jack he'd just poured himself.

I wait under the deck, out of view as the TV goes on and stains the backyard with flashes of blue and white. The light shows our half-finished backyard. It's mostly dirt, with a few clumps of wild grass and weeds and the occasional huckleberry bush. There are still little popped zits in the earth where the tree guys carved out our old stumps. That was the last step. Once we had the twins, we said, we'd plant sod, and we'd have half a football field of flat yard here. The kids wouldn't remember anything else growing up, just that they grew up in a perfect home with a perfect yard and with perfect parents. And I don't blame myself for thinking that way. Back in those days, tree stumps were my biggest worries.

The whole fantasy doesn't feel too far away. Wyatt is watching TV and I am in the backyard, listening to the chorus of cicadas declaring the official beginning of night. Ten seconds, twenty yards. That's all that separates us. If I were sitting out on the deck with a virgin daiquiri, it wouldn't look so very different from what could have been.

I am in my last good pair of jeans, which have gone wrinkly from hours in my duffel bag. After dimming my phone down to minimum, I text Tim.

Just barely missed Wyatt. Didn't find me. But not sure I have anything.

What did you get? he asks.

Sending. Tell me if there's something incriminating.

It's an excruciating wait. The TV is still blinking. Occasionally, I hear glass clinking on the granite countertops, Wyatt pouring himself a refill. The light from the TV goes wild and rainbow when there are commercials.

Not looking good, Tim says.

I type in *Oh, God,* but it autocorrects me to *Oh, Good.* Even when I'm typing, the words never quite come out properly.

Just drive back to Alice's, Tim says. *We'll regroup, figure something else out.*

There is nothing else.

I type it, but can't bring myself to send it.

My throat seizes. If it's my word against Wyatt's, there isn't a judge in the entire country who will give me custody of the twins. And if Wyatt gets custody of them, what will he do with them?

They're only safe as long as they're with me.

I text as much to Tim, and the response comes almost instantly.

Then what can we do? We have nothing to corroborate your side of the story.

Inside, the lights flip off.

Maybe I imagine the pit-pat of Wyatt ascending the stairs in his socks. But I know there is silence when he's finally upstairs. The relief nearly makes me squeal. The master bedroom is above the portico, putting the rest of the house between us. When he's gone, there is no sound around me but the hiss of cicadas, the soft kick of my pulse.

Time to go. Except there's still Tim's text to think about: *nothing to corroborate your side of the story.*

My back is against the house and directly under one of the floodlights, so I shuffle as quietly as I can, crab-walking astride the wall. I find a spot in the dark and try to settle my lungs. My harried breathing is so beyond my control, it sounds like someone else's. I glance at the windows again and Wyatt's still inside. I press a wrist into my breastplate to cool my lungs. My nerves are bristling with static.

Even Tim's phrasing makes me sound small. My *side* of the story. As if Wyatt's madness was only the tint in my eyes and couldn't be found in Wyatt's own words. But that's my problem now. Proving it. Wyatt is too smart to leave anything out in the open. He might have already deleted it, which means I've risked everything just to sit uselessly outside his house.

I click my tongue, my brain working numbly. Nothing in the bedroom. Nothing in the office. No tablet, no tablet. But if he'd simply deleted the file, why hide the tablet at all?

And where? I steal a glance through the kitchen window. Inside, it's museum-clean, and just as empty. Wyatt was never one to keep his valuables at home if there was a bank with safe-deposit boxes nearby, some place where he could shake someone's hand and call him *sir* and bring out his treasures for review. He likes his wealth in plain sight. It isn't safe to keep jewelry at home, he told me once.

So I look around the yard. The rectangle shape of our proto-lawn cut into the forest, with the wounds of yanked-up tree stumps. And in the distant corner, a Vesta Brands toolshed.

Hiding in plain sight. That sounds like Wyatt.

I sneak away from the fluttering gold of the floodlights. A spectacular week of sales is replaying in my head: ten thousand licensed *Perfect Home* toolshed kits sold in one week—one week!—and how we'd been so excited, we forgot about the shed itself. I don't think we ever used it again.

Nope, never once, I think, approaching the double doors and their digital lock.

Our cut that week was $900,000, Wyatt told me. You don't forget numbers like that. And you don't forget the name on the upper-left corner of a check that large. Vesta Brands. The company had done everything for us, the manufacturing, the marketing, the kits themselves, everything prepackaged.

Including the password.

CHAPTER 18

DAWN

The CHECK ENGINE light pops up on the way home to Alice's, but I barely notice. I feel equally elated and exhausted, my joints twitchy and road-weary. For once, my hip is down to an ache.

VESTABRANDS1. I got it on my second try, remembering the password had to include a number, and what the man from Vesta Brands had said about that: "Might as well be number one. You can change the password when I'm gone." Once the lock clicked, the doors butterflied apart like two big welcoming arms. The only tool out of place was the screwdriver. Phillips head, just like the screws for the corkboard. Wyatt was hiding it from guests, not from his wife, so the tablet didn't need to be hard to find. Once I got to the safety of Alice's car, I flipped through the tablet's files for the document, and sure enough, there was Wyatt in all of his ASB-manic glory, predicting a future of tragedy and funerals for the twins. Whoever said Wyatt Decker never made mistakes? He must have believed me when I said I had a copy, and that somehow it would look bad if investigators saw him hiding evidence.

What, like locking a tablet in our toolshed?

The drive into the city is full of stops and starts, every traffic light turning yellow when it sees me coming. I don't rush it. I drive easy, windows down, music on. There's a wormy smell in the air like after a rainstorm. It is the first time in a long while I feel like something hard is past me.

Alice's house casts a wan glow on the yard, its living room window shuttered and dimmed. Inside, Tim hunches over the make-shift command center he's assembled on the coffee table. He hoots when he sees the tablet I'm carrying.

"Shh," Alice says from the adjoining kitchen. "The twins."

"Sorry," he whispers.

I hand Tim the tablet so he can see the document for himself, then I collapse into the recliner and gaze at myself in the TV's matte reflection. A complete mess looks back at me. Tatty jeans, crimped Volunteers sweatshirt, hair knotted in a lazy, two-humans-once-came-out-of-me-in-the-same-day bun. Yet my grin hasn't gone away. How long has it been since I've felt safe?

"How'd y'all do?" Alice asks as she hands us glasses of ice water. She even put lime wedges in them.

"Barely did my part." Tim rubs a bottom rib, like the memory's giving him pains somewhere deep. "Held him up as long as I could. Bought him a drink, but he barely touched it. When I got there, you know who he was talking to? Drake Jennings."

We both look at him.

"The telecom billionaire," Tim says. "Owns four of the stations you get with basic cable? I looked him up. He's a minority owner of HLTV, so technically, Dawn, he's one of your bosses. They didn't walk out at the same time, but they were both in the same room for quite a while."

Tim flips the laptop around. A Google Images gallery of Drake

Jennings photos shows a seventy-year-old man in power suits, walking red carpets and wearing microphones at hoity-toity tech conferences.

"Doesn't ring a bell," Alice says.

But it does with me. The same white hair in a cadet's cut, the still-taut waist, the giant Rolex. He was the man golfing with Wyatt that day a car hit me outside the store, the only one untagged on Wyatt's Instagram story.

"Dawn," Tim says. "You all right? You look like you're about to throw up."

I shake my head. "I've seen Wyatt with him before. There was one day—and I don't think I told anyone about this, because I thought it was nothing—but I found a note of his that said *fifty million dollars.*"

"So what are they up to?" Alice asks.

"If it's Drake Jennings, who knows?" Tim says. "A new long-term deal? A stake in HLTV?"

Alice squints. "Wyatt would have told Dawn."

"No," I say. "I don't own any piece of the show. Technically, Wyatt doesn't have to tell me."

"Whatever it is," Tim says, "it's hinging on how this all turns out. No one's going to make that kind of deal with Wyatt if they think he's a potential baby-killer. Anyway, Wyatt is clearly well-connected. I think someone must have tipped him off that we were back in Nashville because he got a text while I was talking to him, and once he read it, he seemed pretty set on getting home right away."

"You didn't tell Vic, did you?" I ask Alice. One word to Victoria and her two hundred thousand followers would be on the case within minutes. Victoria had broken the news about me being pregnant with twins, taking my family-and-friends-only ultrasound text and sending it out via Instagram Stories. *Oopsie,* she texted back. *I'm so sorry. I thought that was your announcement. But look at the response you're getting!*

"No," Alice says. "But it doesn't mean she didn't find out somehow. What about you, Dawn? How did it go at the house?"

Tim holds up the tablet, showing it off with a wrist wiggle. "We got what we needed."

"Seriously?" Alice sits next to him. "What's on it?"

"Wyatt's plans for the twins," I say. "Funeral speeches, even. Everything I read that made me leave that morning. You know what he did with it? He hid it in the toolshed."

Alice nods, making her lips a grim line. "So, what now? Can they arrest Wyatt?"

"First, we need the world to reconsider its opinion of Dawn," Tim says. "Everyone's looking for her. If we bring the twins back and show this to the world—maybe the police won't be looking so hard. She hasn't technically done anything illegal yet."

"Yet," Alice echoes.

"Hey," I say, "I'm not planning on it, either. Where are my babies?"

"In the spare bedroom. Both asleep. Which you should be, too. You've been driving all day. Dawn, I made up a bed, and, Tim, I have a camping cot set up in the hallway. It's not comfortable, but I put a pad on top of it, if that helps."

"One minute," Tim says, absorbed in his laptop.

Exhausted, I only manage a quick swing of my neck vaguely in Alice's direction. I should hug her, if only I had the energy, if only I was one of those people who gets energy from hugs—people like Alice. She deserves it. Everyone outside this house has gone along with Wyatt's version of events. The clerk at the hotel. Judy Rutledge. The general viewing public. All they see is a psychotic woman stealing her husband's twins. No one is interested in what really happened. And here is Alice, giving us shelter, giving us her car to use, a few hours of babysitting. If I ever win an award for something, she's going to be the first person I thank.

"Alice," I start. "You're my—"

"Thank me later." Ever the mind reader, Alice. She stands, hands on hips, and tosses me a blanket I didn't ask for but desperately need. "We're not out of the woods yet, are we?"

Then I fall asleep in the comfort that my guardian angel just called us *we*.

Bump.

It's still dark out. I wipe the soreness out of my eyes, but the amnesia doesn't leave as quickly as that. A recliner, a small living room, someone snoring in the hallway—a hotel? No. Alice's. The sixty-year-old snoring on the cot: Tim Fremont. My father, but not my father. What about my babies? Both asleep, from the sound of it.

A figure stands over me, but it's so dark, I can only tell its movement from how it blots out little lights: green dots on the wireless router, a phone charging on the coffee table. I try to pull myself out of the recliner and the faux leather crunches loudly as it folds.

"The twins . . . ," I murmur, still sleep-delirious.

"No," Alice says. "I'm sorry, hon. I didn't mean to wake you. Go back to sleep."

The bump was her. A shin on the coffee table? She sits on the sofa, and I'm envious of how she makes no noise. When I move, I always make furniture sing. "Are they sleeping?"

"Perfectly," she whispers. "Doesn't look too hard, raising twins."

I try to throw a punch at her shoulder, but my arm flops, still creased and sore from the recliner. "Everyone says that when they behave for two minutes."

"You want more water or something? I'm already up."

"Sure."

When she comes back with it, I set it down on the end table, too tired to trust my limbs. She filled it almost to the brim.

"I was thinking before," I say. "You're my guardian angels, you and Tim. I don't know where I'd be without you."

She clicks her tongue and says something, but I'm already drifting. Like a parent reading to her children, she seems to be waiting for me to go to sleep. Is she wearing jeans at this hour? Did it make the thumps of shoes on wood when she walked over to the sofa? What went *bump*? Her hips face mine, her legs folded tight and ladylike, and that has me thinking of Momma Harlene when I was a child. How she'd say, "Knees closed, you aren't a wacky dancer," whatever that meant. As images of wacky dancers hang cartwheels behind my eyelids, I start forgetting everything again.

WYATT

The knocking is loud enough all the way from the portico to wake me. I jump out of bed, underwear only, and jolt to twelve-noon alertness. Police. Fire. EMTs. They're the only people who knock like that. I throw on a Volunteer tee—there's time enough for that, at least, to look decent for the world—and check myself in the mirror. My hair has tumored into a poof on the side of my skull. No amount of rubbing will comb it flat. All right, this is my mugshot then, I think, spitting into my palm, scraping uselessly. I run downstairs and open the door.

"Alice."

Her eyes are wet. She's wearing a gray sweatshirt and jeans and looks unshowered, her gunny hair as frazzled as mine. And underneath her arms, she's set two carryalls on the ground. The twins.

"Dawn came—" Her voice quivers between gasps. "Dawn—"

"Easy. Come in. Catch your breath."

And easy as that, breezing past me and into the house, Alice gives me the handles to the carryalls. Harlene Mae is cozy and resting with her chin bobbing on her own soft neck. Wyatt Junior is rubbing the back of his head against the fabric. It takes me a moment to catch my breath, too. My heart is still pumping, sprint-ready. Only about sixty seconds separated dreamless sleep and the possibility the police had finally come. Instead I have the twins. My heart doesn't know what to do.

Alice already knows her way around our house, knows where the coffee is. She's so jittery she can barely press a pod into its place. I bring the carryalls into the living room, make sure I coo loudly enough over the twins that she can hear me, and get Wyatt Junior into a bouncy chair. I had it out near the end table. If anyone visited, they'd see my empty, hopeless chair: *awwwwww.*

"Okay," Alice says, a mug steaming in her tiny hands. She sits on Momma Harlene's old chair. "Sorry. My nerves."

"Not at all. Thank you—thank you for bringing my babies home. What happened?"

She sips the coffee and tells me the whole story. A phone call from a strange number. Wouldn't have picked it up, but it was Tennessee and didn't set off the spam filter. It was Dawn calling from a new phone. Dawn explained the story—the true story, but Alice doesn't need to know that—about driving to Indiana and back. Alice felt queasy the whole time Dawn was in her house, waiting for the time to dial the police, or me, but never wanted to risk Dawn walking in on her. And why, I ask, does Alice suspect Dawn is lying? "She looks so strange. Her hair's the wrong color and her eyes are all puffy."

I lean forward. Alice couldn't have teed me up better. "That's how I've been feeling, too. I haven't known her the past few weeks. She's not the Dawn I married."

"Right? And you know what made it worse? She had a strange man with her."

"Strange man?"

"It's not like that. I guess it's her father. Stepfather. I don't know how they found each other."

"Kind of trim? Couple inches shorter than me, thin hair, notch in his nose?"

She tips her head. "Exactly. You knew?"

James Rockford. The man from the Sevens. Nothing about that conversation ever felt right, even by random-fan standards. Like he had held an invisible lasso around me and never wanted to let go.

Alice is staring into space. "I mean, watching it all online, I didn't know what to believe. When she called, I still wasn't sure— maybe I did believe her. But to see her. She was all splotchy. Her voice was kind of hoarse. I don't know. It rubbed me wrong. She wasn't Dawn. Not Dawn like I've known her."

"Well, you did the right thing. I'm meeting with the police this morning. I'll call ahead, let them know the twins are safe now."

Alice nods, a sad hurricane twisting all the wrinkles of her forehead. She is too expressive to be a good liar. Her face spells everything in detail: I have her. And if I have her, all my public relations carpet-bombing is paying off.

I wondered about Alice sometimes. Victoria and Dawn didn't always make for obvious friends, not since I've known them, but

Dawn had been a drinker once and they'd been roommates with a lot of shared stories, so if you got those two together, it was impossible to get a word in between all the remember-whens. Alice had been Victoria's friend first. I always got the sense Alice had been convenient to keep around, a designated driver. I don't think Alice ever got so much as a speeding ticket in her life. Over time, when Dawn gave up drinking, they grew closer. Dawn finds Alice admirable. And now Alice finds me admirable. Maybe I'm further ahead than I thought.

"What can I do to thank you?" I ask. "You want a refill of that coffee?"

"Sure. Thanks."

From the kitchen, I can hear her playing with the twins. I like the little uh-oh sounds she makes as she bounces Junior's seat. I was never quite as good at the nonsense conversations one has with infants. She's got whatever skill that is. But when I come back to hand her a mug full of coffee, her perpetually honest face is wrought. "You all right?"

"Just tell me I did the right thing."

"You did the right thing." Best not to hesitate. I push the coffee at her.

"There's something else of yours."

"Oh?"

Alice walks to the portico and returns with a backpack. She slips a flat device from it and hands it to me. I hold it a little while, lips locked. I'm not sure how I should react. Clap? *Well done, Alice?* Deny I knew what the thing even was? It feels like she's pulled some sort of magic trick. This should be in the toolshed.

On my look, she purses her lips. "It's yours, right?"

"Maybe." I fire it up. The home screen twinkles, flaring into a wedding photo: me and Dawn in black and white, our foreheads pressed together. It's almost funny, in retrospect, how I'd chosen a stare down.

"They were talking about your tablet," Alice murmurs. "What's on it, what they can do with it. It didn't seem right to me. It belongs to you."

Dawn, then. And Mr. *James Rockford*, so eager to keep me talking at the Sevens.

"Thank you," I say. "It does. Did you see what they were talking about?"

Alice shakes her head. And I finally breathe. She seems satisfied with my answers and sits for a sip of coffee. She nudges a foot against Harlene Mae's carryall.

"Look at them," I whisper. "These two babies are safe because of you."

"They are cute, aren't they?"

"Apples of my eye. A lot of people are going to be very happy because of what you did. In fact, there's going to be a press conference this morning. You should join us." I think Alice nods her assent, but I'm not really paying attention. There is a document on this tablet that needs scrubbing. At this point, I might as well. I press my finger to it, hold until the recycle bin begs me to delete, then drop the file into the void, feeling suddenly grateful for Dawn's friends.

Part Four

BEST FRIENDS

CHAPTER 19

DAWN

"They're gone." Tim stands over me, shaking my shoulder. Morning now. A misty-gray light slivers through the curtains. When Tim sees my eyes open, he throws the curtains apart. My ice water has melted and left a sweaty ring on Alice's end table. I was sure I'd dreamed that.

"What?"

"Alice. She's gone. Her car's gone, she's gone. And so are the twins."

Panicked, I launch myself off the recliner and down the hall, almost tripping on Tim's cot, until I reach the bedroom. Alice left her bed unmade. The floor is bare. Then, the guest bedroom, the one intended for me until I conked out on the recliner, and there's even less to see in here. No car seats and no twins.

"Maybe she went out to pick up breakfast and didn't want to leave them with two people sleeping," I say.

"This was on the fridge." Tim hands me a folded piece of paper. I recognize Alice's handwriting immediately, cursive with frilly swirls at the ends of words.

I'm sorry.

"No—" I gasp. "No, no, no, no—"

"Let's sit down," Tim says, holding me by the shoulders.

He guides me down the house's one hallway, back to the sofa and the tiny living room. There's a touch of spray on the windows, a summer rain making everything cloudy and pearly, or maybe that's just my eyes. Tim looks like he woke up only a moment before I did. He's wearing a white T-shirt with webs of wrinkles under his ribs. His laptop is still on the coffee table, and he unfolds and boots it.

"I saw her," I realize. "Last night. I heard her leaving."

"Why didn't you stop her?"

"I didn't *know* she was leaving." I'm so stupid. Jeans, shoes—everything was right there, if I hadn't been too drowsy to think. "I didn't hear the twins. I haven't slept through the night in so long. . . ."

"It's not your fault. Let's just—let's just figure out our next steps here, okay?"

"Next steps? The twins are *everything*." I catch my face in my hands before I start sobbing. "Wyatt. She took them to Wyatt."

Tim nods. "Sorry to say it, but I'd agree."

"She believes him. Believes what everyone else is saying about me . . . We need to leave. If she really thinks I did this—"

"Pack up."

Without the twins, there's not much to pack. A sweaty load of clothes and a gym bag full of toiletries we'd bought on the road. When we're patting our pockets by the door, I ask Tim, "Did you pack the tablet?"

"You must have."

"No, I didn't."

He scoffs. "Quite the friend."

We're on the road in a few minutes, the hour of the busy morning drive, the city slick with rain. There's not enough moisture for the wipers, which makes every swipe a wail of rubber on glass.

"We'll have to get you out of this car," Tim's saying. "We have to assume Alice took down your plates."

"Drop me off at a car rental," I say.

"Really?"

"What are they going to do? Deny me service?" My heart is thumping with every notch in the road, but strangely, my nerves are fine. What once seemed like a major risk—renting a car in public—has shrunk to insignificance next to getting the twins back. That's the thing about worry. Worry is the thousand needles of everything that could go wrong. But once the real blade enters your flesh, once there is only one wound to mend, everything else falls away.

Without asking, I look up the nearest car rental on Tim's GPS. He doesn't stop me. In fact, he seems relieved when the voice spits out instructions for his first turn.

"Where will you go?" he asks.

"To see if I have any friends left. You?"

"I'll find some place. This stuff with Drake Jennings—there's something there, I know it. I'll dig around Wyatt's past, too. Keep your phone—"

"On and charged, got it."

After a few minutes, we pull into a car rental service near the highway. The parking lot is sparse; for most people, it's an ordinary do-nothing weekday. Tim reaches in the back and hands me his one umbrella. "Godspeed," he says. "If I don't see you for a while, just know . . . I'm sorry I didn't find you sooner."

"Me too." My chin quivers. "You're the only one who helped me."

"I don't know about that." He points up. "There was a moment or two I felt Harlene kicking me from up there."

Wet from rain and snot and tears, I give the door a tap goodbye and turn to the parking lot. The big glassy façade reflects me storming up to it, still in the tatty jeans and Vols sweatshirt from last night. The door announces me with a ding, and I walk straight up to the fresh-faced, scrawny teenager behind the counter.

"May I help you?" he asks.

"I'll rent the cheapest car you have."

The job means too little for him to hesitate at a request like that. It's only when I hand him my driver's license that he shows any pause, two hard lines forming between his nose and his brows. I wonder what a teenager might know. Dawn Decker. Famous celebrity whack job. The woman with the twins. All over Cable Headline News. One hundred and thirty-five make-believe pounds. Blonde in the picture, brunette in real life. Everything about it is wrong, but I no longer care. He will give me a car or he won't.

Finally, he hands it back. "Compact okay?"

"Perfect."

A few moments later, I am driving a maroon Kia Forte through the Gulch, feeling new steel hardening in my spine. I look around at a red light and enjoy how invisible this car makes me. A woman with a flower truck is throwing canvas over her bouquets, the rain getting too thick for sales on the street. A tour bus stops behind me, but none inside even have their cameras out. There's no announcement on the speaker: *And in front of us, in the Kia Forte, is Dawn Decker of TV's* The Perfect Home! *She's currently on the run, so this is a rare treat, folks—get your cameras out while you can.*

I duck out of the rain and press the buzzer for Victoria's penthouse. There's a faint crackle. "Dawn?"

"Vic—yeah, it's me. Just me. Can I come up?"

I don't know how long she waits before she buzzes me in, but it's long enough that when the lock finally shakes open, it startles me.

The elevator dumps me out into the small lobby that splits the two penthouses, east and west. Victoria is standing outside her door. From the looks of it, she's either coming or going. It's about 10:00 a.m., but she's wearing a black sheath dress, heels, and silver earrings that dangle like saliva. She's clutching her purse.

"Your hair!" Victoria pulls me in.

"Trying something new. Road-greasy chic. What do you think?"

She doesn't hear the joke in it. "You were so great as a blonde."

The rain gives Victoria's penthouse a dusty, solemn feeling, like Easter vigil in a cathedral. The sky is pale now, a rolling boil spitting rain at the windows. What light breaks through is dim, filtered. It's the kind of rainstorm that makes you forget the time. Victoria pulls out a glass, fills it with tap water, then presses it to the ice maker in her refrigerator door. No ice—only a dead wheeze. She drinks it facing the fridge. I sit on a barstool at her kitchen island, face on my fists.

"Alice took the twins," I say.

"Alice?" She turns. When Victoria swings around, her hair always drapes onto one shoulder, pageant-perfect. "What happened?"

"Did she say anything? Have you seen her, heard from her? She took the twins back to Wyatt, right?"

She turns to place the glass in the sink. "Why would I know?"

It's a good question. Why *would* she know? Yet it feels right to ask her. I'm leaning forward, an interrogating stance, the recessed lighting turning her kitchen into one of those desolate rooms from cop dramas. How many times have I been with Victoria and wondered aloud where Wyatt was, only for her to dial up something on social media and know the answer before I did? I scan her, drinking in the incongruity of her dress, the weather, the hour.

"Long night or something?" I ask.

"Why?"

"You're dressed for a walk of shame."

"Dawn. Ouch. I look that bad?"

"No, of course not. You never look bad." The words come out as one long groan. I don't know why *walk of shame* was my first thought. She couldn't be more put-together. Painted lips, bright alert eyes, her satiny hair tight and obedient. All colors perfectly within the lines. If Victoria needed money, she could do makeup for weddings. But Victoria never needs money.

"Well, are you gonna stay?" she asks, filling a new glass under the faucet.

"You got anything stronger than that?"

We look at each other.

"Dawn—"

"Kidding, Vic. Only kidding."

"I was asking if you're going to stay, because I do have to be someplace, as it happens, but of course you're welcome to stay here as long as you want."

She slides the glass to me. I cradle it in my fingers, both hands, like a mug of cocoa. Lukewarm. Or maybe it's that my fingertips have felt cold and bloodless for weeks.

"Thanks," I say. "Where are you going?"

"Oh—press event."

"Press?"

"You know. One of those things."

No, I don't know, but I pretend to, sipping the lukewarm water like she poured me coffee instead. Victoria had press events all the time. Lots of local charity events with red carpets. I used to poke fun at those. What kind of press showed up to watch a few Instagram influencers hawk energy-drink sponsorships? But photographers always did. I'd see her timeline later and there she was in the photos, giving smoky stares, hand on hip, like Fashion Week had landed in Nashville. Before *The Perfect Home*, I thought of red carpets as the stuff of Academy Awards and Manhattan galas. Turns out carpets are cheap.

Feeling my eyes boring into Victoria's skull, I twist on the stool, surveying her apartment. It's like a hotel. Everything is gleaming and freshly dusted. There's not so much as a wet teaspoon on the coffee table. Victoria probably hasn't touched a remote since the last time she had it cleaned. I wonder how often she even sleeps here.

"Well, you can have the guest bed," Victoria says. "I mean, if you're staying?"

"Can I?"

"I'm not like—harboring a fugitive, am I?"

"No. And you don't have to do anything right now." I notice one of her heeled feet is pointing toward the door. "Don't let me keep you."

"No! I was early anyway. I'm not going to abandon my friend when she needs me." She walks to the couch, shooting me a grin. It makes her lips snap back. She's giving me her beauty-pageant smile. One of the things I always liked about Victoria was how unassuming she was to talk to, how she always pulled the curtains back for her friends. The world saw Miss Chattanooga; I saw the woman who cusses out rude fans and burps while she scrolls her phone. But she's giving me Miss Chattanooga right now.

"Maybe you want to use my bathroom, freshen up," she says.

"I probably should, huh?"

"No offense. You're so lovely, it's just that you've been through a lot." Pageant grin. World peace and education for America's youth.

The light in her bathroom is harsh and medical. Like the rest of her apartment, it's polished and modern and full of sharp, un-childproofed corners, trimmed with black. She could sublet the bathroom to an avant-garde Berlin nightclub. I splash my face and wonder if she keeps any makeup in the guest bathroom. If anyone does, it would be Victoria. But I only find hand soap and a bottle of perfume.

Everybody has a scent, and Victoria's is gardenias, spicy and grassy and faintly something else, maybe coconut. I spray some on my wrist and rub, wondering why else it seems so familiar. Where else did I smell this?

My heart starts pounding.

"You feel all right, Dawn?" she calls from the other room.

I am hovering. It feels like my feet barely graze the floor. I turn the corner and manage to float into the guest chair across from the couch, fists balled.

"Dawn. What is it?"

Thump. "You slept with Wyatt."

She freezes.

"You slept with Wyatt." The way it comes out of me, it's not an accusation. It's a realization. "Are sleeping with Wyatt." It makes too much sense. His random trips to see *Tom Dale.* The way Victoria always knows where he is, always bothers knowing where he is, whom he's with.

Victoria shoots up and grabs my hands. "No. No—Dawn, listen to me—no. It's not like you're thinking. I never meant to."

"You didn't *mean* to?" I stand, shouting. "You didn't *mean* to?" I am dizzy with rage. I size her up, feeling monstrous, like I could do to her what the world thinks I could do to the twins. "You've been lying to me this entire time. This was the first place I went for help with my kids and you've been—what?—colluding with my husband?"

"It wasn't like that."

"What was it like?"

"I don't know. Not close to like you're imagining. Not at first." Her voice slathers with uncanny calm. "For a long time we didn't do anything. We went for years ignoring the spark between us because we knew what it would do to you. You remember how it was when you introduced us?"

Years ago. A different epoch of my life. Back when I was simpler and only wanted the people around me to get along because I couldn't imagine anything worse than a tiff among friends. Wyatt took us out for steak and cocktails while I went on about how important it was to win over the best friend, bragging out loud how famously they'd get along. Then they met and both seemed to go limp. Instead of them laughing and telling embarrassing remember-when jokes about me, they barely spoke to each other. I still remember staring at the perfect lacy fat of the Wagyu she left untouched. I was certain he rubbed her the wrong way, so afterward, I promised her that she'd come around. Promised *her*.

"We kept our distance," Victoria says, "at first. We'd just avoid each other because I think we both knew. I don't even remember when the dam broke. But by the time it did, we'd been saving it up for years. And I told myself afterward it was just sex. He promised that, too."

"I'm sure he did. Told you everything you wanted to hear, right when you needed to hear it."

She ignores my volley. "Then when it happened twice, we talked about it like a bad habit, how easy it would be to quit if we could just avoid each other. But do you know why I could barely speak to him at first? Because we both knew it the instant he shook my hand and looked me in the eye."

"Knew what?"

"He'd met the wrong woman first."

My stomach feels like she's thrown it across the room. There they are: the unspoken words that have itched us for years.

Victoria swallows. "You used to complain to me about the show—still do—and you're right to. People were always so cruel—they felt like Wyatt was their brother and they had a say in who he married. But if I'm honest, you blowing up hurt me. You *knew* how much I wanted what you had."

"To be the public's whipping girl?"

"To be famous. I wanted it and you didn't. I worked for it and you didn't. You know it would have suited me better. You even told me a few times."

I don't say anything.

"I think Wyatt knew, too," she goes on. "This thing between the three of us was all warped because we'd gotten the timing wrong. I knew one day, everything was going to blow up. When you came to my place that morning, I thought it had. But then I talked to you on the phone and you still didn't know. And for a second, I didn't believe him. I was ready to believe you." She opens a palm at me. "But look at you, Dawn. You're exactly how Wyatt described. I don't recognize you."

That may be fair. My eyes sting, my hair is the wrong color, and for the past few days I've been living on fryer oil and pseudo-sleep. I unball my fists. The violence slides out of me, scraping a hole as it goes. Only bitterness fills it.

It's a long time before either of us say anything. "Anything else I should know?"

She sniffles. "He wants to get a restraining order on you."

Of course. The headlines write themselves. Decker twins reunited with their concerned father, finally freeing him to take legal action against the insane mother. I can practically hear his quote in the *Daily Mail*: *It's just a temporary protective measure until we get her the help she needs.*

Then I will become the crazy wife with the restraining order, who must stay one hundred yards away from her twins and husband at all times. What happens after that? Ugly divorce? Maybe Wyatt will get his Modern People story after all. No more *Perfect Home*, no more store, no more house in Belle Meade, but most important, no more access to my kids. There are plenty of good divorce lawyers in Nashville, but I won't be able to hire any better than Wyatt can. If I don't end up in jail, I will be lucky to have supervised biweekly visits with the twins. The next time I tickle Harlene Mae under the arms, just where she likes, it will be in some government facility with a camera on us. I can hear the doors buzzing now, announcing my entrance and exit. *In. Out. Next parent, please.* That's assuming the twins survive that long.

"What did you talk about?" I ask wearily, sliding back into the chair.

She slumps down to the couch, wiping black flakes of mascara from her cheeks. "Wyatt says your dad has come back into the picture and you've all been spying on him. That you've been sneaking into your own house trying to steal things. With everything on the news and the way you looked . . . Alice thought the twins would be safer with Wyatt."

"You honestly believe that?"

She rubs her nose and pauses before answering. "We do."

We. Victoria and Alice? It doesn't matter. Victoria might as well speak for the entire world, not just my friends. And what is friendship, really? An unsigned agreement, voluntary siblinghood. Volunteers don't have to stick around. Sometimes I wonder about how we became friends in the first place. We had so little in common. Just our ages, our shared seclusions. One has to be careful about that. If you get lonely enough, anyone can become a friend. Just anyone.

Sometimes Wyatt had a habit of talking about our fans as though he were narrating a nature documentary. *The average* Perfect Home *fan likes to be teased,* he'd say. *Pull their tail just before the commercial break, and you've got their attention for at least five minutes.* You'd half expect him to talk about moon cycles and mating seasons. Sometimes it bled out into people he knew. He didn't like talking about his mom, but the one time he did, he said he believed she fell asleep at the wheel on purpose. His father's lung cancer was easier to hate—Wyatt could blame him for smoking his way out of Wyatt's life. Figure out why people let their favorite habits kill them, Wyatt said, and you'll figure out people. But I knew what he meant. People, in groups, are little better than roving herds of your average beast. For years I thought he was wrong. I think I understand now.

There is no sound but the steady tinking of rain when I walk to the door. And no matter how much I want to rush out, I can't help but turn and brush my hair from my eye. It may be the last word I ever have with her.

"I was first, Vic, that's true. But it means everything he's telling you now—whatever he's promising—is all stuff he said to me. Don't ever think you're anything to Wyatt but another face in his audience."

I don't wait for her reaction. I bound out of the room and mash a woozy hand to the elevator buttons and make sure I'm out in the rain before I finally let myself have enough air to cry. It's a clumsy sound: a spit and a gasp. Then I slip in the car, sliding my hand through the purse in the passenger's seat. The lips of the gratitude journal's cover kiss my fingertips. I pull it out and find the last entry before everything started being about ultrasounds and healthy twins. Back when it was just me and Wyatt.

Mostly, I'm grateful it's over, I wrote.

I want to cross it out. I want to cross it *all* out, every entry that chronicles Wyatt's descent like some horrible true crime show I used to watch on Netflix and make fun of, because *how can people be so stupid that they don't see what a monster their husband was becoming?* The ones who didn't see the cheating husband and the beautiful friend right in front of their face.

Now that's me. I am the *people so stupid.* I want to throw the journal out into the road and watch the rain pull it into the sewer, where it can be with its own.

But the earthy smell of paper and leather stops me. There's my handwriting. There's Wyatt's descent, line by line. Every thought dated.

Sliding the pen from its strap, I pull it into my fingers and write, *I'm grateful for the truth.*

I wonder who else might be grateful for it.

The main lobby is an echo chamber of conversations and clacking heels. The high ceilings make it sound like a swimming pool, the way voices carry in big open spaces, taking on the gloom of the air. Under the escalators, there's a big desk counter bordered by speakers and bulletproof glass. I join the shortest line.

A maple-haired police officer barely looks up when it's my turn. "How can I direct you?"

"Well—I don't know. But if it helps, my name is Dawn Decker. I'm the one who ran because my husband was going to murder my children."

CHAPTER 20

WYATT

Outside the room they call the conference hall, the police station is full of noise. Landlines and conversations and clacking smartphone keyboards. Press is filtering in, Altoids tins are popping, ties are adjusting. Someone in a starchy blue uniform shakes hands with me and makes small talk about the Titans—didn't like their first-round draft pick—and it's only when an assistant whisks him away that I realize I was talking to the chief of police.

Everything has become much, much more official than I planned.

With the time I have left, I duck into a bathroom and shake out my nerves. An old routine from *The Perfect Home*: the psych-up. Dawn thinks it all comes naturally to me, but that's just because I don't let her see the weirdest thing I do. No one should see it. It *should* look natural.

"You're the best, Wyatt. The greatest. The world's most famous person."

It's not natural to tell these things into a mirror. But either you tell yourself or no one will.

I return to the hallway. Hattie Wright is rocking Junior on her lap. It's a miracle that he's not screaming. Guzman has Harlene

Mae, who's fretting from all the noise, which makes a sergeant light up and say, "Awwww."

I feel a nudge at my elbow. Victoria hands me a minibottle of vodka.

"I'm not nervous," I say.

"Tell that to your face."

But before I can drink it, it's time to walk in. Camera operators are tilting and panning, making their last-minute adjustments. I wish there was something more police-like about the space. Rooms like this always look bigger on TV. It's almost nothing. Behind the podium there's a curtained wall lined with Old Glory and the three stars and scarlet field of the Tennessee flag, and on the other end, there's only enough seating for a handful of crime reporters. They're already inside, faces ghostlike in the blue glows of their phones. Wearing this monkey suit—I've always chafed in ties—I feel like someone in an airport hotel teaching real estate seminars under a pseudonym, making promises of getting rich by age thirty with *no money down*!

The chief's assistant herds us in and assigns us our positions, like arranging a family photo. Me, then Hattie and Alice with the twins. The publicist thought it would look better if we stood together like a family, nailing down just how darn concerned we all were about Dawn. The police didn't object. After Alice, it's Guzman and a handful of other officers, then, at the end, a beauty queen in a black sheath dress. I avoid eye contact with Victoria. There can be nothing there that ends up on camera, nothing so much as a glance. There is bound to be at least one reporter who is watching my reactions instead of Twitter's.

Behind us, an easel displays a poster-size promo shot from *The Perfect Home*: me and Dawn in each other's arms, some mansion-y front yard blurred behind us. The photo must be at least a year old. Dawn looks thin again, her soft eyes crimped and smiling. I don't know why the police chose this photo instead of the deep-sea-fishing one from our honeymoon, and I hate that I'm in it. The public should see themselves as either Team Dawn or Team Wyatt. This will just confuse them.

The police chief—a couple of bear claws shy of three hundred pounds and his voice a deep, dark shade of bass—kicks us off with a statement. He confirms Twitter rumors that the twins are back in dear old Dad's possession. Everything sounds credible coming out of him. That Old Testament voice, the gold badge, the stripes on his sleeve. "If anyone has any information on the whereabouts of Mrs. Dawn Decker—" Chef's kiss. Perfection. The way he pronounces *whereabouts* is enough to make Dawn sound guilty.

He turns it over for questions. As reporters clamor to be the first, I keep my hands folded, that genital-guarding look all men get when they're wearing suits. A balding reporter in a gingham shirt stands up. "For Wyatt—how did you manage to get the twins back, but Dawn is still missing? Did Dawn bring them back?"

"Last night," the chief says, "Mrs. Decker showed up at the home of Alice Wright, an old family friend." Alice smiles, dimples going hard as cement. "Miss Wright did a very courageous thing. She waited for an opportunity to bring the twins back to safety. Back to their father."

This sends a flurry of questions, but one pops out over the others. "What prompted the kidnapping?"

Guzman steps up for that one. "We don't throw around the word *kidnapping* lightly. Dawn is a legal guardian. What we do want, urgently, is to speak with Dawn as soon as possible. There is a hotline people can call. . . ."

The next question is for Alice. "To clarify, you've seen Dawn within the last twenty-four hours?"

"She turned up at my home last night," Alice says. "I can't really comment further."

"So she came to you—for help? What exactly happened?"

Alice searches our faces, any face, for someone to jump in. I can't, or else it will look like I'm managing the story, playing the role of PR specialist instead of concerned husband. So Alice slinks away, murmuring, "No comment."

The next question is for me. "Were there any indications Dawn was going to do this?"

I make my way to the podium, feeling the awkwardness of my height, the people I blot out by standing in front of them. I have memorized every aspect of my story, even watched my own interview on CHN a dozen times, to know the answer to this question.

"There were no indications—not really. She just wasn't herself after the birth. I know that much."

Yes, I know I'm lying. Lying to America. Who wouldn't, if it meant keeping custody of the twins? Keeping the whole brand? *The Perfect Home* keeps at least three dozen editors, producers, and crew in full-time employment. If it was between you and your wife, and the country had to hate *one* of you, wouldn't you rather shine the spotlight on her?

A woman in a black pantsuit sneaks her way through the door, then whispers in Guzman's ear. I try to ignore it.

"But everything I read at the time suggested it was a perfectly normal form of postpartum depression," I continue. "It's only now, looking back, that I feel I should have recognized the signs that something more serious was developing. . . ."

I trail off. Most of the reporters aren't looking at me anymore, but at Guzman, who has just snuck through the door. The police chief ignores this and takes my place at the podium. "Ladies and gentlemen, I'm sorry we don't have any more information at this time. We're going to have to cut this short since this is still an active situation, but here's what the public needs to know. The twins are with their father and in good spirits. Dawn Decker is still missing, and while we don't believe she represents a threat to the public, we're all very concerned for her health and her safety. If anyone has any information, please call the hotline. Thank you."

A few minutes later, when the conference is over and half of us are back in the hallway, a few of the reporters stop trying to squeeze answers out of the police and form a semicircle around me.

"I just wanted to offer a legal update," I say. "This morning, I filed for a restraining order against Dawn. This is precautionary. I think after everything the twins have been through, and given what happened last night, it's for the best until we can get everything figured out and get Dawn the help she needs."

"What happened last night?"

"I'm sorry, guys. That'll have to be all for now."

This, of course, doesn't stop them asking, so I have to walk away. I go down to where Alice and Victoria are regrouping in a side room. Alice's cheeks are flushed and she's gripping a ruined tissue. Victoria eyes me.

"What?" I ask. "And what's going on with the police? They all disappeared."

"I don't know," Victoria says. "But I saw Dawn this morning. When I went home to change. She came to see me. Alice, do you mind?"

Alice nods and leaves, shutting the door behind her. Ever-faithful Alice. For a second, I think about how lucky Dawn was in her friends—that she actually had *friends* instead of a thousand acquaintances, like me—but I can't imagine Dawn would consider herself lucky just now. What is she writing in her gratitude journal these days?

I go to the window blinds and close them, starting a timer inside my head. I'm not going to let anyone see me alone in a room with Victoria for more than a minute.

"Dawn knows," Victoria says.

"Knows what?"

Victoria makes a you-me gesture, finger flicking. The way she does it strikes me as slightly obscene.

"Did you call the police?"

"Of course. But I only could after she was gone. I don't know where she went. She was in some strange car."

"Is that why Guzman left?"

"I don't know why Guzman left." Victoria leans in, high in her heels and like she's about to whisper, but she backs off. It's a primal move, like she just wanted me to pick up her scent.

"I should walk out first," I say.

"Okay."

I turn and reach for the knob, but Victoria squeezes my wrist and turns me back. "Vic—I can't—"

"Wait," she says.

I'm ready to moan my annoyance. But rather than kissing me, she takes my hand, unpeels my fingers. Inside them is the bottle of vodka she had handed me before the press conference. I had it on me the entire time and barely felt it, the hard squeeze of my fingers, the sweat in my palm. There for any reporter to see. Wyatt Decker, drinking vodka before noon.

It makes me wonder what else I forgot.

CHAPTER 21

DAWN

They move me quickly up the hierarchy: first to a supervisor whose job seems to be answering receptionists' questions, then when she doesn't know what to do, upstairs to a conference room with a view over Lafayette Street. The room is smack-dab in the middle of police operations, all windows and offices and cubicles. An assistant brings me a cup of coffee that tastes like charcoal. Near the watercooler, lieutenants huddle together in a half circle and glance my way. That would once have frightened me, as every cop did. My heart used to skip when I saw black SUVs parked at speed traps. But now I don't care. My stomach might be one big coffee-bitten, twin-missing knot, but I don't pay it any mind. Dawn the Worrier is dead.

"Mrs. Decker." A short, fleshy woman shoves through the door with a folder under her arm. She extends a balmy hand. "Lieutenant Eliza Guzman. I've been conferring with your husband on this case."

Your husband. Great. Another Wyatt Decker fan. I rub the cover of my gratitude journal with my thumbs. Please, please be enough.

Guzman asks all the obvious questions: Where was I, what was I planning, why did I take the twins and disappear? The whites of her eyes flash when I tell her I was protecting the twins from Wyatt.

Clearly she hadn't considered that possibility. She scribbles everything down, leaning an ear my way, and I'm almost startled by the sudden attention. I have gotten used to my words dying in the void between me and other people.

"How are my twins?" I ask.

"They're safe. Alice Wright brought them to Wyatt early this morning. They had a press conference. That's where I was when someone came up to me and whispered in my ear that Dawn Decker had just turned herself in."

My neck flinches. "I didn't commit any crimes. There's nothing to turn myself in for. That's not why I'm here."

Guzman nods. "Can I ask what the book is?"

I slide it across the table. "This is a gratitude journal I've been keeping for the past few years. I date every entry. I want you to see what Wyatt has been doing these past ten months."

She flips it open to the spot I marked with a ribbon. *I am grateful that my husband wants kids so much, he would risk his life. He would do anything. . . . I'm grateful there is a healthy baby growing inside me. I'm grateful Wyatt can stop the ASB now. Mostly, I'm grateful it's over.* Guzman must be good at poker. The blood leaves her cheeks, washing emotion from her face.

"ASB is Angstrom Supplement-B," I say. "It's banned in the United States, or couldn't secure FDA approval—one of the two. Wyatt took it without doctor supervision, and the side effects say without weaning, it can cause hallucinations, paranoia, aggression . . . everything Wyatt was giving me. One day, I logged into his tablet and found a document that outlined his plans for drowning the twins and blaming it on our nanny, Hattie Wright."

Guzman writes everything down. "Hattie Wright—Alice Wright's younger sister, correct?"

"Yes. The document even mentioned buying a small pair of gloves to leave at the scene. Hattie's not very big, and the gloves obviously wouldn't fit Wyatt.

"You don't happen to have those, do you?" Guzman closes the book carefully and slides it my way, then leans back in her chair, hands folded. Apparently, there is no longer anything worth writing down.

I grind my front teeth together. "No."

"And you dated every entry."

"I'm meticulous like that."

"I know. I've seen the show. You're the meticulous one."

Blood cooks in my cheeks. "I mean—it's just a show."

"A *reality* show, right?"

"You'd be surprised how little reality there is to reality shows." I lean forward. "I didn't do anything wrong. I wouldn't just up and leave with my twins without a very good reason."

"Do you have an idea when Wyatt stopped taking the ASB?"

"Not exactly. But you can see he started getting worse after I got pregnant and had the twins."

"We could ask Wyatt to hand over his medical records on this, but as you said—there wouldn't be anything on record, even if he cooperated."

"No," I say. "I don't think he told his doctor."

"So even by your admission, there wouldn't be any pills for us to find, any evidence it was ever in his system. And even if there was, the potential for side effects doesn't constitute a crime."

"Isn't *buying* ASB alone some sort of felony?"

"It would be, sure. Do you have any evidence of that? Bills, packages with his name on them? And before you say it—this, I'm sorry to say, is not evidence." Guzman taps the journal with an index finger. I hate how carelessly she flicks at it. She might as well be tapping on my heart. "There's no way of knowing when you might have written what."

"Test the ink or something. These entries will show up nine months, ten months old."

"Even then. When you wrote it is immaterial. All you're showing me is that you wrote down that Wyatt was taking pills and acting strangely. Maybe it's even true. It's still not enough evidence to charge him with attempted kidnapping, attempted murder—especially when he never attempted anything in the first place. Did he?"

I cross my arms. "Would *you* have waited around to find out if he would?"

"I don't have any children, but, no, I can't say I would have. And this document you spoke of—the plans. You say you're meticulous. I'm assuming you have this document with you, some means of proving it was Wyatt who created it?"

I sigh. Of course I had it. Just a few hours ago, I had everything—the twins, Wyatt's tablet, the knowledge that he'd hidden it in the toolshed. One night of misplaced trust, though, and Alice had taken it all. Alice, the sweet one, the one whose sister I had trusted around my twins just by virtue of sharing her blood. I pull the gratitude journal back into my lap, feeling the cheapness of its faux leather, the paper gone crusty. I haven't thought about it in a while, but it was Momma Harlene who bought me this. "So you'll worry less and be thankful more."

Guzman opens the folder that's been waiting on the table and shuffles some of the papers around. "Several years ago, you were arrested under suspicion of a DUI. Do I have that right, Mrs. Decker?"

"They threw it out."

"But you did have a problem with alcohol, Wyatt told me."

"I haven't had a drink in several years. Lots of people struggle with alcohol."

"Of course. You don't have to tell me that. My father, sweet-heart that he was, he'd have one beer and get this look in his eye sockets like he'd aged ten years." Guzman traces a line of my file with a finger. "But I should just be clear. You aren't drinking again, right?"

"No."

"Because I look at you now and you don't look well rested. Your hair is different than the description. What else has changed?"

"As I said. I haven't had a drink in several years."

"Not even around the time you took the twins from Wyatt?"

"I didn't *take* them from Wyatt. I was *protecting* them from Wyatt."

"All right. I have your answer." Guzman puts her palms up, faux surrender. "Mrs. Decker, do you have a history of mental illness?"

"No. After the DUI—the one they *threw out*—I had a couple of sessions of therapy."

"I mean diagnoses. Bipolar disorder, suicidal ideation. Nothing serious? Nothing in your family history, maybe?"

Family history. For most people, it's such a complicated phrase. We assume everything that came before us—great-aunts with par-anoid schizophrenia, grandmothers who lived to a spry old age—is part of our genetic stew. But I don't know what my stew's made of. To me, it's just a question about my mom. "My mom never saw therapists and never saw the need to. If she was ever diagnosed with anything, it would be a surprise to me."

"And your father's side?"

My mouth pops open, a reflexive answer about Tim in the chamber. Normally I would tell her what little I know about Tim's side of the family. But Tim isn't my father, is he? I only know half of who I am. My biological father is a ghost, a man who could be a bipolar serial killer with a history of hypertension or a churchgoing saint who donates time at the homeless shelter, his family history full of spry octogenarians. I can't say. All I know about him is that I'm blonde with brown eyes, and except for my five feet and ten inches, I don't take after Harlene.

"I didn't know my father," I say.

"Sorry to hear that. Wyatt told me a little bit about the history there. It must have been hard, your father leaving you so young."

"Yeah. It was hard." The last word turns to mist in my mouth. My lips are quivering. Something thick and mucusy snags in my throat. Yeah, it *was* hard. It was hard not knowing my father, and even harder losing my mother, my only real friend, and finding out she'd lied to me about him, too. And I can't talk to her about it, ask her about it, cry with her about it, hug it out, and hear one of her "wipin' mah butt" jokes she'd make about how she hated getting old. Without my mom, without my twins, yeah, it's hard. Without them, the world is empty.

I swallow the thickness down, feeling a tide of tears subside. Wyatt used to complain about the same thing for himself. Not really *knowing* anybody. Wyatt's gift is breadth—a thousand people think they're his best friend, and none of them really are. Mine is depth. Momma Harlene, my twins, even Alice, once. Love sticks in me like an arrow between my ribs.

Guzman slides a box of tissues my way. The small mercy of the gesture makes me want to weep again.

"Wyatt was sleeping with Victoria Weatherly," I say flatly. "Still is, maybe."

Guzman's eyebrows pop. "You have proof?"

"From Victoria's mouth. This morning. It's not evidence for my case. I just want you to know everything I know."

She writes something down, shakes ink through the pen, the words unable to keep up with the trembling in her hands.

"You didn't know?" I ask.

"Mrs. Decker, there's a lot about your case I haven't known." Guzman licks the pen tip. "Your husband's been cooperating. In fact, he came to us."

I shrug. "He always has to look like the good guy. On TV, I'm the funny one who throws out our client's tacky clocks and pretends it wasn't her. That's how America knows us. So people assume I must be the shifty one. But it's not how it is."

The door opens. A young, straight-backed officer nods at me, then whispers in Guzman's ear. Guzman shoves up from the conference table and starts searching for words. "Um—will you excuse me a moment, Mrs. Decker?"

"I'd rather just go."

"Just do me a favor and stay right there, please."

Then she leaves me in silence, with nothing to do in this awful room but sip the last awful ring of their awful coffee out of their awful styrofoam. Police coffee. It strikes me how little I like about the police. I built them up in my head so differently, either total monsters or total saviors. It's easy to forget they're just people, too, capable of the same prejudices as all people, the same biases and blind spots. Guzman may as well be every woman who's ever shown up to Wyatt's book signings. Her tight ponytail even reminds me of a woman once who didn't realize she was standing in line for me. When it came time to sign her book, she went stiff, deer in headlights, pointed awkwardly at Wyatt, and then skipped over to his side of the table. I wasn't even worth the effort of mumbling an apology.

Every problem—even legal troubles, even talking to the police—is a different version of the same basic problem I've always had.

Guzman comes back through the door but doesn't sit down. The stiff-backed man waits behind her. Her hands hang limp around her pockets, swaying.

"Am I free to go?" I ask.

"Mrs. Decker. Where were you last night?"

In my own house. In my own yard. Gathering evidence you don't think exists. How to say it? Everything that happened with Alice sounds like a poor excuse, like a dog ate my homework. "I went to my home to look for the evidence that backs up my claims. I found it. I then went to Alice's, where the twins were, to sleep."

"You admit you were at the Decker home?"

"It's the truth."

Guzman nods, sending the other officer on the awkward walk around the conference table.

"The Decker home. Our home. Mine and Wyatt's. You know, my name is Dawn *Deck*—"

"Yes, Dawn Decker," Guzman says, turning my name into an announcement as the officer nudges me out of the chair, then swings my wrists behind my back. "You have the right to remain silent."

CHAPTER 22

DAWN

I have been in lines at the DMV that lasted hours beyond how long it takes to process me. A young judge, his hair inky and Sicilian-slick, scans me with wary eyes and doles out pronouncements like he's hungry and hard-pressed against lunchtime. Charge? Breaking and entering. Bail? Ten thousand dollars. Flight risk? Of course; we're talking about the infamous Dawn Decker here, who was in Indiana just a few days ago. We good? Okay, that's lunch.

As soon as I post ten grand in bail, I will have to wear an ankle monitor.

I try to tell my court-assigned lawyer, a woman with upsettingly large bangs who looks two months out of law school, that you can't break into your own home. She sweeps through my file and reminds me that an LLC owns my home. That LLC is registered to a shell company registered to a holding company registered to Wyatt Decker. That was for our anonymity, Wyatt and I once agreed, but now it amounts to one thing: I broke into somebody else's house. No, not somebody's. The property of The Perfect Home Productions LLC.

Jail isn't as bad as you might think. My freshman dorm room in Knoxville was smaller. It reminds me of the hotel in Indiana:

twin bed, papery sheets, a hard-cast window you can't open. It only looks up at the sky. By late afternoon, I am rocking Harlene Mae in its light, bouncing her on my good hip, and I am about to swirl her feathery hair with my finger when I realize there is no baby hair there to swirl. My twins have become ghost limbs, as real to me as missing body parts. It's so silent here. The occasional keyboard tapping of a guard down the hall, the hum of air conditioner. What I would give to have Junior screaming in my ear.

A few hours later, Guzman comes down the hall. I stay on the twin bed and make a point of not getting up.

"How we holding up?" she asks.

"Is that like a tease? I'm not great with ball busting."

"No. Sorry. Considering I've been fielding phone calls about you all day—press, mostly—I thought it'd be a good idea to see you're treated well."

"Everyone's treating me well. Except that one cop who arrested me."

"If Wyatt wants to press charges, he can press charges," Guzman says. "Legally, he's in the right."

"I'm noticing there's not much of a difference between what's legal and what people just want to be true."

"It's just charges now. You don't have to keep your lawyer if you don't like her."

Finally I sit up. "What are you, helping me?"

"You said a thing or two about Wyatt that made me think." She leans into the bars, sees a notch of metal she doesn't like, and picks at it. "How long do you think Wyatt was cheating on you?"

"Since the time he started taking the ASB, I assume." That was one of the side effects I read about: *intense sexual appetite*. Technically it was the word *Gefräßig*. Voracious, gluttonous. It barely registered to me as a side effect. Wasn't that the point of the ASB? I wanted him good and *Gefräßig*. It hadn't occurred to me until talking to Guzman that it would explain sleeping with Victoria, too. Maybe ASB explained everything. "Why?"

"If he's willing to lie to the police about that . . ."

"Then what else?" I shrug. "Everything. Meet the real Wyatt Decker."

There's no helping the smile that sprouts at my lips. I'd already mentally sorted Guzman into the bin of *Wyatt's fans*—the place where I sort most people—but that has become a bad habit, a self-fulfilling prophecy. There is a point at which people rise or sink to what you expect of them. Alice, Victoria, Wyatt: I expected the worst, I got the worst. No more.

While I am deep in thought, probably making a wrinkle at the top of my nose that dices my face in half, Guzman steps back, dangles a key chain, and unlocks the bars.

"What are you doing?"

"Letting you out. You posted bail."

Despite a chafe from the ankle monitor and the wrong color in my hair, I limp through the police lobby feeling more like myself.

"Dawn!" Kelly shouts. "Look at you. You are an *awful* redhead. Or is that supposed to be brunette?"

"I don't even remember."

"We'll fix you up," she says, smiling.

Kelly Maynard, my first hire at *The Perfect Home* store, fifty-odd years old, antiques lover, coffee bringer, and now bail poster. I barely recognize her in the puffy jersey dress and her summer hairdo, her curls all cropped now. But despite *my* ridiculous hair, she recognizes me. She wraps one of her elbow pits around my neck, giving me the mama-bear hug I didn't know I needed.

I try to make light of it. "I knew there was something about you the day I interviewed you. I said to myself, 'Dawn, one day, this woman is going to bail you out of jail. Hire her.'"

"We'll talk about my Christmas bonus later." Kelly's smile goes soggy. "But in the meantime, um, I should probably warn you."

"Why?"

"There are photographers outside. I had to practically shove through them." She throws a thumb toward the metal detectors and the smeary glass doors beyond. An entire crowd has congealed. Women in sleeveless dresses pat their microphones—basically props for TV, in this day and age—and pasty men keep recorders and phones at their hips, coiled like duelists about to draw. A few heads bob when they see me looking over. I can feel it hitting social media already: the grainy image of Dawn Decker in an ankle bracelet, paranoid expression, hair gone crispy, skin splotchy and red from her diet of highway burgers. Meanwhile, I'm sure Wyatt is coiffed somewhere, wearing a fresh haircut that makes him look utterly sane. How could I blame anyone for thinking I'm guilty?

"Oh, God, help me," I say.

"The police said they can clear the entryway, but the reporters have the right to the sidewalk. Earl's idling the truck for us. So it'll just be quick. Door, crowd, door. You think you can handle it?"

Kelly's husband has dropped her off at the store while her car was in the shop, so I know what he drives. I'm about to cut through reporters as I'm photographed getting into a 1989 Chevy Blazer with flame decals on the front. It's almost comical.

"C'mon," Kelly says. "We gotta do it. It's like ripping off a Band-Aid."

She gave my hand a squeeze. I hadn't even realized I'd been hold-ing hers.

Outside, the reporters rush me. Cameras flash. Questions fly. Someone accidentally elbows me in the ribs. *Dawn, what was your plan? Dawn, did you harm the twins? Dawn, have you spoken to Wyatt? Dawn, Dawn, Dawn.* Instead of screaming, I keep my mouth flat. Anything—a smile, a scowl—can and will be used against me in the court of public opinion. A strange memory sparks: the locker room after eighth-grade gym class, when I'd put on the wrong person's underwear and everyone found out about it. It was when I discov-ered how naked a person could feel while fully clothed.

Then comes the faux-woody scent of Vanillaroma air freshener. Kelly shoves me in, follows, shuts the door. Kelly's husband waves the reporters away gruffly and takes off. We get loose of the last few stragglers, back into the strange silence of the road.

I finally let out the breath I'd been holding in since jail.

"I thought I knew a famous person before," Kelly says. "But lately, it's on this whole other level."

"Infamy," I say.

"They've gone ravenous. There was a reporter looking through our recycling this morning. We saw that press conference with Wyatt and the police. A lot of talk about 'getting Dawn the help she needs.'"

"What else did he say?"

"It was all about a restraining order—here, I'll show you." Kelly leans over, squishing me against her husband, and pulls out her phone. A headline from Twitter pops up. Beneath it, there's a video of Wyatt and a crowd of friends—people would assume they were his friends, anyway—standing right next to the Nashville chief of police.

WHAT WILL DAWN DO NEXT?

Then the phone buzzes.

"Uh-oh," she says.

"What?"

The photos are already up on social media: me, Kelly, the half-peeling doors of the Chevy Blazer. Everything looks worse than I thought. Puffy cheeks, saggy chin, and nothing in my eyes but deer in the headlights.

"Wyatt just shared this," Kelly says. "There's a caption. 'As you all can see, Dawn is not well. It is with her own well-being in mind that I ask everyone to respect our privacy as I . . .'" Kelly lifts the phone. "'. . . I ask everyone to respect our privacy as I initiate divorce proceedings. For the long-term good of Wyatt Junior and Harlene Mae, I have come to this decision.' Should I go on?"

Divorce should have been my move—if only to get the public wondering why I was the one filing for divorce. Wyatt couldn't even wait until I'd driven home to steal it from me. He knew the ankle bracelet photos would be a disaster. Divorce had been in his chamber for who knows how long, and he pounced on the first opportunity to make me look bad after I'd turned myself in. He is quick, he is smart, and he stole my best move. I just hope it's not my only move.

It's afternoon by the time we've reached Kelly's home, a ranch Craftsman in Nolensville. Over a dinner of squash casserole and corn pudding, I fill them in on everything I've been through. Wyatt's ASB. Indiana. Dad—but Tim, not really *dad*. About sneaking into my house, which I guess is technically Wyatt's house. Alice taking the twins. Kelly and I go out to her back porch to watch the sun set. Her fenced-in yard is Tennessee picturesque—clear night, fireflies glittering, the air as thick as gravy.

"I'm sorry I left you in the lurch," I say. "With the store."

She makes a *piff* sound. "I heard everything in the news and knew something was up. Something had to make you want to protect your children. I didn't know how to help. But you hired me to be manager, so I figured I'd just keep managing. Although I can't say it's been business as usual."

"Place is probably a ghost town."

"Just the opposite. Everything picked up. We've been doing double the business, triple some days. We're something of a curiosity. A few customers asked me if they could interview me for their podcasts. Others take pictures, document everything."

"Like a crime scene," I say.

"I always say no to the podcasts, of course. I just say I know you, and I know you're not crazy. But that disappoints people. They want the story Wyatt's tellin'."

"They want to hear something juicy, right? Like how I yell at my employees, or I was never the same after having the twins."

"Well, as long as they buy some antiques."

I sip my ice water, feeling suddenly ungrateful for everything Kelly's done for me. "Kelly—that bail was ten thousand dollars."

"Oh, it's nothing. We'll get that money back at some point. It's out of my emergency fund, just sitting there. Figured this qualified as an emergency. Anyway, you stay with us as long as you need to. It's not like it's hard on us. You can have my daughter's old room. Comfortable, as long as you don't mind the Bieber posters. They're sort of caked into the walls."

"I don't mind," I say. "Listen—I don't mean to lay too much on you, but I think this makes you my best friend now."

She pats me on the hand. "That's good, Dawn. Maybe I'll bump you from number four to number three."

We laugh, but as I sip the last of my ice water, I think, Works for me.

There is one advantage to being infamous: everyone takes your calls. That night, I schedule a meeting with Carol Hopkins, the best defense attorney I can find in greater Nashville. An assistant answers her phone and tells me Hopkins isn't available, but once I drop my name, I get patched straight to her cell.

The next morning, I am in her downtown office. The room is so big it has sections—the big-desk-and-computer section, the leather-books-on-the-wall section, the couches-and-sweet-tea section. Hopkins invites me to couches-and-tea and sits with her legs folded, twisting her hair extensions around a finger, beginning midconversation as if she's been racking her brain for days already.

"I didn't do anything wrong," I say after explaining my version of events. "Even the break-in . . . that was my house."

Carol pulls glasses out of her sleeve like a magician and starts reading from a folder. I have time to drink in the sight of her. She reminds me of a renovation Wyatt and I did in Mount Juliet: so much plaster you can no longer guess its age. Fake hair, Botox-smoothened eyeline. Up close, I can see the cracks in her lips. But only up close. I hope she will be as good at changing the way people see me.

"Wyatt owns the house through an LLC chain," she says finally. "In the future—always get your name on the house. But that doesn't help us now. Breaking and entering, I'm not so convinced they have much there if they want to play the long game. You lived there for years and he never explicitly denied you permission. Hell, we can use episodes of *The Perfect Home* to prove you had a reasonable right to be there."

It soothes me that she says *we*.

"Nothing valuable was taken," she continues, "unless they want to bring up this tablet you say you found. In which case, they can go ahead and bring it up. I'll hash that out with Wyatt's lawyer, tell them to bluff us, see if they want Wyatt's dirty laundry aired out in public. I'm about ninety percent certain Wyatt'll drop charges once he gets a whiff of that."

"Then how do I get the twins away from Wyatt?"

"Well, that's the trouble. The judge has granted the restraining order, and pending a hearing, Wyatt has full custody. Then you're talking psych evaluations, he said, she said, and all sorts of things that could get very ugly. There's even a chance he could try to have you committed. It won't work," she hastily adds at my groan, "but obviously it would gum things up. And even if he doesn't get that, he's going to secure a divorce that leaves you with nothing. No house, no kids, no show, at least not for you. And a country that thinks you lost your mind."

"He can have everything, as long as I get the twins."

"Is there such a rush?"

My throat squeezes and for a moment I can't speak. *Such a rush?* Yes, there is such a rush. What will he do with the twins once he has a moment alone with them? Now that the world knows Dawn Decker was sneaking around her old house? Whom will they blame? And Wyatt will still have his cover story ready: insane, jealous wife, the twins he couldn't protect, his perfect life shattered by a postpartum monster. My twins will be dead and he won't care. He will finally have his pick of magazine and website covers.

Hopkins reads the desperation on my face. "Sorry. Not the right question. But he won't take the deal, not if he's confident he doesn't need to. With the restraining order, all you can do is talk to the police and ask them to keep an eye out. And we've already seen what that's done for your case. Are you really worried he might harm them?"

"I saw it typed out in his own words."

"Well, he's got the eyes of the world on him now. A single dad, two twins. There are going to be people at the house, I assume, helping him watch them. Maybe he'll hire a nanny. And if he's ever alone with them, he'll be the primary suspect."

"But he had all sorts of ideas for pinning it on someone else. We have to get them back as soon as possible."

"Then I'm going to need more," Carol says. "Leverage. Something I can show a judge. This tablet you were talking about. Where is it?"

"Alice took it when she took the twins to Wyatt."

Carol's brow furrows and she hums. "All right. What about your stepfather—what was his name again?"

"Tim Fremont. He's a private investigator in Nevada now."

"Do you have a number where I can reach him?"

I pull out my phone and dig out the latest text thread. It makes me look a little crazy—I send about six messages, each a paragraph long, to every one response I get. It's been about twelve hours since Tim last replied. Only one message: *Still on it.*

Carol copies the number down into my file, then closes it, throws it to the table, and sighs. "We can work on the charges. Maybe even the restraining order. Defending is what I do. But I can't make any promises about how we get the twins. Usually there's an advantage in family court for moms, but I think you'll agree this is a special case. People know Wyatt, they trust him, they can't picture him losing his mind—well, I don't have to tell you. Family court is all about what a judge thinks about you. And from what I surmise, Wyatt is very good at managing what people think of him."

"God."

"I'm sorry," Carol says. "If it means anything, *you* were always my favorite. That time Wyatt knocked down a load-bearing wall and you told him he's basically a stick of dynamite with legs? If you ask me, you're the whole reason that show is any good. *Was* any good." She points at a ceramic teapot on the table. "You know, I got that at your store about a year ago. I went one day, but you weren't there. I was so disappointed."

"Believe me, you would have been disappointed if I was. I clam up with fans. It's like this . . . allergic reaction. I wish it weren't the case."

"You seem perfectly charming to me."

"Well, I didn't know you were a fan. Now that I do—" I make a cringing face like I'm trying to swallow an ice cube. "It's all over. Nice knowing you."

Carol laughs, a nice laugh, throaty and brassy. "Here's my advice. While Wyatt is relying on babysitters and friends, while there are witnesses in the house that keep him sane . . . work on your custody case. Follow up with your stepfather, see what you can bring me that can force Wyatt's hand. And in the meantime, manage your image. Be more like this. Like how you really are. Let people see you're the best possible mom for those twins. No one likes to admit it—we all want to believe in blind justice and all that—but good PR does wonders for your legal situation."

"Like it did with Wyatt?"

Carol nods. "But he has judges, police, and half the population of the country all eating out of his hand, too. If we can reverse that, there's no telling how it ends up for you."

"Forget me. Just pretend you're the lawyer for my twins. Before we do anything else, we need to get them out of Wyatt's hands."

That night, the doorbell interrupts key lime pie at Kelly's. I'm picking at my slice when Kelly's husband comes back into the kitchen with Tim Fremont behind him. Unable to help myself, I kick the chair away and race over to hug him. Every friendly face is at a premium now.

Once everyone is introduced, Tim pulls out a laptop from his bag and fires it up. A few clicks and taps, and Tim brings up a photo gallery that starts with a picture of Wyatt behind glass somewhere. It's shot on a long lens, all the tree limbs gone blurry in the foreground.

A second photo shows Wyatt behind glass again, but this time, there's a second figure walking through the door. I think I recognize him. He's older. His hair is bright and gray, his midsection taut and barrel-shaped in a way that reminds me of movie stars from the fifties. Tim presses an arrow key again, and in the next slide, Wyatt and this man are clinking glasses.

"Drake Jennings," Tim confirms. "He's been organizing a group of investors to make a majority bid on HLTV. Publicly, at least."

"Wouldn't surprise me. Wyatt's always talking about owning more than the show." I blink. "What do you mean, 'publicly'?"

"I cracked the emails of Jennings's assistant. You didn't hear that from me, darlin'. Turns out the HLTV bid is a public feint. What they really want to do is buy Wyatt off them and make their own channel. And Wyatt will get a hefty stake. He never mentioned anything to you?"

"Never."

But even as I say it, I remember the day from months back, before I knew I was pregnant. The day I went to a signing at the store and a car bumped into my hip. A note he'd left in the trash. *$50,000,000.*

I tell Tim as much and his brow tightens. "I'd reckon that's about what his stake would be. Maybe more."

"My lawyer is putting up a defense against breaking and entering, and working on the restraining order," I say. "But she says it's even more important that I win in the court of public opinion if we're going to get the twins back. And without the tablet—"

"Not the tablet, but at least his words." Tim reaches deep into a pocket and pulls out a USB drive. "Every good private investigator always makes copies, then copies of copies."

Kelly, who has been fidgeting with the settings on her dishwasher so it will give her the look of someone with something else to do, finally presses On. She turns to us, drying her hands on a rag. "You mean to say you have the file?"

"The police said even if I had the document, I'd need to prove Wyatt created it," I say. "They won't care about a copy of a file. It doesn't mean anything to them. In their minds, I could have typed it up myself."

"Maybe in a court of law," Tim replies. "But the court of public opinion is somethin' else. Wyatt has been all over CHN and they're taking his side. So who haven't we talked to? Who might be interested in your side of things?"

"Kat Cameron." The name leaves my lips before I can even think. Cameron had won about a dozen Emmys doing hard TV journalism—oil spills, Ukrainian refugees in Eastern Europe, toxic-water crises in the Midwest—before doing a career U-turn and becoming the cohost of *Early Bird*. She is to modern celebrities what Barbara Walters once was, bringing the validation of the *real journalist* to grocery-aisle stories, pretending the latest actress's struggle with husband-free IVF was as harrowing as the war in Yemen. To score a feature interview with Kat Cameron is a stamp of approval on your celebrity. If you weren't famous before, you become famous the moment it airs.

"Wyatt practically used to stalk her," I tell them. "He wanted an interview with her so badly. But he thought it'd make him look bad if he was a beggar, so he'd try to get featured on all the news she followed. Last I remember, he was talking through something with the *New York Ledger* because he found out she reads it every day."

"The woman with those Intriguing Celebrities lists?" Kelly asks. "I'd say you qualify now. Both-a you, for different reasons."

"I'd start smaller," Tim says gently. "Something manageable. Kat Cameron only talks to people who are already established, and even then, she barely does those features once a year. Any one of the other talking heads would be thrilled to get the first exclusive with Dawn Decker. It's a national story."

"Sure," I say. "But I know from Wyatt that Kat Cameron doesn't watch cable news. May I?"

I sit down and slide Tim's laptop my way. God bless modern technology—it's only a few clicks between me and an email to the editors of the *New York Ledger*. I type in an attention-grabbing subject line: DAWN DECKER WITH AN OFFER OF AN EXCLUSIVE. In the body, I leave only the gentle tease of a story, but I let it slip that Wyatt Decker isn't all he seems and click Send. It's off to the general editor's account, the one that probably gets a hundred tips a day. But it's a start.

Kelly peers over my shoulder, still drying her hands on that rag.

There can't be any moisture left in them by now. "What's this, like fishing? You dangle the bait and Kat Cameron comes calling?"

"That was always Wyatt's idea," I say. "He just never had good enough bait for the *Ledger*. Their media team always viewed HLTV stars as backwater famous. But now . . ."

"Is the file going to be enough for the interview?" Kelly says, thinking aloud. "Maybe you should say some things about Wyatt. Did he ever beat you?"

"No, but he basically threatened to."

"Well, there you go. You could say he beat you anyway. Give him a taste of his own medicine."

"I'm not going to lie." A bubble breaks up my throat, strong as a cramp. Lies got me into this mess. Wyatt's lies. The show's lies about our marriage—me the nagging killjoy, him the ideal American husband. And having no way to tell the country the truth only reinforced those lies. No, I am not Wyatt Decker, even if lying is the easy way out.

"That's okay," Tim says, "because you don't have to. I did some more background on Wyatt that I wanted you to see."

I slide the laptop his way. "Have at it."

"Nope. This one I promised not to copy online." He hands me a rolled sliver of paper with an email address written inside. "And she said she'd only talk to you."

When Wyatt first showed me a picture of Myra Tenney, I remember thinking, Oh, I'm not his type at all. She was a woman of sharp edges: high cheekbones, a straight jawline, and narrow, slicing eyes. Even their color was sharp, a shining-metal flare of blue. In the one photo of her, she had her hand on his chest with one finger extended and curled. Her pointer, scything near his heart. As if holding it hostage. I was glad when he said she'd moved a continent away. If she was ever going to be competition, I wanted none of her.

But when I send her an email tonight—this time at the right address, the one Tim's somehow collected—I don't feel that way anymore. This is the only other woman in the world who knows the full Wyatt Decker experience. Would she be willing to tell her story in the news, I ask, if only to corroborate mine? I don't even ask what her story is. I just ask for the truth.

Hi. Dawn. Sure, I'll talk to you, but if it's all the same . . . not in writing.

Below that is a link for a teleconference one hour from now. As far away as she is—Peru? Colombia?—the time zones aren't too far off. It's late for both of us. Kelly brews a fresh pot of coffee before lumbering up to bed. Tim stays up as long as he can, but by the time eleven hits, he's dozing in the living room. I check into the teleconference ten minutes ahead of time, just in case, and find Myra Tenney already waiting on her end, a single lamplight painting her in shadows.

"Dawn." Her voice is not the sexy whisper I expected. It's got a little more bass and a ton more smoke.

"Hi, Myra. Thank you for doing this."

A sad nod. She is a haunted version of that old photo. Her cheeks are concave, like someone's scooped them out. She's wearing a buff over her forehead so tight she looks bald.

I clear my throat. "My—uh, Tim said that you wanted to tell your story with Wyatt. Do you mind telling me what you can from the beginning?"

"Okay. Well. Where to start?" She breathes in, sagging deep into her chair. There's only a wall and window behind her, a few sharp green leaves visible outside. "Wyatt's a charming guy. I'll get that out of the way."

"I know. And not the kind of charming that sets off alarms."

"No. No, he doesn't." Myra chews on that. "When he turns it on, he's like this beautiful innocent creature. Childlike, in a way. He charms you by letting you think that you've just said something that impressed him. You know that feeling you get when you talk to a kid and blow their minds with some fact? That's how good you feel in any conversation with him. And in most people, that'd get tiring, because you'd think. 'Oh, any old thing impresses him.' But occasionally he drops it, or he'll ignore some pretty woman around you, and you'll think *you're* the magic. You're the one charming him. It's never that way. He's always charming you."

Goose bumps come cascading up my arms. She is describing my experience dating Wyatt, almost exactly.

"You were only married for two years," I say. "What happened?"

"I can't speak for him. But I was used to a lot of attention from men. I always got the sense that once he got married, he lost interest. It was like an insect collection. Once he had me, there was nothing else to do but pin me by the thorax, place me behind some glass, and say, 'Job well done.' He stopped charming me, stopped caring about charming me. And what was left after that? It turned out there was nothing more to our relationship. So we did nothing but argue. That was the two years I had with Wyatt. Really just different types of the same argument, over and over."

"How bad did these arguments get?"

Another pause. Shivering, Myra rubs her arms, though it can't possibly be cold there. "Bad."

"Did they ever get violent?"

"Not on my end."

"Did he hit you?"

"I'm sorry. Can we . . . ?"

"Take all the time you need."

Myra's eyes go skyward as she tries to squint something from across horizons in her mind. "No. Wyatt's not as simple as that. I think unconsciously he's always viewed himself—and I know how crazy this sounds—as a Southern gentleman. What Southern gentleman would ever hit a woman? I think he *wanted* to, maybe. But he's Wyatt Decker, All-American, so he can't entertain those thoughts. It suppresses something in him until . . . darker things come out."

"What darker things?"

"Towards the end of our marriage, I was at my sister's. She'd left Facebook Messenger open. There was a conversation with Wyatt. I was surprised to find *any* conversation between those two, but then I kept scrolling—it just went on and on. And they'd talk about all sorts of things, but it kept coming back to me. Wyatt made up the strangest things. Said I'd been talking about committing suicide, which wasn't remotely true. But he gave all these specific details that made it all sound so real; I started questioning whether I was the one suppressing the memories. He told her he found Google queries about how to strangle yourself. Or that he'd found weird knots in socks, like I'd been practicing tying rope. Of course none of it was true. When we had our last big blowup argument, he threatened to strangle me. It all clicked. He'd been seeding my sister, somehow, with the idea that I was going to hang myself."

"What happened?"

"That was the last night I saw him. I had told my sister the truth, but at that point she was so concerned for me I don't think she really believed my side of things. She recommended I get help. My own sister. By then, Wyatt had his show. Everyone who met him or saw him on TV thought he was just this nice, handsome, helpful guy who surprises people with wheelchair ramps. When he got my own sister to turn against me, I knew I had to get out."

"He said you cheated on him with his attorney."

"No." Her eyes return to the camera. "But I should have guessed he'd say something like that. That's why I agreed to speak to you. When I heard about what happened and saw how they were interpreting it in the news, I never bought any of it. I've been wanting to put that part of my life behind me, but here it was, back in the headlines. The part that scared me most was it sounded like my Wyatt."

"I didn't see this side of Wyatt until he was taking a medication. He never took anything like that with you, did he?"

"You mean ASB?"

My heart slams into my throat.

"I only found out about it when I saw a package in the garbage," Myra continues. "Which is when he tried to explain everything. He said he'd never done anything illegal in his life, but he saw how badly I wanted children and couldn't stop himself."

"He told me you never wanted children."

She shakes her head. "Then he lied. We were trying the entire time."

I can hear the oceanic drone of blood pressure in my ears, as if my head is stuck in a seashell. *It's me,* he'd said in the doctor's office that day. *It's my sperm. . . .*

As if hearing it for the very first time.

"He went on and on about how good it made him feel," Myra says. "About how it made the world brighter, made him love me more—made him feel more like the man I deserved. That's how he packaged everything: it was for my sake. But he obviously loved what it did to him. He said something about being complete."

Tom Dale took it, and now they have three kids. No side effects. No more secrets.

"But why take it again?" I ask. "If it destroyed your marriage."

"There's no *if*. But what else can I say? Wyatt can't feel incomplete. He has to be perfect. Obviously, ASB made him feel like he was."

Entire months roll through my head, smoking like ruins. Fertility appointments and ovulation calendars and late-night Web searches like he really wondered what the problem was. Either he convinced himself the first round of ASB had cured him, or it was all for my benefit. "But he made such a show of it all—"

"Couldn't say. Maybe he learned something from my experience. Maybe he learned he needed the wife on board, too. And if you were just as desperate as he was—"

I'm with you, I said to him. *Let's try.*

"All the while, he knew exactly where the road would take him," I say.

"Maybe. The thing I've noticed about good liars is they lie to themselves, too. I'm sure he told himself he'd get everything right this time."

"Another thing. Why have you been so hard to reach?"

"I didn't want to be found. When your own sister doesn't take your side, it messes with your head. You can argue and argue your point of view, but it just makes you angry, and the angrier you get, the worse you sound. I don't know. People are strange." She clears her throat. "All I knew is I wanted out, I didn't want any part of Wyatt's fame, and if I could do some good in the world while I was at it, I would. I'm not even using my Wi-Fi right now. I didn't know

Wyatt had remarried until the past few days. Your dad's quite the detective, by the way."

"My—" I nearly correct her. "Yes, he is."

"I'm sorry, for what it's worth. I should have known he'd remarry. I could have saved you a lot of heartache."

"Maybe. But a year ago, I don't think I would have believed you."

"I can imagine what Wyatt would have said. 'Crazy Myra. Don't believe a word she says. . . .'"

Pulling a Myra. Had our oh-so-hilarious inside joke started with me, or with Wyatt? I don't remember.

"Would you be willing to tell your side of the story?" I ask.

"To who?"

"I'm trying the *New York Ledger.* They're going to want multiple sources. If they have both of Wyatt's wives, maybe people will finally believe us. I know you never wanted to revisit this part of your life, but—"

"Of course."

"You sure?"

"I owe you that much. Give me a time and I'll talk to whoever asks. As long as the Wi-Fi isn't cutting out."

And that, for the first time, is the whisper of a smile tugging at her lips. The relief of a breath held for too long—for years—rushes out of me. This woman was never my enemy.

We hang up after half an hour and I wake up my email tab. The inbox has dinged bold.

RE: DAWN DECKER WITH AN OFFER OF AN EXCLUSIVE.

CHAPTER 23

WYATT

I hate doorbells. Not just the noise but the intrusiveness of them. The idea that someone, anyone, can walk up to your doorway and ding-dong their way into ruining your evening. Meanwhile, you're watching TV, spread-eagle on the couch, a bowl of ice cream at your crotch, in your most vulnerable and least camera-ready state, and now you're expected to turn on the charm and socialize? Doorbells are absurd. Now, without Dawn, I'm the one who has to answer it. I check the porch video.

It's Victoria. She's dressed casually for her, white blouse and jeans. When I greet her at the door, she seems unrested, her hair yanked up in a lazy ponytail. Her eyebrows flitter when I don't say hello.

"There's no one watching your house," she says. "It's a private driveway. And anyway, so what? Can't I visit a friend after a few days?"

Several days, actually. It's been better for everyone. I shove the door open and let her walk through. Her heels clack on the floor. I almost say something about the scuffing, but she picks them up and tosses them into the closet like she's been invited over for the night.

"How are the babies?"

"Asleep." I wave at the monitor on the kitchen counter, feeling uneasy. Something in her tone has gone lie detector.

"Something wrong? You don't seem happy to see me."

I grab my phone from the couch and toss it to her. It's already set to the *New York Ledger*. "I was in negotiations with the *Ledger*. We were *this close*. Then Dawn hits them up out of nowhere and they decide she has the better story."

Victoria swipes through, too fast to really absorb it, but it doesn't matter. The headline is enough. DAWN DECKER: WYATT THREATENED VIOLENCE.

"But that isn't a real story," Victoria says. "She's making it up, right?"

"Man bites dog. I have nothing new to give the *Ledger*, just another interview like I've been doing on CHN. But if Dawn says something like that—it's *new*."

"But is it true?"

"No. Of course it's not."

There's something mournful about the way her eyes idle on my lips. What is she reading in them? I don't flinch. She needs to see our story as she always did—this long, romantic journey, with Dawn as nothing but our mutual obstacle. Victoria had been onboard with that once. To that Victoria, these national headlines would just make a funny anecdote at our wedding speeches. "Before you, Vic, my life was just a *little* rocky. . . ." Laugh, laugh, chuckle, chuckle. Once it was all she could have seen in our future: champagne, slapping wedding cake in each other's mouths, whisking away in the JUST MARRIED limo. Roll credits on her fantasy.

Now? I don't know what she thinks.

"I'm sorry if I'm being weird." I sit next to her, sliding an arm under hers, hoping the gesture is intimate enough. "It just doesn't feel good being lied about."

"I'm surprised you didn't call me." The words sound rehearsed. She tucks a strand of hair behind my ear. "I'm your best friend, Wyatt."

"What?"

"Aren't I? You're my best friend. That's how couples should be."

I look at her for a beat. Is she testing me? "I guess I just thought of us as—we're not *friends*, exactly, are we—"

"Think about the last few years. Besides Dawn, who have you spent more time with?"

She's right. There's been no one else. A thousand text messages, sure, but that's the thing about being famous—a world of false friends is still an empty house. Janie doesn't have a show to produce, so she's taking her vacation early. Is that what a best friend does at a time like this? No. She's a colleague. Drake Jennings? Our relationship is all business. What about *actual* Tom Dale? He texted me a few days back. Well-wishes. Polite, cordial, warm, as he always is. A quick "sorry about Dawn" and "if you need anything," and that was it. My thumbs hovered above the phone for a while until I just typed, *Thanks. Means a lot.*

It was the most we've texted in six months.

Distance does that to people. Tom was the best man for two of my weddings—you can bet he gave me the exact occasion-appropriate amount of ribbing for that—yet I can't think of the last time I saw him. I was even a little self-conscious about asking him the first time, like he would think, Gosh—Wyatt doesn't have *one man* in his life closer to him than me?

Truth be told, I asked Tom Dale because he was the one least likely to say no. I never had a best man in my life. We were part of a circle of friends in college, and he was always the most well-bred, the one I was always proudest to say I knew. But when he got married, I was the groomsman standing at the end. The steps hugged the altar at a strange angle, so the highest step cut off right at my feet. For half the wedding, I wasn't sure whether to climb to the highest step and breathe down his youngest brother's neck or be the only one in the wedding party standing on the second tier. So I planted a leg on each step, hoping no one noticed how awkward I looked. Second-tier Wyatt. Three brothers and three friends ranked ahead of me. That didn't surprise me. Tom was the one always driving home on Sundays in fall, and when we gave him crap for it, he would just say, "The three Fs, boys." Faith, family, football.

I envied Tom Dale. He was a man who knew what to do with his hands.

I thought I would get there, too, setting my goals, hanging my vision boards, getting on the best websites (though Modern People still eludes me). Shooting *The Perfect Home* made me feel like a man of Tom Dale's good breeding. The Perfect Man, The Perfect Job, The Perfect Life. But reality TV isn't real life. What if you had met Victoria Weatherly first, instead of Dawn? What if you spent several years on TV cultivating the image of a home renovation superman, but your sperm count is low? What if the only medication worth a damn is illegal? What if a woman you barely know, except for biblically, comes over and declares herself your best friend? And what if she has a point? What does it say about you?

It says I am not Tom Dale. And like the bad tux I wore to his wedding, I only ever rented his friendship.

"No," I say aloud. "I don't have a best friend."

Victoria stares at me, lips slightly open. "You have me."

You don't understand. I don't want to have you. "I always had girlfriends," I say. "Or a group of friends. Five guys with nicknames.

I always lied to Dawn and said this guy Tom Dale was my best friend. I haven't seen him in years."

"But—the whole world cares about what happens to you."

Victoria still doesn't understand. She is my mistress. My former mistress, I hope, because my best play might be to get Dawn settled and set the stage for our reunion episode. Victoria won't like that, of course. I'd promised her a spot in the next season. I don't know how I'm going to pick up the pieces if I shatter that dream.

If I had a moral code like Tom Dale does, I could tell her to leave right now. Faith, family, football. Faith—that comes first, so of course I'd dump Victoria, confess my sins to the world, ask forgiveness, go to church. It all sounds so easy that way. That's the beauty of codes. At least they're clear.

"You're right," I say. Victoria's two favorite words. I smile stiffly, forcing my mouth open, but the lie feels nice—like I am handing her a plump piece of candy, like she's the crazy one if she turns me down. "I have you."

Victoria reaches under my arms and gives me an awkward half hug. We sit next to each other, arms knotted together, the TV flickering on mute, a commercial for alopecia medication. I lean into the corner of the couch. On the far end is Momma Harlene's old chair. It rocks in the edge of my vision, but when I look at it, I see it's the blanket swaying in the air-conditioning.

And just when we're about to speak, my phone buzzes. Then her phone buzzes.

And mine starts buzzing again.

It's repeating: not a text but a full-on phone call. The publicist. I send it to voicemail, but then a text alert brightens the screen. *Seeing this?*

"Turn on NBC," Victoria says from the glow of her phone.

• • •

The photo of Dawn with the pink snapper splays out in a green screen. In front of it, sitting on a stool as the camera wheels around her, is the silhouette of Kat Cameron.

My heart sinks.

She did it. She got there first. Dawn, my PR-averse wife, the one more comfortable *behind* the camera, landed Kat Cameron.

Stomach squirming, I unmute. Kat Cameron's husky, everything-I-say-is-hard-news voice is in full deployment. ". . . believes it was the only course of action she could take to *protect* her children from the real threat. She maintains that threat was her husband, America's favorite handyman, Wyatt Decker."

The TV cuts to a still photo of yours truly. It's a publicity shot. I'm dangling a sledgehammer over my shoulders—gee, what could be Kat Cameron's message *there?*—and giving a squinty smile, a row of veneers showing. The camera zooms in slowly, and as it inches closer to my eyes, I can feel the opinion of millions moving with it. Everyone looks more sinister if you slowly zoom in on the eyes.

"What the hell?" Victoria mutters.

I shush her.

Dawn's voice, lifted from their interview segment, cuts in off-screen. "Wyatt is an expert at making people like him. That charming person you see on TV—yes, that's him. But over the past year, he dropped that. At least, he did at home."

"According to Dawn, the couple had long struggled with fertility issues before pinpointing the problem: Wyatt's low sperm count." Cameron is speaking as stock footage shows laboratory technicians dripping needles into test tubes. More appropriate than showing some guy masturbating in a windowless medical room, I suppose. "Wyatt, image-conscious and determined to have children, turned to experimental fertility drugs from Europe. This, Dawn claims, is when she saw another side of her famous husband."

Now it cuts to the interview itself. Dawn, already red-faced and bleary-eyed, sits on a hotel sofa. The skyline of Nashville is sunset pink in the background. Nashville. Kat Cameron even flew out here.

Dawn looks like she's been weeping. But it's not ugly. I'd forgotten how well Dawn cleans up. Her hair is the old color again, sandy blonde. With lipstick on, the frown lines in the corners of her mouth disappear and any flicker of a smile shows the heart shape I used to love. Kat Cameron's production team relish their extreme close-ups, so you can see every lash when Dawn blinks. I have never seen someone look so innocent.

I am screwed.

"'Angstrom Supplement-B,'" Cameron reads, holding her glasses up. "Illegal in the United States. These are serious accusations."

Dawn nods. "He told me he okayed it with his doctor. And I never doubted it. Everything Wyatt says sounds credible. It's part of his charm."

"You were married for nearly *five years* before this. You never saw this side of him before?"

Dawn chews on that, tonguing something behind her lips, then sags into the chair. Kat Cameron has the best editors. They leave Dawn's silence in. Five seconds, ten seconds, drowning us in her anguish. It is the anguish of being married to me.

"Wyatt's always been cynical. He's good with people, but only because he doesn't have a high opinion of them. When he started the show, he wanted it to be educational content, mostly. I think he was always resentful that people didn't like it at first. So he would watch the number one reality shows on cable and see how they did it. He's the kind of guy where if someone else tells a joke and everyone laughs, he has to go write it down. And as the show got more popular, and when I came on, he focused more on the season arcs. Our wedding episode, there wasn't any renovation going on at all. He and our producer, Janie, milked the drama of my missing father for an hour-long special. And it worked. We got better ratings than cable news that night. But I constantly try to tell people that it's all engineered. It's just a show. Nothing gets broadcast that doesn't fit Wyatt's public image, or that he hasn't drummed up on some spreadsheet months before."

Kat Cameron taps the tip of her glasses to her chin, oh so serious. "And what *is* the public image your husband is so concerned with?"

"The brand," Dawn says, as if it's obvious. "*The Perfect Home.* The perfect husband."

"And what perfect husband is infertile?"

Dawn shakes her head. "Wyatt views us as fantasy avatars for our audience. He knows his audience all has kids, and he didn't. I never thought that mattered. People can handle it if we don't have kids. Yeah, we got a lot of pressure, but that's like any other couple. But I think now, looking back on it . . . he just wanted new material."

The screen cuts to more clips of medical facilities, doctors sitting down with patients, scenes of people waiting in fertility clinic waiting rooms, their faces obscured and out of focus. "Research into Angstrom Supplement-B is difficult to come by in the United States," Cameron narrates, "but what we could find suggests a wild array of side effects. Aggressive tendencies. Increased libido. Suicidal ideation, homicidal ideation. Yet for the people we asked, it's the intensity of the side effects that makes ASB so dangerous for fertility treatment."

"They did one clinical trial in the United States," a gray-haired doctor tells Cameron in his office. One glance and I hate him. He looks completely credible, the face you imagine when you hear the phrase *nine out of ten doctors recommend.*

"It was a disaster. Half of the men had exhibited such profound changes in behavior, their families intervened and made them stop. And we've found ASB is so intense that those who don't properly wean exhibit long-term effects."

"What about the other half?" Cameron asks.

"It did work for them. Those subjects didn't exhibit the mood changes. Their sperm counts increased. In fact, many of them had children as a result of being in the trial. But even so—the first rule of medicine is 'do no harm.' You can't help people have children if there's a fifty-fifty chance the medicine destroys them in the process."

Now the screen shows footage of Cameron walking with Dawn outside on the grass, a bright Nashville afternoon. I recognize Dawn's old house, the white two-bedroom ranch she shared with Momma Harlene for eighteen years.

"Dawn tells us she was reticent about the medication, especially after researching it online. But within a month, she had gotten pregnant—and Wyatt promised to wean himself properly. Then, over the next nine months, Dawn claims, Wyatt's behavior slowly went off the rails."

Smash cut to Dawn in the interview now. "Nothing much at first. Ignoring me. Not laughing at the jokes he used to laugh at. But over time it got more serious. Threatening me on set one morning when he had a nail gun in his hand. Calling me a word I can't repeat in front of your audience. Suggesting violence. And then, one day, he left his tablet out and I found a document with all sorts of strange notes."

I have to mute my phone or it will buzz and dance its way off the coffee table. Over the baby monitor, I hear the static cut with a screech that can only be Junior waking up. Let him screech.

As the screen fills with zoomed-in selections from the infamous *document*, Victoria scooches close. "This can't be right."

Cameron narrates, "The document was all but a confession to Wyatt's plans to drown his newborn twins and pin it on a new nanny, Hattie Wright. In it, Wyatt fantasizes about being the top story on Modern People. He even wrote his own headline: 'The Long Road from Tragedy.' Wyatt also wonders if the murder should happen after baptism, so the children can, quote, 'go to Heaven.'"

"Is she making this up?" Victoria asks.

I can't look away. "Vic—please."

"The police don't consider it evidence," Dawn says. "Because anyone can create a document like this. But Wyatt's charged me with breaking and entering into my own home. I'd just ask the country to think about this: Why was I breaking into my own home unless it was to find *this* and show it to the world?"

"Dawn says she can't prove her husband's behavior," Cameron's voice-over announces, "because Wyatt has gone through household security tapes and deleted footage of his worst offenses. But NBC was able to corroborate some of Wyatt's behavior through a second character witness, who claims that the Wyatt whom Dawn Decker describes is all too familiar to her."

Another cut, but this time, the screen starts out blurry. It slowly culls into focus as a cheap camera auto-adjusts. Cameron's editors are masters, letting us hold our breaths for just a little bit, wondering who the mystery guest will be, but my heart is already thumping in my throat. I know exactly who it will be.

Myra.

With the camera under her and in bad lighting, she looks ten years older. She looks thin and hollowed out. That hurts my image, too—people will imagine it is the stress of being married to me that did it, and not ten years of volunteering in South America, ten years of raw jungle fruits and tapeworms.

"Myra Tenney was Wyatt's first wife," Cameron tells us in voice-over. "Both in their twenties, the two shared what was by all accounts a tumultuous two-year marriage. Tenney ended it suddenly and moved to the Peruvian Amazon, where she provides nursing and medical care to children in Christian missions."

Great. Yes, mention that. Saint Myra of Peru.

"I wanted out," Myra says in her conference with Cameron.

"Out. Why?"

"What Dawn is describing—and I say *what* instead of *who* for a reason—reminds me of my time married to Wyatt. It's exactly what he did."

"You mean the threats, the homicidal ideation, the ASB—"

"I mean the ASB. He took it with me, too."

I lock eyes with Victoria. Hers are usually narrow, slitty, like they could spit at you. But now I see the whites. She slides away, putting the crack of cushions between us. I don't have to wonder what she's thinking. It is what America is thinking now. Not *Is it true?* No one is wondering that anymore. No. They've rearranged the words.

It is *true.*

I didn't take Myra with me to the fertility clinic all those years ago. If it was true—if the problem was on my end—it felt better walking into the waiting room alone, thumbing a magazine, whistling like everything was fine. Fake it till you make it. Then the test came back and the doctor told me—if I can translate his overpriced language—that a toilet seat had a better chance of getting Myra pregnant than I did. I suppose I could have told Myra and the two of us could have weighed the options. Instead I spent that night in a wan computer glow, sliding from the Mayo Clinic to social media threads and finally to message boards where men shared their sperm hacks: *Have you heard of ASB?* No, I hadn't, but I was a sucker for simple-sounding acronyms. My numbers flew higher at the next test and I stopped taking it. I felt as if a distant part of me had clicked into place. If I got a little irritable with Myra, so what? It healed what needed healing. And after Myra left, after I'd weaned, I held out hope I *had* been healed. That's why I resisted the new tests with Dawn for so long. For months—years—I thought I didn't need pills to be complete. I enjoyed that time. Even I didn't want to see the thread at the magician's thumb.

"I saw it in the trash," Myra says. "And it scared me. Not only his changes—which were exactly like Dawn describes—but what it meant about me. Maybe I committed a felony, aiding and abetting, or maybe I'd be legally complicit if I didn't turn him in? I didn't know."

"One day," Kat Cameron narrates as a slow-moving shot of a generic-looking cell phone beats steadily toward the camera, "Myra discovered messages between Wyatt and her sister. Wyatt had been planting the idea that Myra was thinking about suicide—an idea Myra strongly denies."

The interview cuts back to Kat. "How long had he been speaking with your sister, introducing this idea that you were depressed?"

"Months, I think. He was so patient with it. And he always steered it in a way so it was their secret—that if she told me what Wyatt was saying, maybe I'd go and do it. But I never said anything about killing myself."

"And that's when you left Wyatt?"

Myra shakes her head. "In the messages, he talked about me googling ways to hang myself, or strangle myself. Then one day we had an argument and he threatened to strangle me, and that was when it all came crashing in on me: this had been his plan for months. And those months aligned with when he came off the ASB."

Kat shuffles some papers. "That's exactly what Dawn describes."

"Even my own family didn't believe my side. So I did the only thing I thought I could. I left Wyatt, left the whole country, to try to do some good with the rest of my life. But then I heard about Dawn. I heard about what she said, down to his specific choice of words—"

"Which words?"

"He said, 'You—'" Myra starts, but the word is bleeped out. If I know the American audience—and you bet your ass I do—the bleep will sound more threatening and heinous than if she had just said the word, clear as day: *cunt*. "And talking about her being in the hospital. That was his go-to phrase with me. It's exactly how he was coming off the ASB. I don't know much about Dawn, but I can tell you this. She is not lying."

Back to Dawn's interview now. Kat Cameron asks her to tell the world what it was like going from one of America's most envied brides to its most tortured.

Another second or two of pause. The TV goes so quiet, I can hear my refrigerator buzzing. It's as if the editors are torturing me— *me* specifically—with all the silence. I can feel the ratings go up with every beat of dead air, as tangible as the blood pounding in my neck. Dawn smacks her lips, and what she says comes out whisper quiet.

"I didn't question why his first marriage ended. I don't think I wanted to know. It could only be something I didn't want to hear. I just knew I had the man of my dreams. A husband the whole world idealized. And he charmed me into thinking that I had been so special to him, that he thought he was the lucky one."

The TV intercuts Dawn with silent photos of our home—the one I'm sitting in, right now—and I feel self-conscious. Middle America will want me to live in a house like theirs. A farmhouse, maybe, or an old corner Victorian we renovated. Viewers have seen the house on TV, of course, but I've always had a say in the editing room. We've never done wide angles. Now someone stole a drone shot of the entire property. The world knows what a nouveau-riche behemoth I live in.

"But what about *you*?" Kat asks Dawn. "Did *you* want kids?"

"Of course. Especially his kids. A year ago, my biggest problem was worrying whether *I* was enough. Enough for the show, enough to make people want an autograph at a book signing. And, the big question, enough of a wife for the most eligible man on TV. But then when he looks you in the eyes and tells you that not only are you enough, but that he wonders the same about himself . . . you don't want to hear anything else. You don't want to know what went wrong with the first marriage because you're worried whatever it was will stain his second."

"Well, you were certainly enough for the show. A lot of people say you were the missing element that made *The Perfect Home* the runaway success it is today. In your first season, there was an immediate uptick in female viewers."

The next cut is an extreme close-up of Dawn. Every time they cut back to her, she seems to have added a wrinkle around her soft eyes. The sympathy builds. There is strength behind those eyes. If I see it, the entire country will see it, too. They will know that if nothing else, Dawn has never lied to them. And they will see something

I have never been able to do. Dawn is willing to open her veins on national TV.

"I liked to think it was the chemistry," Dawn says. "You know—the witty repartee. And it's the perfect word, *chemistry*, because if you get one ingredient wrong, none of it works. So when people said it was our *chemistry*, I loved that. It meant I was the only one who could have possibly made that show what it is today. But now I don't think that's true."

"Why not?"

"I think Wyatt is a freight train, a success machine. He was going to figure out the formula eventually, with or without me. I just happened to be the one he met at that time, the one he scooped up. I'm not as good with people as he is. People come to my book signings and they're disappointed I'm not as quick-witted and sassy as I am on TV. Well, that's TV. We get to reshoot if I bungle something. Meanwhile, Wyatt, he's the kind of guy who practices witty repartee in the mirror. He *likes* it. I never did. I wanted the perfect home, lowercase letters. He only ever wanted the show."

Cameron shuffles some papers she's holding in her lap, adjusts her glasses. I've never realized until now how much of a show it is. Rather than a television journalist—which is what she is, all she is—she looks like the district attorney conducting a prosecution. "And now, you're facing a restraining order, the possibility of losing custody of your twins?"

Dawn tries to speak, but her chin starts wavering. She weeps. Real weeping, her chest bobbing, her eyes red, the tendons taut in her neck. The kind of weeping where, if we were watching these interviews the way we used to, we'd point at the TV and go, *That woman is definitely not faking it.*

"I don't want his money," she says. "I don't want the show. I don't want to be famous anymore. I just want my babies back. If something bad happens to them, I will never forgive myself."

There's a clacking sound on the floor. Victoria has gone to the closet and started putting on her shoes. I come out of the spell and hit Mute. "Where are you going?"

"It's true," she says, stashing her purse under her arm. "Everything she's saying is true."

A faint hiss bursts in my ears. I've lost Victoria. And if she's abandoned me, then *The Perfect Home*'s audience is next. No. It's not just that audience, is it? It's all of America now, the Twitterverse, the readers of Page Six, the millions who watch every Kat Cameron special. It's *Middle* America. Flyover country. My country. Nurses and hairdressers and supply chain coordinators and church ministers and HVAC repairers and EMTs and small-town doctors and servers who top off your ice water. All the people who need a silly home renovation show at the end of the day, something humming and harmless on the TV while they put up their aching feet. All the good people I've been pretending to be. That's the thing about good people—they'll forgive you anything except lying. It's the only thing that takes advantage of their goodness.

"She's delirious," I say. "You know what mother lions will do to get their cubs—"

"No!" Victoria shouts, and points at me. "No more, Wyatt. I can't believe I was on your side. Every time I let you pull me back in. I should have known better." She pulls out her phone and dials three numbers.

"What are you doing?"

"The twins are here. If I'm leaving, I'm going to make sure they're safe."

I jump from the couch and slap her phone to the floor. The audible *crack* of the screen freezes us and our eyes lock. Victoria's thin hand dangles in the open air, her fishy mouth open and out of water. In the silence, there's no doubting that's Junior screeching on the monitor, that staticky knife in the ears. I slap Victoria's hand again, catch one of her rings on a bone, then take out my pain with a backhand to her pissy fucking Miss Chattanooga face.

She turns away and grabs her broken phone, dodging out of my hands until she's out the door, into public air, the one place she knows I can't go. Paparazzi. They bring telephoto lenses and shoot you from miles away if they have to. Then, at the armpit where the walkway meets the driveway, she stops and turns. "I'm going to the police."

"Go ahead. They'll find a good man sitting at home with two happy twins."

We stare at each other awhile, the gusty night tugging at us. But her eyes are what get me, sharp as cracked glass, gold specks gone hot in the light of my house. Crisp and clear. "Happy twins, maybe," she says. "But no one thinks you're a good man anymore."

The fog of the next few moments takes ages to clear. Somewhere a car door slams, an engine chugs up, the car trails off. A thump of heartbeat brings me back. I am still standing in the middle of the foyer, an awful hiss in my ears. I weep. Real weeping, and I know that because there are no cameras here. When I bring my hands to my face, I feel a cool metal slap. I don't know when I did it, but I've grabbed my key chain: Ford remote and Swiss Army knife. And somehow, seeing that little white cross as I listen to Junior's wailing makes me feel better.

I know what I need to do before the police arrive. I know where I need to go.

To the twins' room.

Part Five

THE PERFECT HOME

CHAPTER 24

DAWN

A fuse has blown inside me. This time, the world has seen it. After the interview airs, my phone becomes the fireworks: pops, sizzles, buzzes, *Dawn that was amazing*, flash, flash, flash, *Dawn why didn't you tell us??* Darren Paulsen of CHN wants to devote all of next Monday's hour to telling the Dawn Decker story. Indira Chakhsar of CBS is already looking into Wyatt's past and asks if I'll confirm some of her findings. Modern People asks who my publicist is. (The irony of that isn't lost on me.) Alice leaves three missed calls and just as many texts. *I was so stupid. Can you ever forgive me?*

Just as I'm reading that, a call from Victoria lights the screen. I roll my thumb in the direction of voicemail.

After cutting a notch of Kelly's banana bread in the kitchen, I head to the back porch. I leave my phone out on a table and let it keep dancing in the light of new phone numbers. There's only one contact I need to see. When my phone announces TIM FREMONT, when he gets back from Belle Meade and tells me the twins are still okay, I'll rest easy. He said he'd be back at nine thirty if he could confirm that someone else was at our house with the twins besides Wyatt.

Nine thirty. Maybe then, I'll have won.

Two evenings ago, it was me, Kat Cameron, her camera operators, and her army of handlers, all of us in a hotel suite Cameron's team had booked downtown. And then there she was: hair extensions, TV makeup, her pantsuit far too thick for the Nashville summer. Kat Cameron is one of those famous people who made you wonder, Why *her*? She has narrow-set eyes and a neutral, flat mouth she keeps perfectly level with the horizon. Her main skill—interviewing—always struck me as too easy, like painting by numbers. But when I confessed to her I was nervous, she told her cameraman, "Hold off a few minutes," and started telling me about all the troubles she's been having with her summer house in Kennebunkport. After a few minutes of her giving me a riveted stare while I ran through tips about using high-contrast throw pillows to pull a room together, I realized my heart rate had slowed. I would have been comfortable telling her my Social Security number. Oh, never mind, I thought. She's a genius.

By the time the lights clicked on, hangover harsh, I was ready. I was me. Not Wyatt's me, not the *Perfect Home* version. The real me, Momma Harlene's daughter, Junior and Harlene Mae's mother. And I realized then that the lights were never the real enemy. It was my own cringing instinct. For the twins, I could overcome any of it.

When it was finished and Cameron's team was disassembling her like a NASCAR pit crew, she touched my arm. "I'm so glad you connected with the *Ledger*," she said. "I came across it one day—"

"That was Wyatt's idea."

"Oh?"

"Well, months ago. He used to stalk you on Twitter. He always tried planting stories in the *Ledger* because he knew you read it. So I just . . . remembered that. And I knew we had something you might want."

"I'll say." She kept her eyes on me, then reached out to pull me in for a hug. "I usually don't hug. But, God, you look like you need it. Go get your twins back."

I couldn't say anything back through the tears. That was for the best, because if I could, it would have been something like *I love you, Kat Cameron.*

On the table, my phone brings so much good news, I switch it to silent mode. Success is like chipping a piece of granite, Wyatt always said. You can chip and chip and chip and not make a dent, until one day, a whole chunk falls away. Right now, it's as if the whole chunk has shattered in a thousand pieces on the ground. Janie texts that she tendered her resignation to HLTV—unless *The Perfect Home* proceeds without Wyatt. Carol Hopkins sends about fifty clapping-hands emojis and says this is exactly what I needed to do to win my custody case. My email inbox floods with new interview requests. It's all as Wyatt always said: The truth doesn't matter. It's what people believe. And rarely do the two intersect.

Well, they're intersecting now.

A knock at the door jolts me out of my phone hypnosis. I check the time. Ten after nine. For a moment I wait, expecting Kelly to answer the door, but then I remember she and her husband are out at their favorite sundae shop—"Don't wait up."

I snap up the last of the banana bread and roll myself out of the chair with a groan. I'm exhausted, but I'm so happy, so buzzed in the afterglow of the Cameron interview and the idea of getting the twins back, I walk to the door without thinking to ask who it is.

Wyatt's dressed in a T-shirt and track pants—pajamas to him, unwearable in public. Kelly's porch light cuts his face into hollows. His breaths are tight like he jogged here. But his Ford is parked on the curb. Silently, he points into the house, and even though my heart is hammering, I move aside. It seems pointless to shut the door now. If he really wants in, there's nothing I can do to stop him.

Kelly's decorated a console table with so many picture frames that it's like a booby trap—pick up one the wrong way and the rest will topple over. But Wyatt is able to sneak one out. He lifts it to his eyeline: Kelly, her husband, their kids locking shoulders in front of EPCOT, each of them ten years younger, glowing in turquoise light.

"I was going to suggest Disney," Wyatt says hoarsely. "When the twins were old enough to want it. Junior was going to love dinosaurs and Mickey. And Harlene Mae would love Cinderella. At her sixteenth, I was going to have our glass guy make her a shoe. I had it all planned."

"That's not what you had planned, though, is it?"

Wyatt doesn't say anything. He pinches the picture frame and slips it in with the rest, all too conscious that one wrong move will send the whole house of cards tumbling.

"How did you find me here?" I ask.

"Where's Kelly?"

"Out."

"I was thinking maybe you'd like to call a truce."

"A *truce*." I grind the word between my teeth so he can hear how childish it sounds.

"Yes. Don't act like you don't know what we've been doing. Launching ICBMs at each other through the media."

"Maybe that's how you see it. I told Kat Cameron the truth."

"Oh, the truth." Wyatt wipes his forehead of whatever invisible sweat he seems to imagine and goes to the living room sofa, but doesn't sit. He shakes his fingers and bobs on his toes, like a man about to take a long dive.

I start scanning the room for blunt objects. There's a miniature bust of a dragon on the bookshelf, guarding a few high fantasy books, but Wyatt's closer to it.

"Everyone thinks they have a monopoly on the truth," he continues. "But when they open their mouths, all that comes out is some version of what they always wanted to believe."

"Not everyone lies like you."

"How do I lie?"

"By instinct. Maybe I can't prove it's yours, but I have a copy of the document you made, and now Kat Cameron's seen it, published it. Myra confirms everything I say. And now Janie, who remembers when I started complaining about you on set. Victoria admits you were having an affair. Everything about you that you tried so hard to keep hidden."

"Yes, that's what people will think. I agree."

"They'll think it because it's true."

"It doesn't have to be."

"It *does* have to be," I say louder. "That's the thing about the truth."

As if my words shoved him over, Wyatt falls back into the couch. He rubs his knees. So, so tired, his movements seem to say, aching from all his hard work, holding up the entire world.

"The truth, then. I'm better, Dawn. You were right about the ASB—it was wrong for me. I should have told my doctor. But I've been off it a long time. I'm the same Wyatt you married now. And I'll never take those pills again."

I don't sit with him. Arms crossed, I lean under the arch frame, making myself small. If I run for the dragon bust, will the coffee table get in his way? "Where are the twins, Wyatt?"

"Safe."

"Safe where?"

He doesn't answer. His thin lips broaden into a smile. It's a gummy smile, not like his smile when we first met. I remember that smile. Big, wide, unconscious, an involuntary reaction. This is not the same. There is something stitched-off about it, like his teeth need hiding.

The cover headline he'd thought up flashes in my mind. THE LONG ROAD FROM TRAGEDY. Goose bumps sizzle down my arms.

Tragedy. His word.

"What do you want?" I ask.

"To rebuild our family."

"No. Why are you really here?"

The smile fades, and without the light, I can see how hollow and dead eyed it had always been. "You probably heard that I've been meeting with Drake Jennings."

I nod.

"He's got an investor group that's ready to buy out HLTV. He wants to spin *The Perfect Home* into its own brand. Perfect Home TV, a digital magazine, a line of pots and pans. Everything. He offered me half to star. I'd sign over the name, and as a sweetener he'd throw in six percent of HLTV, too."

"Congrats. Enjoy. Where are the twins?"

"I'm not done." He pounds a fist to the coffee table and holds it in place. A red streak slices across one of his knuckles. It's too dark to tell if it's fresh blood. Following my eyes, he rubs his fingers together, wiping it off. It reminds me of how flies clean themselves. "You burned the chance of this deal going through. So I see no other way out. Here's my offer. Half."

"I don't want your money. Where are the twins?"

He ignores me. "Half of my share. Half of my stake in HLTV. Do you know what that's worth? Last time it sold, it went for four billion. Drake Jennings wants to buy it for ten. Then there's twenty-five percent of *The Perfect Home*—"

I laugh. "You think I'd *own* something with you now?"

"What you do with it is up to you. But I need you to go on TV and recant the story. I'll drop the restraining order, the custody challenge—"

"I don't want your money. I'm not going to recant." My stomach boils so hard, I taste banana bread and acid. "The *twins*, Wyatt."

His face goes cold as he stands in the middle of the room. The dragon bust might as well be miles away now. I give it a stupid, futile look—my stupid, futile mouth probably open, my stupid, futile eyes probably showing everything I'm thinking. But it doesn't matter. He puts his hand under the back of his tee, at the small of his back, and pulls out a handgun. My neck tightens and my teeth bite and my hands move up instinctively. Wyatt gets in, kiss close. His gun at my temple, his eyes swept in a hurricane of tears and veins.

"Do you know how many women would trade places with you?" he whispers. "I'm offering *millions*. Just to be my wife for a few years. I'm not even asking you to try. Just to pretend. And you can't even do that."

"Where are they?"

"They're with us now."

A wail belts through the room. It's only when I try to catch my breath that I realize it's mine. "What did you do to them?"

I feel the barrel of the gun leave my temple. Wyatt waves at the recliner. "Sit down. And stay there."

He goes through the doorway and I hear the locks of his Ford beep awake.

As I slink back in the recliner, feeling heavy and numb, the Hobbiton clock on the mantel shows nine twenty. I think of Tim and the thought of him brings me back to my pocket. The things he said I should always carry. Keys, wallet, cash, phone finder, recorder. I lift the recorder out of my jeans just enough to hear the button go click.

Wyatt steps over the threshold, two carryalls under his arms. I have never been so happy to hear a screech coming out of Junior. Those feed-me moans. He is alive. *They* are alive. Wyatt sets them on the sofa and puts the gun on the coffee table, the barrel pointed my way.

"I'll recant," I say. "I'll do it. Just take the gun and walk away from here."

"Aww," Wyatt says, singsong. Then he unfastens Harlene Mae and pulls her out of her carryall, his two meaty, veiny hands big enough to collapse her rib cage if he wanted. Harlene Mae's head bounces around, searching, but as always, she is the calm one. I want to close my eyes, cringe away from this agony. But I can't let her out of my sight.

Wyatt bounces her on her feet, play-dancing, making up some goochie-goo song. Harlene Mae keeps her arms at her face, guarding. Her head bobs, but her neck isn't strong enough to find me. Mama's little girl.

I reflexively reach out but Wyatt flinches. "Don't you move."

"You wouldn't."

"Wouldn't what?" The look he gives me is bright-eyed, innocent. Harlene Mae knocks her nubby hands to his face, trying to connect with him, make sense of him. There is more humanity in her than him already. Wyatt closes his eyes and lets her explore the notches of his face. Then he pinches her little wrist and sweeps her up and cradles her in one arm, feeding position. She is so small in his arms. I want to rush up to his gun, turn it around, and send a bullet straight to his spine. But Harlene Mae is wriggling under him, I'm on the wrong side of the room, and he's much stronger than me. Far too strong. My eyes water, my throat turns to mush. There is only one thing to say.

"I'll *do* it. Okay? You win. Just put her down."

Harlene Mae relaxes and pinches one of his fingers. I look at the clock. Nine twenty-two.

With his free hand, Wyatt spins the gun on the coffee table. "You'll do what, Dawn?"

"Recant. On TV."

"And what else?"

"What else *is* there?" I want to be calm—strong for Harlene Mae—but my eyes burn and my lungs seize. "Just put her down, I'll do whatever you want."

"Oh, it's not all I want." Wyatt dabs a finger on the gun to stop it spinning. He pulls it up, shakes it a bit, and feels the weight of it, reveling in the power this gives him. "I need you on board until the deal goes through. You've done a lot of damage and it's going to take you a long time to make it right. You're going to have to do a lot of embarrassing things. We'll do a few double interviews, both of us in the same shot. I want the country to see you agreeing with me when we talk about how crazy you've been. And how it was your fault to think any of it could be true. Unresolved trauma with your dad, maybe. And we'll talk about how you're getting help for it. I don't know if you can convince Myra to recant, but you're going to try. Can you do that? All of that? It may take years. And when the deal's done, you can't take any of it back."

Years. The word is so small and easy in his mouth—as if he is describing folding the laundry for a little while. But how old would the twins be when Wyatt's *years* are over, if those years ever do end?

What kind of home would they grow up in, with this monster? What he's asking for is impossible.

Still. The gun sits heavy on the coffee table. I can feel its gravity pulling words out of me.

"Okay. Three years. Will three years work? But please—hand me Harlene."

He draws back. "I can't say if it'll be three years. Six months after the deal's through. That's what I need. You'll get your cut, I'll get my cut, we'll sign some NDAs, and then we can both walk away. It'll be clean. But it has to be after the deal."

"Okay. Okay, Wyatt, do you hear me? But I need you to put Harlene Mae back and put the gun away."

"It's not going to explode. It doesn't have a mind of its own. But if it makes you feel better." He looks at Harlene Mae, still soft in his arms. "Mama's gonna stay right there now, isn't she? She wants us to be a big, happy, safe family together, so she's gonna stay right where she is while I put you back."

Harlene Mae knocks her hands in the air. Sweet thing—she still wants to touch him. Has no idea who he is, what he's saying. She only sees a giant, friendly face. Wyatt walks over to her carryall and slips her back in, watching her awhile. Tipping the handle to rock her.

The clock. The damn clock, so slow it might as well run backward. Come on, Tim. Wyatt's here, not in Belle Meade. Where are you?

"The gun now, Wyatt." I swallow. "I assume it's loaded. I'd like you to take the cartridge out, please."

The words barely register with him. He's still rocking Harlene's carryall, lost in fantasy. But it's real to him. He really can see our family living in our fake bliss for the next few years. How would that work? Every time a baby is out of my sight, I'd panic that he'd done something horrible. And while we give those interviews and talk about the path to healing (*my* path to healing), wouldn't the camera pick me up as I bite my tongue to shreds? Even if I promise him what he wants, there's no telling how long I'd be able to stay in that hell.

Wyatt makes his way back to the couch and dabs his fingers on the coffee table. "Not much point in an unloaded gun, but if it makes you feel better . . ." He pulls it into the air, makes a show of releasing the magazine, which pops into his palm. Then he yanks the slide, which spits out an amber bullet from the top. It rolls on the table until Wyatt plucks it up and holds it to the lamplight. And after staring for a while, his eyes work back over to me.

"What?"

Wyatt shrugs. "I was just wondering about Tennessee's self-defense laws."

"I can't do anything. I don't have a gun."

"No. You don't."

He stuffs the magazine up through the handle, pulls the slide. A bullet rolls into the chamber with a hefty *thwick*.

"I said I'd do it." I can barely hear myself over my heart. Blood is howling in my ears. "I'll *do* it, Wyatt."

"I know. You said that."

He grips the handle, folding each successive finger. Aimed at the wall behind me now, but the gun is steadying in his hand.

"Twelve months after the deal goes through," I promise. "One full year."

"Yeah? That's nice of you." His words are soft and flat. The barren look in his eyes reminds me of when I found him in the twins' room staring into an empty universe.

The gun tips toward me.

Bright yellow lights shine through the window behind him. A car parking along the sidewalk, brakes squeaking.

"That's Tim," I say.

Wyatt spins around to look.

Across the room, over the coffee table, I jump as far as I can until I'm bear-hugging Wyatt around his elbows. He shrugs out of me like I'm wet paper. My teeth knock hard, shooting pain through my skull. When I press my hand to the table to reach for the gun, Wyatt boots me in the ribs. A metal thud, a wood scrape. I don't see where the gun slides. I only hold on to Wyatt's legs, keep him from moving, keep him from turning toward the twins again.

Then I go deaf.

Nothing at first. Only numbness. My right ear rings back to life with a whistling version of sound, then yields to the low scuffling noise in the room. When I close my eyes, I see white, not black. I only feel my body in the faintest sense, the way you feel a puppet's body, but I throw it over the carryalls, over Harlene Mae and Junior.

Through my right ear, I hear my breath against Harlene Mae. Her face is covered in blood. No, no. No, no—nothing hit her, I know it. It can't be. I pull away to wipe her off, but a mucousy string of blood sticks to me. I almost cry in relief. The blood is mine. I press a finger to my face and find my cheekbone is slick with it. A searing, root-deep pain comes just as fast as the realization, a burn from neck to temple.

"Dawn!"

Tim's voice, hot in my right ear.

The two of them are wrestling under the frame of the front door, snaking and rolling. Wyatt mounts on top and grabs Tim's wrists, leaning to pin them. They're both reaching for the gun. It's sitting near a vent in the hallway.

I can only crawl. Every step paints blood onto the floor. Wyatt grabs my ankle as I go past, but I kick free of him. He pounds my ankle again, and something between the bone and the floor catches. But I am closer to the gun than he is. The burning in my ear, the wailing of the twins—it's all nothing now because I am no longer me.

The gun is near an air duct. I grasp it, but my hands shake. They're so full of blood I can barely grip it.

"Dawn!" Tim shouts again.

Wyatt is free of Tim's grip and is barreling toward me. Once he's on his feet and sees me lying on the floor with the gun, he freezes. I don't know if it's the angle, or the top-heavy light of the hall, but it seems like there is some appeal for mercy in it, a crimped look of atonement. Is it regret? Regret toward me, or regret that things simply didn't work out like he hoped? I can't say, because soon the look melts away and he leaps at me.

The shot rings out.

CHAPTER 25

DAWN

When I come to, it is in an ambulance. I have the vague sensation of stretching out my arms and asking about the twins, only for someone to strap me down and whisper in my good ear that everything will be all right. I float from space to space. Then I am turned sideways on a hospital bed and a doctor pokes a needle into my cheek and asks if I can feel it. I murmur that I can't and drift back to sleep. The memories become a thin slurry at the edges of my brain. But after a long, drooly sleep that feels at least twenty hours long, I start to feel like my old self.

The next time I am alert is in a hospital room. A summery blue light seeps from the window. It could either be early morning or the next evening. Or, judging from how I feel, it could be next year. A pug-cheeked nurse is standing at my IV, checking levels.

"Murruroreurrur," I say. *Morning or evening.* When I try to talk, something tugs the entire left side of my cheek. I finger at it and run my thumb along spiny quills that can only be stitches. I am beyond dentist's-office numb. It feels like rubbing someone else's face. And there's still no sound on that side.

"Morning," the nurse says, somehow translating my nonsense.

"Merrwavies."

"Sorry, Mrs. Decker?"

I try to clear my throat. "My . . . babies . . ."

"They're safe," someone says at the door. Tim steps inside and nods as the nurse leaves. He's wearing a fresh polo shirt and jeans, but his arm is in a sling. He looks exhausted, his face a flood of red blotches, his eyelids more crust than skin.

When I try to speak, more gibberish pours out of me, so I just put my arms out for him. He dips his head in for a hug. He's on the wrong side of my face and I can't feel him, but I still remember the sensations it should bring, his sandpaper cheeks, the ripe tang of his sweat. Even in only one of his arms, I am a child again. My heart sinks into the hole of remembering Momma Harlene is not here.

"Oh, don't cry," Tim says, patting me like he once patted Harlene Mae. "Don't cry. It's all over now."

When he lets me free, I club my wrist at the unfeeling skin of my jaw. "Over?"

"Wyatt's dead." Tim's small eyes seem to want to retreat into their sockets. "Can I sit, darlin'? I'll sit. I'll need to sit for this. How are you feeling? Up to it?"

"Just tell me."

"I already told the police what I saw. We were fighting for the gun. You got to it first. He charged at you, and that's when you shot him." Tim winces. "You passed out after that, so I don't know how much you remember."

"It's a bit blurry."

"You shot him in the chest. Must have got his heart because he went down like a sack of potatoes. I called the ambulance as soon as I could, but he bled out before it got there. Dead on arrival."

Bled out before it got there. A feeling of massacre swamps my stomach. I shot him. I shot my husband. Yes, he'd become a monster. Yes, he'd had his gun pointed at our daughter only a minute before that. But I shot *all* of him. I shot the Wyatt he had been. I shot the guy I once saw on TV and wondered, Why isn't this charismatic man who's two inches taller than everyone he meets a star yet? I shot the Wyatt I'd met, too, the one who looked at me like I made him forget other women existed. And I shot the Wyatt who eventually cheated on me. I shot the Wyatt I'd married, the Wyatt who paid for Momma Harlene's living facility. The Wyatt who insisted on putting up our Christmas decorations himself, the Wyatt who once fretted about the twins and all our living room's sharp corners. The father of my children. Of Harlene Fremont's grandchildren. I shot the man who nearly killed them.

Every emotion slams me now, guilt and relief and horror and morbid satisfaction. Most of all, the feeling of untethering from what had tied all my worries to the world.

Tim's lips are pursed. "You all right, darlin'?"

"I really killed Wyatt?"

A slow nod. "Self-defense. Don't you worry. Witnessed and recorded."

"Recorded?"

"I told the police to search your pockets. What did I say to always have on you?"

"R-recorder."

He nods. "I talked to this lieutenant—Guzman? Told me it's all there, everything backs up the story. Me, what's on the recorder, what the paramedics found." Tim's head dips, hunching over. "You're the last witness, of course. There are going to be some tough questions. You just tell them what happened, what you remember, don't leave out anythin' to make yourself look good. They know the twins were in danger. *We* were in danger. Just remember you did nothin' wrong. Fact is, you saved all our lives."

"I don't remember much. But I do remember a man in his sixties holding Wyatt down so I could get the gun."

Tim smiles. "I ain't so strong, but I'm pretty good at being dead weight."

We share a laugh at that, my smile half-numb. After a while, the sound settles until it's just the beeping of my heart rate monitor coming through my good ear. The other ear only gives a seashell drone.

"Mrs. Decker?" A doctor appears at the foot of my bed, gazing at my chart. She's small and mousy, which must be why we didn't hear her come in. "How are you feeling?"

My first instinct is to make a joke about my numb, bandaged face. There is the faint sensation of burning in my cheek, the soreness of being sewn up. Something is wrong because I shouldn't feel this good.

"Um . . . high, I think."

"That'll be the oxycodone. You've been through a lot. We're gathering a gun went off right next to your ear. Most likely, you're in for a round or two of reconstructive surgery, I'm afraid. Ruptured eardrum—"

"The gun went off?" I look at Tim.

"Wyatt got a shot off," he says.

The doctor nods. "To you it probably just sounded like your hearing went out."

"She gonna lose her hearin' in that ear?" Tim asks.

The doctor raises a hand next to my ear. Her arm shakes twice. Two finger snaps click faintly in the wrong ear. "You hear that, Dawn?"

"Yeah." I point at my right ear. "But only from this side."

"There's no telling with noise-induced hearing loss. But if the cells of your inner ear are damaged, there's no way of bringing them back." She thinks. "You'll have options. Hearing aids, cochlear implants. We'll have to see the extent of the damage."

We'll have to see. I flick my fingers at Tim, who digs out his phone and hands it to me in selfie mode. And there is the fish-eye view of my face half-bandaged, my chipmunk cheeks swollen up to boulders. A mound of gauze outside my left ear hides most of it, but even the exposed skin shows bruisy streaks threading from the same wound. This isn't going to go away anytime soon, like ears popping in a plane. "Oh, no—"

"I thought you'd be happy," the doctor says. "You lucked out, all things considered."

All things considered. Could she pick a more cavalier phrase to describe it all? I killed my husband. I'm going to be infamous. Yet I'm supposed to feel better because I turned out all right, *all things considered*? I'm inches away from asking for a new doctor, but I swallow down the annoyance. "Is there any chance it comes back?"

"You'll know more when you talk to the surgeon." The doctor pauses on her way out the door, giving a flimsy smile. "Oh, by the way. I just want to say how sorry I am about everything you've been through. I really loved your show. And as long as your pain level's okay, I have nothing else. Feel better, Mrs. Decker."

Mrs. Decker. But I'm not Dawn Decker anymore, am I? I am now the infamous Dawn Decker née Fremont. The future answer to a pub trivia question. In ten years' time, people drinking IPAs and eating bar nuts will be googling, *Whatever happened to that HLTV lady? Remember? The one whose famous husband went crazy until she finally had to shoot him?*

"What do I do now?" I ask.

"Just rest," the doctor says. "You have a lot of healing ahead of you."

Understatement of the century.

Kelly pats Junior, who is sleeping over her shoulder. "He just went down."

After an hour-long session with Lieutenant Guzman, it's a relief to talk about anything except Wyatt Decker and bullet wounds, about how the gun was positioned, where and when. Now Harlene Mae is in my arms, sucking on my pinkie. I love the doey look in her eyes. I envy her infant ability to forget. My sweet, beautiful, un-remembering daughter. One day, when she is old enough, I will tell her all about the last few weeks—the last few months, really—and explain everything she wants to know. Like me, she will grow up without a father. But unlike me, she will never remember him. She will not know any better.

There will be no repaying Kelly for the kindnesses she's done me. Yes, I gave her a job, once. That doesn't make up for her and her husband posting my bail, for me freight-training my way into their lives, for turning her whole house into a bloody scene of nearly killed children and justifiable homicide. Yet here she remains, bringing the twins and watching over them for my sake. It is true what they say about hard times showing you the difference between friends and the people who have just been pretending.

"So next steps," Kelly says. "We don't want you to worry about a thing. Tim's moving to Nashville. He's going to stay with us until he gets it all sorted."

"No, Kelly, I have a house—"

"I won't hear any of that. Man's got one good arm. He needs someone to cook for him. And we'll watch the twins until you're out."

"It's too much to ask."

"Please. It's not like I'm busy with work. Besides, after all you've been through—" She stops herself. "We've. After all *we've* been through, you think I'm going to stop now? I'm feelin' a little invested in how you turn out."

My eyes water. Harlene Mae frets at losing her latch to my pinkie, so I give it back to her. I am becoming a drippy, sobbing mess, overwhelmed with Kelly's kindness and the thought that my twins are finally safe. But I'm usually a worrier, not a crier. Maybe it's the syrupy feeling of painkillers in my veins, or the weight of Wyatt falling off me all at once, but I'm not sure if a human being could be any happier.

Then there's a knock. "Dawn?"

"Oh, no," Kelly says. "You can leave right now."

A shipwrecked look shivers through Alice Wright. She's holding a gift bag in one hand and the other braces herself to the doorframe, like she expects that a hurricane of rebukes will blow her back into the hallway. And if I had the strength, it would. I want to tear off the bandages and scream things at her like *Howcouldyoutakemytwins* and *Younearlygotmychildrenkilled*. The thought of it alone is loud enough to register on the heart rate monitor.

I calm myself, push out a hot gush of air.

"I thought . . ." Alice trails off, expecting to be interrupted.

So Kelly obliges. "You thought wrong. Dawn needs her rest. She can deal with you in her own time."

Alice gives a nod of surrender. Her tight, dimpled cheeks look so strange when they're not smiling. Like knobs of butter melting in summer, hopelessly clinging to their first shape. Some people don't know what to do if they can't show the world a cheerful face. But here she is, trying anyway.

"No," I say. "It's okay."

"You sure?" Kelly asks.

"I'm sure." I hand over Harlene Mae. She hates losing the comfort of my pinkie finger, but her whine is brief as Kelly whispers to her that they will go and find her formula. Kelly hovers a bit near the foot of the bed, one evil eye fixed on Alice, then leaves with Harlene Mae and Junior, still fast asleep on her shoulder. I've never seen him sleep so well.

The light from the window cuts the space between Alice and me. She steps forward, her slight body shifting weight as if dangling from something. Even in bed, I am confident I could tip her over. But I don't. The gift bag means Alice is here for contrition. I can accept contrition now, especially from her.

"Is that for me?" I point at the bag.

Alice lifts a lemony cupcake out of it and sets it on my tray, next to the fossils of things soft enough to eat, mashed potatoes and Jell-O. "I know you like sweets, and I thought you might be tired of hospital food. . . ."

I push aside the tray, rolling it away, and do it slowly so she can see just how much I am not eating her overpriced cupcake. I motion for her to sit. She does, pulling up a tiny cantilever chair that still manages to swallow her.

"I guess I'll start," she says. "I'm so sorry, Dawn. I thought I was doing the right thing."

"You snuck away with my children. In the middle of the night. I remember waking up as you were leaving."

"I thought they were in danger."

"From me. You can say it. Danger from me. You thought I was the one who'd lost it, and they'd be safe with Wyatt. You didn't trust me."

"No," Alice says, chastened.

"But *I* was your friend. Wyatt was the guy you occasionally saw, yeah. And he was the guy you saw on TV. And still, despite knowing me as well as you did—as well as you do—you thought they needed to be with Wyatt."

"I . . . I didn't know what to make of it," Alice stutters. "I thought you were so erratic! Getting up and, out of nowhere, driving to Indiana. And these reports of you on the news, how you'd escaped with a police car. The dyed hair. And then you brought this stranger to my house—"

"Tim isn't a stranger."

"He was to me. I thought you hated him, and then you didn't? It wasn't making sense. I'm sorry, Dawn. I had to make a coin-flip decision, in my mind. I honestly thought that when everything was done, you might thank me—"

"*Thank* you?"

"—for keeping your twins safe."

"Just admit it. Admit you fell for Wyatt's bullshit. Because it was *your* sister he planned on framing, and you chose him."

Chin in hand, she nods.

"No," I say. "Let me hear you say it."

"I fell for Wyatt's TV bullshit. And I'm sorry."

The heart rate monitor stirs. I turn away and face the window and all its comfort, the warm gold of summer-evening light. I should be even angrier. I deserve to let myself get hysterical. The twins could have died, and it would have been Alice's fault. Her fault for buying Wyatt's nonsense, her fault for trusting the media over what she could have known just from looking her friend in the eyes and asking.

But I am glad we're at least having the conversation. Me in the hospital bed, her with the peace offering—we are at least closer to equilibrium with the truth of it all hanging between us. The world makes sense again.

"It's just you?" I ask. "Not Vic?"

"She was here awhile. We were going to come in together. But visiting hours are almost up, and I said, 'It's now or never.' We both got up, and she just walked to the elevator. She couldn't face you."

"She's a coward."

"What happened exactly?"

"She was sleeping with Wyatt. For months. I only found out after."

Alice slinks into the chair, deflating. "That explains . . . a lot."

"And how's Hattie, through all this?"

"A little freaked-out. You can understand. I don't think she's going to watch the twins for you anymore."

Despite myself, I have to laugh. "I wouldn't either."

"Anyways, I won't add to your stress. I just wanted to show my face and tell you how sorry I am." She stands up. "I got it wrong, Dawn. That's what it comes down to. I should have trusted you. I *knew* you. And I let myself get swept up in what the rest of the world was—anyway. I'm not saying we have to be best buds from here on out. But I want you to know that I'm sorry, and I'll always regret what I did. I'll be ninety years old one day, in a nursing home, and I'll still be wondering how I could have gotten it so wrong when it counted."

I shake my head. "I know how."

It's the same for all of us. We allow ourselves to fall for the easy stories. That's what Wyatt always knew about people—give them the medicine that goes down easy, because that's the one they'll swallow. *The Perfect Home* did that in every episode. How a wheelchair ramp solved every problem a single mother with a special needs child ever had. How a new bay window made a widow feel less lonely because she could see the neighborhood. Why should Alice be any different just because she knew me? I was the one trying to sell the truth. And selling the truth is always dangerous.

"Alice," I say, before she can step out of the room.

"Yeah?"

I flick a finger toward the cupcake on the tray. "Slide that my way, would you?"

And her dimples emerge again, her smile straight back to sweetness.

When it's done and I'm alone, I watch the sunset through the window. The amber light sundials across the frame of a Monet haystacks print. Every time I look back, I swear the shadow points to a different nub in the wall. There is something both comforting and disquieting about how, with enough patience, you can watch the earth move.

When I tell the twins about what happened these past few weeks, it will only be with regret—*Your father wasn't right in the head*. That will have to suffice. Seems like a stretch now, so soon after seeing him with that gun in one hand and Harlene Mae in the other. But that's the thing about time. It shifts, melts, changes your perceptions. And if I'm capable of forgiving him one day, *that* will be the real end of Wyatt.

Someday.

Another knock at the door. I'm ready to ask the nurse about the stinging in my cheek, but a man is standing under the frame instead. I blink. No, it's not Tim—Tim has his arm in a sling and isn't as tall as this man. But there is something familiar about his taut torso, the strangely smooth face and the ribbony wrinkles at the neck. He wears a crisp single-breasted suit, no tie.

"I'm sorry," he says to my startled look. "They said visiting still goes for a few more minutes, and there was no one else around. I can come back later."

"Do I know you?"

"We haven't met." He puts his meaty knuckles over the edge of the chair, but doesn't sit. "I just wanted to—congratulate you, I guess, on coming out of what you've just been through. I knew your husband for a while, and it's because of you I know he was a very sick man."

"Um—thanks." The wall separating my room from the hallway is mostly glass, cut into shards by half-closed blinds. Through them, I see a registration desk, where not one nurse looks concerned that this man is standing in my room. "I'm sorry, I don't know your name."

"Drake Jennings." He extends one of those meaty hands. "Just giving you my well-wishes. Making my introductions. Because when you heal up and you're ready to talk, I've got a business proposition for you."

CHAPTER 26

DAWN

Three years later

"Oh, look," Tim says. "Mama's here."

Harlene Mae drops from his grip, which she'd been using as her personal merry-go-round, and darts across the grass, exploding into my arms. I'm so glad we named her Harlene. I've looked over the old photos, and she looks just like Momma Harlene did at three, the sandy hair, the wild, lightning-struck eyes.

"Mommy!" Junior ambles his way over and barely makes it down the newly installed porch steps without scraping his knee. But as he picks himself out of the dirt, he doesn't whine, not like he did as an infant. He just keeps running until he can smother himself against my thigh. Then he's off in search of more mayhem.

We are on one of the especially green hills of Green Hills, Tennessee. Behind Tim, a ten-acre lot holds the home I've almost finished, a ranch in the French Country style. It's still unpainted, but it will have tan sides highlighted by ocean-blue shutters and window aprons. Most important (and most expensive) are the fully mature Leyland cypress I've brought in. Privacy trees. If you buy enough of them, you have a wall. The last time I built a house, a man named Wyatt Decker made me compromise on the privacy trees: for the backyard, he said, but not the front. The front would have been overkill.

But now there's only one name on the title. And she says, Leyland cypress for days.

"Grandpa wasn't supposed to show you the house yet," I say, my hand locked in Harlene Mae's sweaty, steely grip. "It's not quite done."

"'Not quite done'?" Harlene Mae echoes. She's a great mimic still learning to speak, and my heart goes soft every time I hear East Tennessee come out of her.

"Almost. Then it's all ours."

"Are we sleeping here?"

"Not tonight, Mae. They have to bring our beds in first."

"Oh." She nods, so wise, so professorial, Harlene Mae Fremont and all of her almost-four years on earth.

"C'mon," Tim says to her. "Let's go check out the livin' room!"

Harlene Mae squeals, unjigsaws her hand from mine, and shoots off to Junior, who's already climbing the front steps. Those are new. The front door's in, too: an arch top with no windows. I like the idea that you can't look inside even if you want to.

I follow them up the steps. Strange as it sounds, I have Wyatt to thank for this. I wouldn't have met Drake Jennings without Wyatt, and Drake Jennings wouldn't have been stuck with a half-finished deal to buy out HLTV and spin *The Perfect Home* into its own brand. After the Kat Cameron interview, after my being cleared by the police, the world became enthralled with the real story. It helped that Showtime made a miniseries about those few weeks, called it *The Perfect Home* (what else?), and sent a beautiful English actress out to follow me for a week so she could get the accent right. Turns out my *s* sounds are just as shushy as Dolly Parton's. After that, after the public watched how things really unfolded—plus or minus a few minor details—Drake Jennings and his group of investors were sure the deal could go through as planned. They just needed a signature from someone at the show, and Janie was officially retired and had never been on camera anyway. Would I lend my (cleared) name to get the deal done?

I would. In exchange for Wyatt's share.

But I'd be a silent partner. Drake wanted Perfect Home TV's flagship show to follow me and the twins as we adjusted to life after Wyatt. That felt wrong. It's hard enough finding moms who want playdates with my infamous twins. It's hard enough keeping the sun hood down on their stroller every time I go out in public and some stranger in a grocery store wants to sneak pictures. It's hard enough scouting preschools when administrators ask you how many hours of therapy you go through a week, just because they saw the Show-time series and they're a little concerned you might shoot somebody if they look at the twins wrong. It's hard enough getting second looks at the DMV or everyone telling you to "Please hold" when you're on the line with customer support and have to give someone your name. I just want to return an espresso machine; to them, it's a story they'll tell the rest of their lives. I don't have to be more famous. I don't want to be. I couldn't imagine if the twins were on TV.

They're America's Twins, someone told me, and people feel invested in their future. Well, good for people. I'm not going to use them for ratings, or to be a TV star. The channel is doing well enough without me. If no one watches Perfect Home TV, I'll sell my share, cash out, and get a place somewhere near the ocean. Somewhere warm and small and not especially prone to hurricanes.

Georgia, maybe. St. Simons, Jekyll Island. I like places with simple beaches and opaque water. I like how every time the tide sucks away, it erases a little skim of earth.

I won't tell you how much my share is worth—Momma Harlene would call me tacky if I did—but let's just say that I don't worry about sending the twins to college.

Nor do I worry where I'm going to live. For now I've got a ten-acre estate with an enclosed garden, a privacy courtyard, a fence, a gate, and now a wall of Leyland cypress.

Things have moved quickly since I last visited. Drywall's mostly in, carpets are installed, even the TV's arrived. Except for a few appliances for the kitchen that still need delivering, and a few licks of paint here and there, Château Fremont is starting to take shape.

Harlene and Junior each pull Grandpa Tim by a hand, dragging him in to see the living room. I know that trick—he's the only one who'll let them watch *The Lion King* for the umpteenth time. While they're occupied, I go upstairs to look at the writing nook. At my request, the desk's already installed. This is what I really came here for. I check emails—ten new ones, none of them spam. I've gotten used to that. Journalists and true-crime podcasts always want interviews, and Drake Jennings's team always CCs me on decisions I will never weigh in on. Toward the bottom of the folder, there is a request from Modern People. Am I interested in a feature with me and the twins? They offer the top spot for a full week. A great opportunity, the editor notes, to promote Perfect Home TV on a website that gets more impressions per month than Weather.com.

Nah.

I tap the checkbox. *Delete.*

Then I'm done with the laptop. I pull out my gratitude journal and get to the real work of blessing this new house.

I'm grateful for my family, I write, meaning Tim and the twins. But I can't write it without thinking of Wyatt. And I am grateful to him, in a way. The danger of Wyatt Decker is long gone. Now there are only his ruins. When I think of him now, it's as a sad and lonely man in permanent need of validation. I do think he would have done something truly horrible, because to him, infamy would have been better than obscurity. I don't regret shooting him. He might have killed all of us. But I don't regret what he gave me, either. Junior and Harlene Mae are here because of Wyatt.

I scratch my ear and thumb the sound processor nestled in my hair. Yes, I have Wyatt to thank for the cochlear implant, too. The therapist suggested I reframe the implant as a badge of honor. "You gave up that ear so your children could live," he said. "It's proof of the kind of person you are."

Next, I write that I'm grateful for my friends. Meaning the new friends I've made since those crazy weeks a few years ago. But some of the old friends, too—Kelly (you can bet I got her a job at Perfect Home TV), Hattie, and, yes, even Alice.

I stare at the journal, the page full of my lazy, giant cursive. This is the same journal I've always had, the one that goes back before the twins, when I was grateful for a husband who wanted kids enough to try ASB, when I was trying to find silver linings in the slow-moving fifty-car pileup of my life, when Momma Harlene was still alive. That was something to be grateful for. She lived long enough to see her grandkids in the flesh. She'd seen what I'd made.

I pack the gratitude journal into the desk drawer. I wanted it to be one of the first items I moved to the new house. Now it is.

"C'mon, guys," I say. "We have to be out of here before the crew gets back to bring in your beds and all that fun stuff."

This makes Junior start to whine, but Tim bribes the twins by telling them I'll buy them ice cream. Thanks for that, Tim. When he's got them packed in my car, I remind him that I can watch them tonight. He throws a suspicious look my way.

"Thought you had a date," he says.

"I canceled it. I'm not ready."

"That's a shame. It coulda done you a lotta good."

"Let's be honest. Even if we'd made it to dinner, I probably would have scared him off with all twenty tons of Dawn Fremont baggage."

"Yeah." Tim closes an eye and sweeps an arm across the property. Surveying my modest Dawn Fremont empire. "Hard to imagine a guy wantin' all this, darlin'."

He means the house and the money, and I want to protest because all I can see are its little imperfections, the incomplete steps between Dawn Fremont as a finished adult product and Dawn Fremont as she actually is. But I meant my social baggage. For about a week or so, Wyatt had the world convinced I was about to murder my children. I've been absolved and exonerated—and my children are with me, thriving—but first impressions leave stains in the bones. For most of the country, the first time they heard the words *Dawn Decker*, it was under the headline WYATT DECKER SHOT DEAD.

Thirty-five, two kids, one husband dead at my hand. I'm not exactly bring-home-to-Mom material.

"Just promise me," Tim says. "Promise me you'll keep tryin'."

"Would it be so bad just being a widow? Living out my days like this?"

He doesn't hesitate. "Darlin', I spent twenty years alone. Yes, it would."

All right, I think. In good time, I can try. But it's been so long since I dated in earnest, I wouldn't even know where to start. An app? My profile would make for one hell of an attention grabber. *Must love kids and trashy reality TV. Oh, and trust me when I say that shooting my husband was a onetime thing.*

After Tim leaves, I secure the twins in their booster seats, flip the AC on, and set the car to blast all the songs Junior needs before he goes nuclear. But I don't get in. I want another moment to survey the property. Everything smells clean and brightly fragrant, like fresh-chopped herbs. I swing around the back, looking for bad news under the gutters (hornet's nests, maybe), finding none. Some things are just as they should be.

Except the BMW 5 that's just pulled up.

The woman who gets out of the driver's seat is tall, lithe, with silky black hair and buggy Jackie O sunglasses that cover half her face. She waits by her open door and slides them off. Her expression is tight.

Because we were born in the same month, I know Victoria Weatherly is now thirty-five. I'm looking for the hornet's nests under her gutters. A little sign of age, worry-weathering—a damned wrinkle, please. But she's exactly as I remember her, exactly as she appears on Instagram when I'm thumbing my phone during my weak late-night stalker sessions.

She calls something, but it goes whistly in my implant.

"Sorry?" I approach, pointing to my bad ear and twisting a finger.

"I can come back if it's a bad time." Victoria dips her head at the twins. Junior's eyes are half-closed, his body hugged in song. Harlene is clapping completely out of rhythm. So like her mother.

"More of a bad place." My arms seem to cross themselves. "Who gave you the address?"

At the same time, we both say, "Alice."

Victoria looks at her feet—in heels, she's completely uncertain on the gravel. The concrete gets poured next month. "I keep sending you DMs and you never respond."

"I know."

"I just—don't want to go any further in life hating each other."

I shrug. "I don't hate you."

"But we're not friends."

"I'm getting a little choosier with my friends. You'll understand why."

She studies her feet again. Gets sick of the heel piercing the gravel, kicks off the shoe. Then the other. She wears heels so much I've forgotten I'm taller than her. "I understand why," she echoes. "I'm not saying we have to be friends. I just don't want to be enemies."

"Okay. We're not enemies." I flick my chin at her car, which is still ringing: door ajar.

"I just wanted to see if we could talk, kind of like the old days. Remember how I used to buy us coffee and we'd hang out at the store? Those were my favorite days."

"Yeah, they were fun back when I didn't know anything. I'm trying to forget."

"So am I. I'm so disappointed by how I handled everything. I had all these crazy ideas about Wyatt and me. I think that's how I spun it in my head—that if he and I had something special, then I wasn't going around your back. I was being hypnotized by a rare love. And there was always part of me that saw what you had with him and thought, 'Why her? Because she was first?'"

She means to justify herself, but all she's done is get a tighter grip on the blade already stuck inside me. "Maybe you're right," I say. Maybe you should have met him first. But I can't wish that on anyone, not even Victoria. I eye her down, the fresh hair, the green maxi dress. "You're all dolled up. Where you headed?"

"Nowhere. This was for you."

"I like you better in pajama pants and Vols T-shirts."

"So do I. God, I loved that—you and I, roomies. I almost thought about bringing some T-shirts with me. Custom-print something, maybe."

The idea comes out of my mouth before I can throw up a wall. "I SURVIVED WYATT DECKER."

We laugh together. And despite the numb death in my ear, I remember that exact sound: our treble chuckles on the sectional sofa of her apartment over ten years ago, when I was an intern and she was an aspiring model and the world had yet to ripen, yet to bruise.

"Maybe I did pick a bad time," Victoria says. "I'm not great at that. But if this is my only chance, I'm sorry, Dawn. If I could take it back, I'd take back everything. And isn't it fair to say he fooled both of us?"

I can only nod, only hold myself against the sudden summer chill. She waits to see what I might do, but that's all I can give her. She crouches down, knees wobbly in the dress she wore for me, and slips her heels back onto her feet, turning to her car.

"Vic," I call.

She spins around.

"Don't stop the DMs, though. Try again."

When she smiles, I'm reminded of a tip she once gave me: smile with your eyes, that's how you know it's genuine. Her eyes are puckered into happy little globs. "How about the occasional text? Still at the same phone number?"

"I'll give you the new one."

After she takes it into her phone—sending me a test text, *We survived Wyatt Decker*—I watch her pull around and wave her goodbye. It feels a little strange that I couldn't say the right words when she apologized. I'm still defrosting to the world.

I check the twins' seats again and climb behind the steering wheel, deciding that I'll work on that. It's not as if I'm short on things to keep me busy. As we pull out of the driveway to go our separate ways—Victoria back downtown, me to run errands with the twins—I steal a last glance at the house. There is so much to do before it's ready. The painter's tape around the doorbell, which isn't installed yet. The absent weather strip on the front door. The sod that has yet to be unrolled and planted. So much work to do, so many long miles between me and perfection. But that's all right, I think, turning my eyes to the road. I'm in no great rush.

ACKNOWLEDGMENTS

My first thanks belong to the reader. Thank you for buying this book, for spending time reading it, for hanging out awhile. I hope we can do it again sometime.

This book wouldn't be in your hands without Ronald Gerber of Lowenstein Associates. Thank you for all your thoughtful work and patient guidance. If you hadn't been this book's representative, it would currently sit under a cloud of digital dust in one of my folders: "Old novels." Working with you changed everything. Special thank you to Barbara Lowenstein for creating an encouraging and supportive agency.

To the brilliant Sabrina Pyun: I'll never be able to say "thank you" enough. Thank you for championing this book, for lending me some of your emotional IQ, and for mining treasure where I'd buried none. Feels like I won the editor sweepstakes.

Thank you to everyone at the magical Scribner as well as Simon & Schuster for making the dream come true. Thank you, Nan Graham, for making this possible. Thank you to Brianna Yamashita, Kassandra Rhoads, Leora Bernstein, Colleen Nuccio, and Amy Rohn for helping share this book with readers. Thank you to early readers and encouragers, especially Ashley Rose Gilliam, Rachel Podmajersky, Paul Samuelson, and Sophie Guimaraes. Thank you, Jason Chappell, and sorry about all the hyphens.

Thank you to the beta readers and fellow writers for feedback and support, especially Austin Idles for critical questions about the third act and my cousin David Salvi for being my writing companion over the years. Thank you to friends, web-friends, and Internet colleagues who've helped make freelance writing a career: John Werner, who always helps me out with what cars a character might drive; Spencer Keller; Kaleigh Moore; Ashley R. Cummings; Alyssa Towns; Kat Boogaard; Emma Siemasko; Nsisong Asanga; and Matt Koulas. Thank you to professors and teachers like John Craig, David Riordan, Barbara Wuest, and Mary Carson.

Special thank you to my kind and supportive family. Steve, Ally, Joe, Kim, Rachel, and the Honorable Michael; Marita, Lyvia, Patrick, Simona, Charlie, Isobel, Teresa, Ky, Reagan, Finnley, Joe, and more to come. I've got an enormous extended family in Wisconsin, Pennsylvania, Arizona, and especially Illinois (Bear down, Chicago Bears). Everyone deserves mention, but I don't think there's enough ink in the world to encapsulate what all of you have meant to me. We're all long overdue for a game of Diplomacy. To my grandparents, Albert, Marita, Curt, and Maryann: I hope I did you proud.

This book is for my parents, Scott and Mary, who gave me a childhood in a perfect home I'm happy to say did *not* inspire the events of this novel. In a family of respectable professions, they easily could have encouraged me to pursue something more sensible than writing, but they never flinched. I can't ever repay everything you've done for me, so hey—how's about a book?